MW00399728

Holding Their Own IX: The Salt War

By

Joe Nobody

Edited by:
E. T. Ivester
D. Allen

PrepperPress

Dystopian Fiction & Survival Nonfiction

Holding Their Own IX: The Salt War

ISBN 978-1-939473-27-1
Copyright © 2014 Kemah Bay Marketing, LLC
All rights reserved.
Printed in the United States of America.
Prepper Press Trade Paperback Edition: November 2014
Prepper Press is a division of Kennebec Publishing, LLC

Other Books by Joe Nobody:

Holding Your Ground: Preparing for Defense if it All Falls Apart

The TEOTWAWKI Tuxedo: Formal Survival Attire

Without Rule of Law: Advanced Skills to Help You Survive

Holding Their Own: A Story of Survival

Holding Their Own II: The Independents

Holding Their Own III: Pedestals of Ash

Holding Their Own IV: The Ascent

Holding Their Own V: The Alpha Chronicles

Holding Their Own VI: Bishop's Song

Holding Their Own VII: Phoenix Star

The Home Schooled Shootist: Training to Fight with a Carbine

Apocalypse Drift

The Little River Otter

The Olympus Device: Book One

The Olympus Device: Book Two

Secession: The Storm

The Ebola Wall

Find more titles at

www.JoeNobodyBooks.com

and

www.PrepperPress.com

Foreword by Joe Nobody

The El Paso Salt War actually occurred in 1877. Sometimes called the San Elizario Salt War, the regional conflict raged for an extended period across the arid lands of West Texas.

The namesake mineral had little to do with the actual cause of the clash. Salt was merely a catalyst for the underlying, long-simmering disputes brewing in the region. The right to access the plentiful natural resource was nothing more than a rallying point, a call to arms, for those seeking to implement a social-political agenda or financial gain by use of arms.

While studying this historical event, it occurred to me that Bishop and Terri's world would face many of the same issues and challenges as our early American ancestors' more basic society. West Texas in 1877 probably wasn't a significantly different environment than the social and financial ecosystem that might develop after a collapse.

Without rule of law, bigotry and discrimination would run unchecked; age-old divides along the lines of race, religion, or heritage might occur. It is very likely, just as in 1877, these segments and sentiments would lead to organized violence and conflict.

In the Holding Their Own series, I have written several different scenarios addressing how the vacuum of leadership might be filled once government hierarchy no longer existed. I think this is one of the most interesting aspects related to the rise and fall of historical civilizations.

It is my firm belief that a pre-collapse organization, with an established pecking order and chain of command, would have a head start in filling such a void. Given that conviction, it has been a natural progression to explore how today's entities might fare if they found themselves in control after an event.

In this work, I use the example of a labor union, more specifically the Teamsters. I am not anti-union, just as I am not anti-church (HTO 7), anti-police (HTO 1), anti-military (HTO 3), or anti-corporation (HTO 5). All of these entities share the characteristics listed above, enabling a rapid rise to power. In some instances, their leadership might be exactly what is needed. In other cases, that power might ultimately corrupt.

And finally, in real life I encounter very few situations where people are either entirely "good," or wholly "evil." The same can be said of life's everyday problems, opportunities, and interactions. The reader will find my fiction mimics the real world in this regard. The challenge of determining right versus wrong, positive or negative, has never been easy. In a state of anarchy, reaching those conclusions is likely to be even more difficult. The apocalypse may alter a lot of things, but I doubt human nature will be one of them – at least not for a while.

    Enjoy,

      Joe

Chapter 1

By the time Bishop spotted the spikes, it was too late. His foot was halfway to the brake when the front tires of the pickup exploded, followed less than a second later by the rear rubber. The steering became mushy, the truck fishtailing as he fought desperately for control. Someone had strategically positioned sheets of plywood across the road, dozens of huge nails pointing skyward.

Terri shouted something from the backseat, but he was too focused on avoiding devastation to digest her words.

The pickup skidded the last 200 feet on its rims, only the soft sand of the roadside desert preventing the tortured machine from flipping over on its side.

Bishop's first instinct was to check on his wife and son in the backseat. Terri was pale, huddled over Hunter's car seat trying to protect the child with her body. She stared at her husband with wide, questioning eyes. "What the hell just happened?" she snapped.

Before he could answer, the passenger window exploded in a shower of glass... small holes stitching across the windshield, bullets thwacking and sparking into the truck's sheet metal.

"Get down," he screamed, reaching for his rifle.

Bishop bailed out of the driver's door, hitting the ground hard, pulling the M4 by the sling along behind him. He rolled toward the back tires, his instincts screaming that the shooters were on the passenger side and to the rear of the truck.

Bullets snapped through the air, their supersonic greeting forcing Bishop to stay low to the ground. Careful not to expose his head, he raised the M4 over the edge of the bed and fired several blind shots. He didn't expect to hit anything; the act was merely a desperate play to keep the bushwhackers at bay and give him some time.

Still crouching close to the ground, he flung open the passenger door, shouting for Terri to get out. The truck wouldn't stop bullets or help them escape. Bishop's beloved Texas pickup was now nothing more than a death trap on wheels. Damn, and I just washed it, Bishop thought.

His wife was already one step ahead of him, a wide-eyed Hunter liberated from his car seat and on the floor, shielded by his mother's torso. "Come on! Come on!" Bishop screamed, reaching to pull the boy out.

Cradling the baby in one arm, Bishop again raised the rifle with his free hand and began firing blind. Keep them back, kept racing through his mind. Give them something to think about.

Hunter, his ears assaulted by the report of his dad's rifle, started screaming at the top of his lungs.

Terri pivoted and twisted her way out of the truck, hitting the ground in an ungraceful tangle of arms and legs. She was reaching back in the cab for her own rifle as another salvo slammed into the couple's pickup-shield.

Surprise was no longer an advantage for the attackers, Bishop recovering enough to begin forming a tactical outline of the situation. There were at least six or seven shooters engaging them. They sported a mixture of weapons. The ambushers were grouped in two separate areas. The most damaging piece of information – they didn't give a shit if they killed women or children.

Slinging her rifle, Terri tugged Hunter from her husband's arm and then scrambled for the front wheel and the protection of the engine block. Smart girl, Bishop noted in a momentary flash of pride.

He chanced a glance around the rear bumper, exposing his head only long enough to take a mental snapshot. His scouting effort was rewarded with a dozen bullets pinging off metal and cracking through the air.

Focusing intensely on the image in his mind, he determined his family was in a completely untenable position. The ambushers were most likely leveraging a small drainage ditch about 70 meters away. A natural bend in the gully allowed the highwaymen two different angles on the road. A strategic location to set a trap.

"We can't stay here," Bishop shouted to his wife.

"I'm listening," she replied.

Bishop looked behind them, thankful the opposite side of the road afforded at least some cover. He spied a boulder field, a few of the individual rocks the size of their truck. Beyond that lay a steep, craggy-looking ridge that might be a dead end or might be climbable.

"We're going that way," he announced, gesturing with his head. "But I need my pack out of the bed. Can you give me some covering fire?"

"Where?" she mouthed.

Bishop pointed with his arm, giving her the general direction to aim.

Nodding, Terri set Hunter down and pulled her rifle around. Her finger was working the trigger as she rose over the hood.

Bishop did the same, this time exposing his head more than before. He centered the red dot where he was sure the ambushers were camped and let loose a hailstorm of fire.

After 20 rounds, he took his left hand off the weapon and reached into the back of the truck. His pack was there, along with a load of supplies. He'd barely managed to pull back before a blizzard of bullets was punching through the bed, exit holes of jagged metal chasing the Texan as he ducked behind the rear wheel.

Hunter was back in Terri's arms, protected by her body and the engine block. That didn't seem to matter to the attackers, a fair amount of lead being issued in her direction as well.

"I'm going to keep them down while you cross the road," Bishop informed his wife. "Once you are on the other side, find some good cover and start shooting to keep their heads down. I'll hustle along and join you. Understand?"

Terri frowned. "You want to use a technique called 'bounding' to cross the road – right? Play leap-frog with our suppressive fire – correct?"

Bishop, despite all the stress and danger, had to smile. "Yes," he responded, "that's exactly what I want to do."

"Why the hell didn't you just say so? I'm not some dumb girl, Bishop."

"I love you," Bishop mouthed, feeding a fresh magazine into his carbine.

"I'm ready when you are," Terri announced, Hunter clutched tightly against her chest, crying at the top of his little lungs.

"Go!" Bishop shouted, rising up and throwing round after round at their foes. He had identified the enemy's position now, the red dot of his optic never wavering. Five shots at group one, six more at group two, and then he was down, protected again by steel of the rear axle and wheels.

He spotted Terri's hair flying around the closest big rock, a few seconds later her rifle appearing over the rim of the boulder. When her muzzle began spitting white flashes, Bishop gathered up his pack, darting half-bent to join her, bullets chasing him across the pavement.

"They might try to get around and in front of us," he barked after drawing a few deep breaths. "As we move toward the ridge, be diligent about what's ahead as well as behind us."

"Gotcha. Where are we going?"

"I don't know… anywhere but here. We're outgunned, and they know the terrain. Distance is going to save our asses today - let's put some between them and us."

"Do you see that big rock shaped like a cow?" Terri asked, pointing to a formation 30 meters behind them.

Bishop nodded, "Looks good. Stay close to the ground…. I'll see you there."

He braced his rifle on the edge of the rock, scanning for any ambushers who were stupid enough to expose themselves. He spied the top of a baseball hat just as Terri's footsteps announced she was making for the bovine-rock. The hat's owner raised his head, swinging a rifle into shooting position. It was his last act, Bishop's red dot centered directly on the man's face.

One of their own going down had the desired effect, the number of rounds hounding his wife greatly diminished from previous volleys. Maybe they only want the vehicle, Bishop pondered, sweeping the gully for another target. Or... they've split up, and some of them are trying to flank us.

A quick glance informed the Texan that his wife had managed cover. Snapping a quick 3-shot spread, he pushed off, humping the pack and zigzagging to join her.

The couple repeated the process three more times before Terri's labored breathing and sweat-soaked hair demanded they take a break. Peering down at the now-calmer Hunter, she chided, "You need to lose some weight, big boy."

"We can't rest for long," Bishop announced, sweeping the desert with his optic. "They still might be trying to get in front of us. Do you want me to carry Hunter?"

Terri eyed the heavy-looking pack on her husband's back. "No, I can pull my own weight. Let's get going. See you at that bush over there." And with that, she was running again, rifle across her back, child clutched close to her heart.

So much for a nice, quiet, family road trip, Bishop thought. I should have listened to Nick.

An hour of continuous movement later, Bishop said, "Okay, I think we're out of the danger zone. Let's hole up here and catch our breath."

Terri looked spent; Hunter was fussing, and it was damn hot. Bishop offered his wife a drink, extending the tube from his Camelbak water bladder. She gladly accepted. After a few gulps, she quipped, "What the hell happened back there? Who were those guys, and what did they want?"

"No idea. Their tire-spike device was well-placed and purpose built. They had identified the perfect spot, right at the bottom of a little dip where I couldn't see the snare until it was too late. I think they've done this before."

"Do you think they want the truck?" she asked after another few more swallows.

"Maybe, but that doesn't make any sense. What good would a truck with four flat tires do way out here in the middle of nowhere?"

Terri considered his statement for a bit and then brightened. "I bet they wanted the gasoline."

"I don't think so," he responded, shaking his head at the

mystery. "They were shooting like crazy, as if they didn't care if they hit the gas tank. And besides, even considering the recovery, there aren't that many vehicles way out here. What would be their chances of trapping a victim? They could sit out here for days and never see a car or truck go by. I don't think it was a gas trap."

"Nomads?" she suggested.

Bishop understood the reference, a term used throughout the Alliance territories for roving bands of displaced people. "Could be," he said. "But they used ammo like it was as common as sand, and that doesn't fit the profile. I don't know. We are pretty close to the border. Could be a group wandered up from Mexico, I suppose. But why shoot up the truck? Why spring the ambush here?"

Terri nodded, accepting her husband's logic. "I guess we might not ever know. The definitive question is, 'What now?' I'm going to have to feed this bottomless pit of a baby in a little bit, and my legs and back are killing me."

"You've done great, babe. Can you make it up this crest? I want to get to the high ground, and then I'll set up camp. We can figure out the next step once we find a good spot."

"Not much further, Bishop. I'm sorry to be a sissy, but I've been spending a lot of time behind desk lately. My bad... but it is the truth."

He brushed a strand of hair from her face and smiled. "No apology needed, and there's no one I would rather have at my back. I'm not exactly feeling like a spring chicken either. We can slow our pace, but I want to get something set up before it gets too hot out here. The sun is going to become our enemy in a few hours."

The couple continued up the ridge, moving slowly through an ever denser rock field. With the incline increasing and the sun rising, they both began to feel the effects of heat and exertion.

Bishop spied a shady outcropping, an indentation in a wall of stone that wasn't a cave, but would provide reasonable shelter. It reminded him of the bat cave back at their ranch. Pointing to the formation, Bishop announced, "There are our 4-star accommodations."

"I hope the pool's open," Terri replied, wiping the perspiration from her brow.

They found the opening to be about 15 feet deep, a crevice formed by a sheet of rock separating from the cliff. The floor was smooth, the air several degrees cooler than in the direct desert sun.

"So here's the good news," Bishop said, dropping his pack to the ground. "This place is very defendable."

"And the bad news?" Terri asked, using the cotton shirt over her camisole to make a nest for Hunter.

"There's no retreat. We get pinned in here, and we're screwed."

Terri glanced around, nodding her understanding. "Should we stay on the move in hope of something better?"

"I don't think that's best. Like I said, the sun is going to be more dangerous to us than human aggressors right now. Let's hole up here – at least until dusk."

"And then? I don't mean to be a nag, but I was kind of hoping for a long term plan, my love. I know you don't have any reservations about crawling around the desert and smelling like a goat. Hunter and I, on the other hand, have more refined tastes and expectations for our vacation outings."

Bishop snorted at her choice of words. Feigning a hurt look, he spread his arms to indicate the bare stone walls surrounding them. "What? This is a great place. What more could you ask for?"

"Diapers. Baby food. Water. Someplace to bathe. Toilet paper. How about sleeping without worrying about a tarantula crawling up my butt?"

"So, I suppose now is a bad time to talk about my plans for a second honeymoon?" he replied sheepishly.

The remark elicited a growl of frustration as Terri reached for a nearby pebble. The projectile bounced harmlessly off of Bishop's body armor, but the point was made. "I suppose not," he mumbled, reaching for his pack.

He began pulling items out of the large ruck, hoping a quick inventory would improve his spouse's mood.

It did not.

Bishop's bug out bag had been carefully stocked to keep him alive for several days. Missing were the items for Hunter.

"We can tear up my spare shirt and pants for diapers," he offered, trying to improve Terri's outlook. "I've got two MRE's (meals ready to eat), with potatoes. We can mash and squash parts of those for Hunter to eat. I've got my water filter – I just have to locate some water."

"Bishop," she interrupted, "How long before someone comes looking for us?"

Sighing, the Texan peered down, suddenly finding his boots very intriguing.

"Bishop?"

"Well... probably three or four days," he shyly answered. "Maybe a bit more."

Terri shook her head, obviously unhappy with the response. "Why so long? What did you tell Nick about this little endeavor before we left?"

Bishop's words tumbled out rushed and apologetic. "I was only doing it for you... for us. You were so stressed after Galveston and the hurricane. You seemed frustrated with having your security guys around all the time. We haven't spent any time alone for almost a year... and... and I just thought we might...."

Terri's fists maneuvered to her hips as he rambled on, her head tilting with "the look."

"Okay. I fucked up," he confessed. "I told Nick I was going to take you to this canyon I knew about – a picturesque little nook on the Rio Grande. I let him in on my plan... that we were going to camp for a while. Swim in the river... you know... vacation stuff. I told him not to worry if we didn't show up at Fort Bliss for a few days."

"And the provisions we were carrying in the back of the truck?"

"That was our camping gear, extra food, and supplies for Hunter. I had the church ladies pack five days of whatever they thought he needed."

Bishop lowered his head, chin resting against his chest. "I just wanted to spend some time as a family. Just the three of us. Like regular people."

"Great," she replied, spinning in a small circle with her arms spread wide. "This is just great. So now we're stuck in the middle of nowhere, with practically nothing to survive on. We've got a bunch of people shooting at us, and no one even knows where we are, let alone having any reason to start a search. Wonderful."

"We've got each other," Bishop ventured, his tone soft. "We're all here and alive."

Something in his words resonated with Terri, a realization that her husband's heart had been in the right place. She went to him, wrapping her arms tightly around his back in a snug embrace. "I'm sorry. I know this wasn't what you had in mind. You're right; we are together, and that's all that really matters."

Bishop pulled her head against his breast and kissed the crown of her hair. They held each other for several minutes, the stillness of the desert providing a relaxing backdrop. Bending slightly lower to whisper in his wife's ear, Bishop prodded, "Now about that second honeymoon...."

Rocco pulled a handful of diapers from the cardboard box, displaying the bounty for everyone to see. "Shit! This is bullshit!"

he spouted. "We lost Javier over diapers? A tent? Baby food?"

"I don't think these people were soldiers," one of the older men stated, peering into the bed of Bishop's truck.

"How were we to know?" someone else asked.

Rocco didn't answer, his scrutiny fixed toward the elevated rise where the truck's occupants had fled. "No matter," he announced, turning back to his patrol. "Take whatever we can carry. Sometimes in a war, there are innocent casualties."

"Tell that to Javier's mother," the old man mumbled, shaking his head.

Stepping in, Rocco grabbed the man's shirt, balling the material in a commanding grip and drawing the complainer close. "I am growing tired of your constant complaining, old man. You bitch and moan, yet I don't hear you offering any solutions. I would advise you to keep your mouth shut."

Fire filled the elderly man's eyes, but his ancient frame was no threat to the younger, stronger Rocco. "Beat me if you will," he hissed. "Shoot me and leave me to die in the desert if you must. But I'm not going to change my voice. This fighting is wrong. There has to be another way."

"Again, no suggestions," Rocco declared to the men now circling around the conflict. "We have tried talking until our lungs were exhausted. We made every attempt to trade and barter, and all we received in return were more demands and higher tariffs. Our people are starving. The village council made its decision. The only choice was to take up arms."

"They made that decision based on your bullying," countered the old timer.

For a moment, the throng of men thought their leader was going to strike the naysayer, but he didn't. Waving off the remark, Rocco pivoted and demanded, "Pack up what is useful. We'll bury Javier with honor tonight."

The men soon gathered, the body of their fallen friend resting nearby, the corpse a motivation to the sullen, angry members of the patrol. Others hefted the cardboard boxes from the back of Bishop's truck, inventorying the contents. It was another hour before the rumble of the bus sounded across the quiet, desert landscape.

The dilapidated, old Chevy finally rattled over the nearest rise, its blue and yellow paint faded and weary. It was the only vehicle in their village that would transport so many, and soon the men were loading boxes and hefting the body of their fallen comrade inside.

Bishop's truck was secured with a tow rope; the shot-up hulk would be pulled back to the village on its rims and cannibalized for parts or anything else of value.

Once inside, the old man shuffled up the aisle and selected a seat beside his leader. Over the bus's less than quiet muffler, he gently pressed Rocco for resolution. "So if those gringos weren't coming to fight with the Salineros, who do you think they were?" he asked in a conciliatory tone.

"There is no way to know," the leader replied. "The only thing we can be sure of is that they weren't coming to help us Tejanos, and that's all that matters."

"So many have died in this war, Rocco. So many wives and mothers mourn over something so simple as salt. It is a shame, but I should not have confronted you in front of the men."

"We both know this is all about more than just salt. The Salineros lord that mineral over our heads to control us. We need salt to survive, my friend," Rocco replied calmly, his voice indicating acceptance of the apology. "When everything went to hell, we lost so many. Our food spoiled, and the well water went bad. Only a modest amount of the crystalline mineral would have saved so many. We must have salt for our people to survive. The Salineros know this... they know we can't live without it, and yet they try to rob us blind for a resource that simply lays on the ground."

"But they believe it is their land and their salt. The gringos have always thought that way. They have held close the concept of individual ownership over all other things, including the wellbeing of their neighbors. The Comanche couldn't understand that way of living either... of personal property, or owning a hunk of the earth. I don't agree with it, but no one should be surprised that they fight to protect what they believe is their God-given property."

Rocco surveyed the passing desert through the dust-covered window glass, bored with what seemed to be an endless debate. He, like the majority of his village, was beyond questioning the justification of the war. Now, his mind was occupied with the burden of leadership and the goal of winning the conflict. It was the only path he could see to end his people's plight.

"Not long ago, after the trucks stopped coming to the village, five pounds of salt cost a pound of meat. Then the Salineros raised the price, doubling the amount we had to pay. Next, they wanted ammunition, tequila, tomatoes, and corn. Our people were already starving, but we traded and suffered while they sat back, hired more guns, and grew fat. Our children worked in the fields with their ribs sticking out while the gringos were stockpiling the results of our labor. And still it wasn't enough. Do you remember, Señor? Do you recall the night they raided the village and took the girls?"

The old man grimaced, crossing himself and mumbling. "God help their souls."

"That was the end of my rope," Rocco whispered, touched by the memory. "That night changed so many of us. Before, I was a peaceful farmer, and now I carry a gun to kill men."

Bishop knew water was the key to his family's survival. His Camelbak held a few quarts, the two additional plastic bottles in his pack doubling their supply. But that wasn't nearly enough, especially considering the bone-dry, hot desert terrain.

Food wouldn't be an issue right away, the emergency MREs sufficient for at least 3-4 days if they were careful.

Keeping vigil at the opening of their shelter, he watched patiently as the shadows grew longer across the valley below. Any concern over pursuit had vanished long ago; now he was waiting for the light and heat to fade so he could scout the surrounding territory.

"I'm going to do a little exploring," he informed Terri. "There might be a huge shopping mall right over this crest, and we'd never know it."

His wife grunted, pointing to a sleeping Hunter. "Be sure to check out aisle 4 while you are there and see if they have some diapers."

"Seriously," Bishop continued, "We're going to have to make a decision very soon. I don't know this area at all, and we are either going to have to stay put and wait for someone to come looking for us or try to walk out."

"I don't like either option," she responded, "but I do understand that we have some hard choices ahead of us."

"I'm going to circle our little hacienda, no more than a half mile in any direction. If there's water nearby or some other sign of civilization, then we can form a plan around that. If not, then at least we'll know. You need to keep watch while I'm gone - just in case."

Terri nodded, kissing him on the cheek. "How will I know it's you coming back in?" she asked, hefting her rifle.

"Do you remember our signal when we were staying back at the ranch?"

Smiling, she nodded. "You would throw a rock onto the camper roof. It used to scare the crap out of me, but then I was always so relieved that you were home and safe."

"That seems like a lifetime ago," Bishop replied, his tone

reminiscent. "This is going to sound funny, but in a way, I kind of miss those days."

Terri considered her husband's remark. "Really? I remember both of us losing weight like crazy, worrying about where we would get our next meal. Hunter was on the way, and we didn't know how we were going to fill another stomach."

"Yes, but we were together. We were fighting our way through side by side. I don't know... I felt closer to you then. That's part of the reason I dreamed up this stupid vacation scheme."

She walked over to her mate, wrapping her arms around his neck. "I remember all those candles you sat out at Christmas and the reflection on the water. That was one of the most beautiful things I've ever seen."

Bishop returned her embrace, his hands circling to the small of her back and drawing her close. "I'll never forget that peppered bacon you somehow found in the market. Damn... that was about the best gift ever."

Terri rested her head against his chest, enjoying the moment. After a bit, she said, "If you want me to resign from the council, I will. Our life together is far more important than anything I'm doing there."

Bishop's hands moved to her shoulders, holding her at arms' length so he could peer into her eyes. "Don't be silly, young lady. What you're doing for the Alliance is a million times more beneficial right now. I'm just an old softie, feeling sorry for myself for not getting as much of your attention as I want. Our time will come, and it will be a better life because of the sacrifices we're making now."

Her cheek returned to his chest; Terri nestling in his strong embrace. "I love you," she whispered.

After a brief, extra squeeze, he responded, "I love you, too."

Chapter 2

"There's no rule that says any person or community has to join the Alliance," Nick stated firmly.

"Then what are you doing here?" came the surly response.

Nick leaned back, the folding chair issuing a creaky protest under the heavily muscled man's weight. Knowing this was a critical point in the mission, he wanted to take his time before responding. He pondered how Bishop would reply. Terri? Diana?

"We are here merely to introduce ourselves to any isolated communities who may be unaware of the recovery. We offer an alternative... a different route. If the people of Cartersville don't want to be a part of our effort, then so be it."

The locals referred to the man across the table as "Mr. Gospel." Nick's team, during its infiltrations, had learned his real name was Henry Standowski.

Mr. Gospel was the area's head honcho, and after trying to reason with the man, Nick was beginning to think the fellow might be a head case, as well.

The two representatives were seated on the courthouse lawn, aides quickly retrieving a card table and several folding chairs to facilitate the public meeting. "We make our decisions out in the open," Standowski announced. "We let any citizen watch."

Word had spread quickly, the temporary conference room of grass and shade soon surrounded by dozens of people. There was a stranger in town, a man who claimed to be from some newly formed government, and he's meeting with Gospel.

Rising from his own lawn chair, Mr. Gospel scanned the surrounding crowd that had gathered to watch the proceedings. His expression progressed from contemplative to irate.

"When civilized society ceased to exist," began the middle-aged man. "I was running the local Teamsters 157. Cartersville had been blessed with one unique advantage at that time - we were smack-dab-center between Dallas, Texarkana, and Shreveport. The interstates had saved what was a dying town. Every freight company operating west of the Mississippi wanted a facility here. The mechanics, truck stops, tire stores, and other infrastructure soon followed."

Mr. Standowski paused, sweeping his arm across the horizon. "These people," he continued, "all the hearty souls left in Cartersville, owe their lives to the teamsters. When I realized the government wasn't coming back, I sent out the word as far as our CB radios would carry – bring your rig to our town; we'll protect you. And they did... by the hundreds they rolled in, carrying trailers stocked with food, tankers full of fuel, cattle cars, and chickens by the thousands."

"And you've done a remarkable job, Mr. Standowski," Nick smiled. "Those were trying times for everyone, and I can see with my own eyes that the fine citizens of Cartersville have fared better than most."

"I spread the good word over the air waves," the man continued, ignoring Nick's compliment. "And then I approached the mayor and city council advising them, 'Let the teamsters in. Welcome those drivers; you'll be glad you did.'"

Nick decided to let the man go, simply nodding in acknowledgment. It was a good play as Mr. Gospel clearly wasn't finished addressing his flock.

"According to the drifters I've talked to, Cartersville is probably the only town in the area whose population actually increased after the collapse. Our people didn't starve like everywhere else. Our folks didn't suffer. But it wasn't easy, young man."

Standowski spread his hands wide, still making his case. "When the stragglers started showing up, I spoke up again. 'Shut the gate,' I told the mayor. 'Those folks have nothing to offer our community. They will bleed our food and medicine stores dry, and when it's all gone, there will be trouble.' But they didn't listen. They were soft men with charitable souls, and we all paid a steep price for their generosity."

Nick was curious now, the man he was negotiating with taking it upon himself to fill in a lot of the blanks.

Mr. Gospel continued, his growing passion obvious in his voice as his tale progressed. "We took up arms. I had my union boys and a lot of the truckers. We even got the chief of police to join us, but it was too late. The first wave was the flu; the second was cholera. Dysentery took its share of lives as well. We were resource poor... lacking drugs for our ill and having no way to process the sewage. We buried hundreds of friends and neighbors."

Cartersville's leader turned and scanned the crowd, his voice carrying to the masses. "You all remember what that was like, don't you?" Then, without waiting for anyone to answer, he continued, "Well, of course you do. How could any of us forget?"

Nick looked around, noting the dozens of heads nodding in agreement.

"My heart ached for the people we had to turn away. They were truly the unwashed masses, hundreds of coughing, begging, sickly souls. But we had to keep them and their diseases out of our town. Some left peaceably; some didn't. It was necessary to deal harshly with the troublemakers."

"I've seen and heard similar accounts from all over Texas," Nick stated. "It was a struggle for every city and town. You all should be proud of how well you weathered the storm. But things are getting better. There is a recovery in process... tens of thousands of like-minded survivors who now have electricity, medical care, fuel for cars and trucks, and full bellies. I came here today to extend the hand of friendship, to invite you to join the new nation we're trying to build."

Standowski tilted his head, digesting Nick's spiel. It didn't take long before he pronounced his judgment. "Not interested," he stated bluntly. Then, addressing the throng, he began to explain his decision. "Most of you call me Mr. Gospel... a man who spreads truth and the good word. So please, listen to my words again. We've seen every con man, criminal, desperado and villain imaginable approach our community. They've all been polished, smooth, and seemingly above board. Yet in every, single case, these charlatans have caused harm to Cartersville. We don't need any Alliance. We're doing just fine. It was big government that caused all of our pain and suffering the last time. Washington and Austin made all kinds of high-sounding promises before, and look what happened. No thank you, Mr. Alliance. We're not interested."

Mr. Gospel's eyes bored into Nick, almost daring the envoy to debate his logic. But the bait wasn't taken.

Spreading his hands, Nick sighed, "As you wish."

Nick rose from the card table, extending his hand to Mr. Gospel. The gesture was ignored. Instead, Standowski turned to his second in command and began whispering orders.

The gathered throng divided, allowing a path for Nick to make his exit, many of the onlookers staring rudely at the foreigner in their town. Glancing at his watch, the big man realized the negotiations hadn't taken nearly as long as he'd planned. Kevin and the rest of the team wouldn't arrive at the rendezvous point for another four hours.

It was supposed to have been a simple introduction to the Alliance, one of a dozen ongoing operations occurring throughout what had been the state of Texas. Small teams were spreading out, scouting the local populations, introducing the new government to any leadership, and extending a friendly hand to let them know that a recovery was in process. Given its fascination with labeling everything with an acronym, the military had dubbed the peaceable missions SAINTs – or Scout, Approach, INtroduce, and Transition. Members of the teams charged with performing such assignments referred to them as "Pandoras" instead, because the emissaries never knew what to expect.

Cartersville also was important strategically to the Alliance's future growth. As Mr. Gospel had stated, the town was located in a prime location for transportation, and more importantly, it was key to the region's most prominent natural resource – timber.

Recovery meant rebuilding, and that required lumber. Trees had to be harvested and milled, the finished product then transported to distribution centers where end users could access the desperately needed raw material. Cartersville boasted massive numbers of semi-trailers, close proximity to major interstates, and resided smack-dab in the middle of the Great Piney Woods.

When Nick's SAINT team had been tasked with the critical assignment, the council's planners had referred to the small berg as a "twofer," meaning the Alliance could receive double benefits from one mission – if they pulled it off.

Since the collapse, the Alliance had encountered a variety of social hierarchies that had formed to fill the vacuum in leaderless communities. When federal, state, and local government collapsed, it was only human nature for some form of organization to occupy the void.

They had confronted everything from escaped convicts combatting church groups to local business leaders using their corporate assets to establish control. Law enforcement assumed command over some areas while rogue military units had become dominant in others.

While the Alliance teams had no way of predicting the specifics for any given town or community, a few reoccurring trends had quickly emerged.

Groups sporting a chain of command and organizational structure before the collapse were provided an advantage afterward. Almost every replacement "administration" they encountered had existed in one form or another before the world had gone to hell. It didn't matter if the chain of command was based on religion, race, gang affiliation, or business... having an in-place hierarchy, known leadership, communications, and some level of trust allowed these groups to rise to power, establishing their positions faster than any random caucus of previously unassociated citizens.

The second trend was the most troubling. In the hell on earth of the aftermath, democracy had ceased to exist. Darwinism had prevailed in practically every hamlet and metropolitan area across the wasteland that had been the United States. The strongest had not only survived, but also subjugated their surrounding areas. Often this resulted in brutal dictatorships enforcing draconian measures on the meeker population. Wolves and sheep, Nick thought. It's always been that way, always will be. Some days, I feel like a sheepdog, leading the downtrodden to safety.

At first, it had been easy for the Alliance leadership to criticize these desperate reformations of society. Brute strength, the best firearms, or possessing the most ammunition seemed such anti-American processes of establishing leadership. But as time wore on, it became apparent that in many cases, there simply hadn't been any viable alternative. The heavy-handed corporate executive may have taken over the town out of desperation, perhaps rallying survivors to bury the bodies so the entire population didn't succumb to virulent plagues. Maybe gangs of nomadic raiders had been robbing the locals blind, picking them off one by one, thus forcing the community to form a militia to defend itself.

The third trend occurred naturally. Power is a seductive temptress, and many of the leaders encountered by the Alliance simply didn't want to give up their hard-won positions any more than they would like walking away from a sensual woman. While there were exceptions, those were far and few between. Once tasted, men develop an undeniable craving for control and influence. Galveston Island had been one of the more notable examples as of late, as were Meraton and Fort Davidson. Even then, the lack of communications, nonexistent infrastructure, and a healthy dose of distrust made initial contact with each of these communities difficult, if not dangerous. Thousands had already died due to early missteps and mistakes in the reintegration process.

"So much for getting lucky," Nick whispered as he negotiated the town. "Figures I'd run into one of the more Machiavellian groups. Damn it, Bishop... of all the times for you to want to work on your tan."

He headed toward the small city park where he'd been instructed to pitch his tent. All of the town's motels or hotels were occupied, converted into apartments to accommodate the influx of truck drivers that descended on the tiny berg. There wasn't a boardinghouse or inn available. Visitors were allowed to camp, the temporary housing area scrutinized carefully by several armed deputies. Everyone referred to the place as "Shantytown."

Deciding he'd grab a quick meal and then catch up on some sleep, Nick was actually pleased with how the operation was progressing. A seed had been planted. Whether or not it grew was out of his control. He'd done his job, accomplishing an introduction without bloodshed on either side.

He meandered across the town square, nodding politely to passersby, smiling at anyone who made eye contact. His path took him through what the locals called the "Exchange," two closed streets that resembled Meraton's now-famous market. Unlike the West Texas community's place of commerce, the Exchange was closely monitored and tightly controlled. Taxes were collected, fees charged, disputes dealt with harshly. Mr. Gospel and his men ran the whole show. They had even taken to printing their own currency.

Wishing he had more time to study and observe, Nick made his way down the bustling street, hawkers offering him everything from dry goods to homemade remedies for whatever ailed him.

It was all so interesting. Here, in rural northeastern Texas, was a textbook example of a city-state under feudal rule of law. Cartersville had a king, noblemen, coin of the realm, and even a castle-keep of sorts – the downtown area being walled off with roadblocks, patrols, semi-trailers, and guard towers. It was a microcosm of Europe's Middle Ages, unveiled right before his eyes.

As he ambled through on his way to Shantytown and his camp, Nick studied the faces of customers and vendors alike. These citizens submitted willingly to Mr. Gospel's rule, supporting the primitive form of government by their mere presence and participation. They all seemed content enough, buying, selling, and browsing through the open-air bazaar.

But Nick knew there was a difference between these people and the residents of the kingdoms of old. He was surrounded by freeborn Americans, individuals who had tasted liberty, had experienced democracy. They accepted the status quo because it was a safe harbor from the anarchy and barbarianism just beyond the walls. But now, if the Alliance leaders and he were right, all of that would gradually begin to change. Now they knew something better was beyond the fortress, an existence that would, hopefully, stir memories of a better life.

General Owens and the military forces under the council's control could take down the local king in an afternoon. Irregular militia, equipped with small arms, didn't stand a chance against tanks and gunships. But the Alliance had learned a hard lesson from previous engagements – the loss of life could be significant, and that wasn't what the new government was all about. Bishop's recent encounter in Brighton, Texas had exposed the unintended consequences of a brash, heavily armed approach. That community was still suffering from the mass causalities, hundreds of families continuing to mourn the loss of husbands, brothers, and sons. Even under Alliance rule, life was severe there, food hard enough to put on the table, despite the presence of able-bodied men in the household. Widows and orphans stressed the resources of the entire community, their struggles significantly more difficult and painful. Resentment still lingered just under the surface of the societal façade.

Nick stopped, the smell of boiling corn drawing his attention. He retrieved a small amount of local currency out of his pocket, smirking at the image of Mr. Gospel's stoic portrait residing on the poorly manufactured paper money. "How much for two ears?" he asked the middle-aged woman working the small booth.

"Aren't you that stranger talking about a recovery?" she inquired, eyes squinting with pessimism.

"Yes, ma'am. That's me."

"Is it true... what they're saying? Are there really towns nearby with electricity and real jobs?"

"Yes. It's true," Nick answered, amazed at how quickly word had spread.

The vendor scanned both directions, checking to see who was within earshot. "Can I move there? Do they allow strangers to settle there?" she whispered.

"Yes, you can. We welcome newcomers. Every town has a relocation committee."

Again glancing both ways and finding the coast was clear, she pulled a significant wad of King Gospel's currency from under her apron. "I've got money," she declared. "People say my vegetables are the best in the Exchange. But I want to get out of here. Mr. Gospel keeps raising the taxes and taking a bigger cut. You have to be cautious what you say here... careful about who might hear. My boy got in trouble for speaking out last week, and now the deputies are watching him real, real close."

Nick nodded his understanding, a dozen questions forming in his throat. Before he could ask, two armed men came into view, one of the many patrols working the outside market. His new friend's eyes dropped down to the pot, not daring to make eye contact with the passing enforcers.

"The maize is two Gospels per ear," she said louder than necessary, no doubt for the lawmen's sake. "I don't give a discount unless you buy at least four."

Nick played along, having no desire to get anyone in trouble with the authorities. "I'll take two," he responded, counting out the required bills.

The steaming corn was delivered, complete with husks still intact. Nick moved on, thinking his extra-large frame could use a little more sustenance and sick to death of the dried food in his pack.

Eyeing a table stacked with tomatoes, he sensed a presence behind him. A slight turn of his head revealed the two deputies, each assuming a tactical position on either side of the display.

Nick ignored the local enforcers, checking the firmness and color of several vine-ripened examples on the table. The vendor, an older gent who had smiled warmly at his approach, backed away. That reaction was immediately followed by the sound of tap, tap, tap... one of the deputies slapping his palm with a nightstick.

"Morning, gentlemen," Nick said politely, turning to face the two men. "Can I help you?"

"We're wondering why you haven't left yet," replied the older of the two. "Our understanding was your business here in Cartersville was complete."

Nick sized them up, the confrontational body language making their intent clear. Both would be considered large men by any standard, their thick shoulders and wide frames so prevalent with law enforcement types. While the ex-operator's 6'4" barefoot height and considerable mass dwarfed either of the locals, he didn't want any trouble. Besides, they were armed – he was not.

"I'm heading out soon enough," he replied with a smile. "My people won't be at the gate for a bit, and I wanted to get a bite to eat and then break camp."

"Mr. Gospel thinks it would be better if you broke camp right now and ate along the road," came the reply.

A frown of concern and fear crossed the big man's face, but it was an act. Inside, he was secretly celebrating, Standowski's loosing of his dogs a sure sign the man was worried. Nick shrugged, "Fine by me, I can wait for my friends outside just as well as on the inside. I'll go pack up my gear."

The verbal deputy seemed disappointed Nick had deescalated the encounter. "We'll tag along – just to make sure you don't get lost."

Nick found his poncho-tent and pack undisturbed. Before breaking camp, he strolled to a neighboring bivouac and pulled out the remainder of his Gospel dollars. "Thanks for watching my stuff, Ray," he said, handing over the small wad of money.

The two enforcers idled nearby, chatting among themselves as Nick stuffed items inside his pack. "Ready," he informed the officers, swinging the ruck onto his back.

The gate was really nothing more than a barricaded street at the edge of town. Having managed the teamsters allowed Mr. Gospel access to a virtually unlimited numbers of semi-trailers, which became the breastworks and parapets of choice.

While erecting a castle wall around Cartersville provided security, it also created the same issues suffered by its European brother from long ago. Agriculture and livestock couldn't exist within the city limits, yet the people inside the protective perimeter had to eat. It was impossible for the town to completely isolate itself - thus the blockaded entrance.

When Nick's team had first been assigned to approach the humble berg, a quick scouting mission had uncovered the rules and procedures for passing through. Countryside residents were allowed access, but they had to be unarmed and possess goods for trade or sale. Anyone displaying the obvious symptoms of a contagious disease was turned away.

Handing off his weapons to Kevin and Grim, Nick had pocketed small amounts of ammunition as his barter. After spending three days checking out the local situation, he'd approached the men in charge and made his pitch about the Alliance. One thing had led to another, eventually resulting in this morning's meeting with Mr. Gospel in the flesh.

In reality, Nick hadn't expected much more from the local leadership. His presentation of the Alliance's goals, history, and future had to be shocking to hear for the first time. Even if Mr. Gospel and his union boys didn't relinquish their iron grip on Cartersville, eventually the people of the town would start to drift away. Freedom, commerce, security, and prosperity were powerful magnets to a distressed population.

Approaching the southern gate, Nick spotted two more deputies idling along the route. When they noticed the big man and his escorts, both enforcers stiffened, their body language indicating a higher level of alert.

Moving to block Nick's path, the older ordered the big man to stop. "I need to see inside that pack," he growled.

Having nothing to hide, Nick pulled the ruck off his shoulders and set it down on the ground. The two new lawmen began pulling his belongings out, a quiet crowd gathering to watch.

As they neared the bottom, Nick noticed one of the deputies try a slight of hand, something bright and red hidden in the man's palm. A moment later, the enforcer raised that same hand, holding a tomato high in the air for everyone to see.

"That's not mine," Nick said calmly. "You already had that in your palm."

"Bullshit!" barked the deputy. "You stole this from the market. We had a complaint."

"Really? Seriously? You're going to plant a vegetable on me and then claim I'm some sort of shoplifter? That's all you got?" Nick responded, his tone making it clear he wasn't taking the charge seriously.

"So this is what your so-called Alliance is all about," boomed Mr. Gospel's voice as the crowd parted to let the local leader approach the scene of the crime. "You come in here all high and mighty, telling everyone that you stand for the rule of law, democracy, and a better way of life. Now we know that's bullshit... you've just proven you're nothing more than a petty thief."

Nick understood the man was preaching to the gathered public. Two could play at that game. "That's rich, my friend, especially coming from a power-hungry dictator who's frightened of losing his subjects," Nick replied. "You're trying to frame me in order to keep your people from moving to a better place."

"Arrest this criminal," Standowski ordered, unwilling to be drawn into a debate.

Nick sensed the two deputies approach him from behind, the closest throwing his arm toward the big man's neck, an attempt to grasp his throat and then pull Nick over onto his back. It was a standard law enforcement tactic and very effective against the average suspect. But Nick wasn't average.

Catching the flying arm with both hands, Nick ducked under and twisted in the same motion. Before anyone else could react, he had the deputy's arm behind the man's back and was reaching for the holstered Glock on the lawman's belt.

The other rearward enforcer tried to step in and assist his comrade, and that was a mistake. Nick torqued on his prisoner, spinning the now howling deputy into his mate, knocking him to the pavement. By then, the Glock was free of its holster.

Still maintaining his grip on the first guy's arm, Nick crouched low, using the enforcer's body as a shield. Both of the forward deputies were pulling their weapons when Nick shot the first man in the leg; the second took a 9mm slug to his Kevlar-protected chest.

Absolute bedlam erupted through the surrounding crowd. Women were screaming, men yelling warnings and the entire populace was trying to run somewhere... anywhere to get away from the roar of gunfire.

Nick pistol whipped his shield, slamming the barrel hard into the back of the man's neck. The fourth deputy had finally managed to palm his weapon, but it was too late. Like a football punter, Nick took one big step and landed his size 14 boot squarely on the enforcer's temple.

In less than five seconds, all four of Gospel's henchmen were disabled. The former union boss stood speechless, fear filling his eyes, watching Nick point the captured weapon at his head.

"I'm going to give you one warning, Standowski... and only one. Don't start a fucking war you can't win. This was a minor league play against a professional, and there are thousands and thousands more just like me in the Alliance. If you ever pull such bullshit again, I'll personally kill you ... and do it slowly."

For the first time since Nick had been around Mr. Gospel, the local leader didn't have any good news to share. In fact, he was speechless.

Nick glanced once more at his attackers moaning on the ground and shook his head. "Shame you ordered these men to do your dirty work, and all because you are a coward. Hard telling how many of your people are going to die if things get really rough," he stated, and then began jogging for the nearby gate.

There were four guards at the barricade, all of them having heard gunshots just a few moments before, none of them knowing what or who was involved. Before Gospel could gather his courage or wits, Nick passed by the armed sentries and was outside the wall.

Kevin, Grim, and Cory were scheduled to meet Nick just over a mile outside of town. With only an occasional glance over his shoulder, Nick casually strolled along the road, seemingly confident no one from Cartersville would be stupid enough to chase after him.

He had completely overestimated Mr. Gospel's intelligence.

Ten minutes and half a mile later, the distinct hum of engines sounded from the receding town. Nick stopped his trek, turning to see what possible dumb ass stunt his former hosts might have in mind. He didn't have to wait long for the ill-conceived plot to be exposed.

Soon the emissary could identify at least a half dozen pickups, the beds piled full of men brandishing rifles in the air. The vision pissed Nick off.

Seconds later, he was running through the pine woods bordering the road, moving at a rapid pace while growling profanities at the ignorance that dominated Cartersville, Texas.

The tracks and manure put Bishop on the trail. A shod horse, maybe two, had passed this way not long ago. Soon, he encountered some older tracking signs, a confusion of hoof marks trotting both directions. Somebody was using this route on a consistent basis. Cresting a small rise, he spotted the riders, the picture-perfect scene worthy of a dime store postcard.

They were 300 yards distant, the blood-red sun casting its matchless pigment on the backdrop of the Guadalupe Mountains from its vantage near the western horizon. Two horsemen perched on their trusty steeds, the outline of their western hats tilted low, their posture indicating they were saddle-weary from a long ride. They were headed toward Bishop.

Were it not for the time and place, Bishop would have assumed they were two ranch hands, riding fence or looking for strays. As the pair ventured closer, the silhouette of battle rifles carried across the saddle horns completely ruined the earlier, picturesque image.

The Texan traced their route, the older tracks he'd been following a clear indication of their intended course. A short distance away, he identified the perfect hiding spot, a rock formation that would allow the armed men to pass directly beneath him.

After a quick, scrambling climb, he was waiting. The gentle hoof falls in the soft, sandy soil confirmed he'd conjectured correctly, watching the armed men pass not more than 15 feet away.

"Evening," he said, startling both men.

The one in front started to turn, his rifle coming up. "I wouldn't," Bishop barked, his tone deep and stern. "I got the drop on ya, fair and square. I just want to talk."

The rifle returned to rest across the saddle horn, both men craning their necks to catch a glimpse of the man who was behind the voice from up in the rocks.

What they saw must have seemed odd to the cowboys. Bishop was above them, his load vest bristling with pouches and magazines, thick body armor and kit swelling the Texan's outline. While the steady muzzle of the M4 rifle communicated the seriousness of their situation, it was the cold, unblinking stare of the stranger's eyes that sent fear racing through the rider's veins.

"Why did you ambush my wife and me?" Bishop asked. "Why did you shoot up my truck?"

"We never shot up no truck, mister. Swear it. We thought we heard some gunfire earlier today, but it wasn't us," replied the older of the two.

Something in the man's voice led Bishop to believe the words, but there wasn't any way to be sure. "Okay, say I buy that story for a minute. What brings you two fine gentlemen out this way, complete with AR15 rifles and binoculars?"

"We ride for the Salineros," replied the younger man, quickly recovering from the shock of Bishop's appearance. "We work for Mr. Culpepper, and you're on Culpepper land."

"Salineros?" Bishop questioned, trying to recall his seldom used, barely passable Spanish. "Salt men?"

Bishop observed the forearm muscles ripple across the

young rider's arm, his grip on his rifle tightening. "I wouldn't, son. I've got a four-pound trigger on this blaster, and my finger is already at three and a half. You'll never make it."

The senior of the two reached across, putting downward pressure on his partner's arm. "Don't," he whispered. His gaze then directed at Bishop. "Mister, I'll say it again; we never shot up no truck. The last fighting our outfit did was two days ago. I'm guessing it was the Tejanos that bushwhacked you."

"The Tejanos?"

"That's what they call themselves. They're mostly Mexicans from a small village right across the river. They've ginned up some of the outlying ranchers and farmers, got them to join their side as well. There's been trouble in these parts for the last four months... kind of a range war, if you will."

Bishop was puzzled. What was there to fight over? The area was remote, with slight population and even less resources. Further south of here, the Rio Grande valley wasn't tillable like so much of the river's shoreline. Vertical canyons and sandstone rock formations were landscaping mainstays of the border area, a heaven for climbers and campers, but not of much value for agricultural pursuits. Still, why hadn't the Alliance been aware of this ongoing conflict?

"Can you explain why these Tejanos would open fire on an innocent passerby?" Bishop asked.

The two riders peered at each other, obviously vacillating about how to answer the question. "Look fellas, I'm not having a good day," Bishop began. "Somebody shot up my new pickup, damned near killed my wife and baby son, and left us to perish out here in God knows where without water or food. Those horses you're riding look like my ticket out of this shithole, so start talking before I decide to knock both of your asses out of those saddles and canter back home."

Sighing, the older man nodded. "Mr. Culpepper has been hiring men to shore up our side. The Tejanos obviously don't like that much. Could be they thought you were new employees heading to the ranch and decided to waylay ya."

"I see," Bishop responded. "And where might this hacienda be?"

Again, the two caballeros hesitated to answer, almost as if they were protecting some military secret. Bishop was growing tired of their games. "Do the Tejanos know where the Salineros spread is?"

"Look, stranger," the older cowpoke said. "Why don't we just give you and your family a ride to the ranch? You can talk to Mr. Culpepper and sort all this out. As long as you're not working for the Tejanos, there's no ill will on our part."

Bishop considered their offer, his first reaction a negative one. He had been chased by hot lead; his pickup had been turned into a hunk of bullet-peppered metal, and he'd been forced to take a life. The thought of strolling into an armed camp, hostile or not, didn't sound like a winning proposition.

But, on the other hand, Terri and Hunter wouldn't last long out here in the desert. Even if his family did manage to hike out, it would be a dicey experience, riddled with agony, fear, and misery. He visualized Terri trekking out of the sandy inferno, massive dehydration headache, blistered lips, and burned skin. I would never have sex again, he rationalized.

Guilt, spawned by the awareness that his plan had landed his family in the middle of this mess, superseded his pessimistic outlook. "Okay, friend, we can do that. Keep riding south for another 200 yards and then cut over the ridge. We'll pick up my wife and son there."

Terri was spooning small portions of what the military called mashed potatoes into Hunter's eager mouth. "Here comes the airplane," she smiled, swooping the spoon through the air to keep his attention. Between bites, she scanned the ever darker desert beyond, wondering how much longer Bishop would be gone.

The single, small stone bouncing off a nearby ledge answered her question, but her relief was short-lived. Two men leading horses were approaching.

Much to Hunter's surprise, the infant found himself being scooped up from his improvised high chair. Now he was the airplane. Setting her child on a makeshift bed comprised of Bishop's spare shirt, Terri darted back to the entrance in a flash.

She had just centered the red dot on the lead man when Bishop's profile came into view. Taking a deep breath to slow her racing heart, she lowered her weapon but still kept it handy.

"Terri," Bishop called, "I've brought home some new friends for dinner."

"Are you going to skin and dress them before I sauté them?" she asked, instantly regretting the smart-ass remark.

Laughing, Bishop responded, "Very amusing. These men work for a local rancher by the name of Culpepper. Gentlemen, meet my better half, Terri."

Both men removed their hats. "Ma'am," the two responded in unison.

"They've volunteered to let Hunter and you ride one of their horses out of here. They claim the ranch isn't far away, and that we'd be more comfortable there."

A thousand questions swirled around Terri's brain, but she suppressed them, still embarrassed over her verbal faux paus. "If you think it is safe, Hunter and I are all for it. We're already bored with the amenities at this rustic establishment."

Bishop signaled for the two cowboys to stop several feet from the entrance. "Be right back," he announced, moving past them to help Terri pack their meager belongings.

"Do you trust them?" Terri whispered as he walked by.

"Not for a second," the Texan replied, bending to refill his pack with the items Terri had scattered around the nook. "But it's the lesser of two evils, I suppose."

Before he realized what was happening, Terri was retrieving Hunter, leaving the two men unwatched. The sound of "Ya!" followed by the pounding of hooves reached his ears before he could make it back to the entrance.

Bishop raised his rifle, zeroing in on the lead rider as the two Culpepper men raced away at a full gallop. But he didn't fire, instead lowering the weapon and barking, "Shit!"

"I just messed up, didn't I," Terri confessed, arriving at his side, watching the two horsemen grow smaller in the distance. "I guess I should have kept an eye on them while you were packing. I just didn't realize...."

"It's okay," Bishop mumbled, "I should have been more specific. It's been a while since we've worked together."

"Well, at least you don't have to pack up just yet."

"Actually, I think we'd better find a new place and do so quickly before it gets dark. They know where we're camped now. They might decide to come back with more of their friends."

Kevin stood in the pickup's bed, scanning the logging lane with his high-powered optic. "See him yet?" Cory asked from behind the wheel.

"Nope. He'll be along... you know dad."

Grim, taking a knee 20 meters inside the tree line, was making sure nobody approached from the cover of the pines. "He's late," the ex-contractor observed, "which these days, doesn't mean squat. We better start thinking about making camp."

"Coming in," a voice from the forest thundered, the sound

triggering two rifle barrels to snap toward the source. No one relaxed until Nick's outline appeared through the foliage.

Kevin, despite wanting desperately to be treated like just one of the guys, leapt from the bed and dashed to hug his father. The embrace was returned with a warm smile.

The rest of Nick's team was happy to see their leader return as well, handshakes all around.

"I'd love to stay and trade recipes with you ladies," Nick stated, moving with purpose to the boxes of supplies in the back of the truck. "But I've got about 40 guys tracking me, and I don't think they're a happy bunch. I need my rifle and the rest of my kit."

Pulling off his pack, Nick began rummaging through the supplies, stuffing his ruck with food and full magazines of ammunition.

Grim grunted, reading between the lines. "I take it you managed to make new friends and influence the locals. Diana is going to require your enrollment in charm school, my friend."

Nick smiled and nodded, "Everything was going fine until today. That's when the road got a little rough."

Kevin, his gaze fixed in the direction his father had come, was worried. "Seriously, Dad? You've got that many men trying to kill you? We better get you out of here, and right away."

"No, son, that's not how we're going to play this one. Gather round, gentlemen, and let me dazzle you with the brilliance of my plan."

Chapter 3

The incessant wailing of the village's women grated on Rocco's nerves. The anger of the men only amplified the leader's own frustration and rage. Javier had been one of the few in the community to finish school, his uncle in Mexico City sending money to the family so the young man wouldn't have to work the fields and could stay in the classroom.

Javier had been an icon of hope... of an optimistic future. His mother would never again good-naturedly chide him for leaving his boots in the hall. His younger sister and brother would never again relax after dinner while Javier fingered a tune on his guitar. The promising, young man was now buried in a hole on the hill behind the settlement.

As was his habit, when the pressures of the world grew too strong, Rocco walked. When a fever ravaged the livestock, he walked. When his wife experienced complications in childbirth, he walked. When he believed the blood of the current war was on his hands, he walked.

His route was well established. Across the knoll, past the oak, along the river, and through the canyon. The solitude, combined with the familiarity of local landmarks, instilled a sense of peace to his troubled soul. He often paused for a heart to heart with the tree, the largest growing plant for many miles. Its shade had provided an oasis for games and play, used by the village's children since he had been a boy.

Sometimes, he saved his confessions for the waterway.

Conversation with the oak was for those moments when he felt his words needed to be remembered, preserved in the record of the tree's fiber and bark. The river was for those times when his thoughts deserved to be carried away by the current or drowned in the muddy, swirling stream.

He reserved the canyon for deep contemplation during times when he was conflicted. Here, the solid stone, precipitous walls, and echoing structure served to reflect his emotions – a mirror of sentiment or angst through which he could achieve clarity.

Tonight, he saved his outburst for the canyon.

"We wanted none of this," he hissed at the unforgiving, inflexible, rocky gorge. "Our only desire is to raise our children, celebrate our festivals, and put food on our tables. Greed is a stranger to my people. Wealth an illusion. Why do pain, suffering, and strife have to find their way to our homes? We are undeserving of this bad fortune."

Concise thought would have concentrated Rocco's anger

on the occupants of the pickup. Reasonable logic would have identified the strangers as the source of his grief. But the war had taken his mind far, far beyond any rational connection of direct cause and effect.

It was the Salineros who were responsible for Javier's short life. It was Culpepper and his band of mercenaries who were to blame. He wanted them to die - and die badly. Images of his enemy's homestead filled his mind, the ranch house engulfed in flames as his men stood and watched it burn.

He hungered to feel the sensation of his skinning knife, peeling away Salineros flesh, their screams of agony and pleadings for the mercy of a quick death music to his ears. His fantasy included bound Culpepper men and watching his soldiers take their turns with the captured women. Those whores, the ones who had birthed such scum, would be tied over barrels while the victorious Tejanos used their manhood as swords, plunging and violating over and over and over again. Their children would be enslaved, whipped to toil in the fields until reparations were paid.

Rocco shook his head in disgust. The canyon provided less relief with each revelation of his malicious thoughts, the rock walls evidently growing bored and dismissive with the continuing confessions of rage. Regardless of how vile his fury, even the stone was becoming immune and disinterested. He heard a message from the ancient formation... a lesson in time and life. "Stop this ridiculous fantasizing," scolded the granite. "You must be as I am, hard and uncaring, impervious to pain. Take action. Control your own destiny."

Continuing on his way, he finished the loop of his walking tour, strolling upon a group of men gathered in front of the church. From their expressions, he realized he wasn't the only one wrangling for revenge.

"We want to mount a night patrol," one of the more aggressive men announced. "Our ears are full of listening to Javier's mother wail. Our hearts demand blood, and we're not going to find it here. Are you with us?"

"Let me get my rifle," Rocco replied coldly.

Samuel Culpepper scanned the corral with a pessimistic eye, a worn and dusty boot perched on the lowest rung of the gate. One of his most robust stallions limped by, the midnight-colored animal having pulled up short two days ago.

They lacked in horseflesh, beef, ammunition, and manpower. "This ain't no way to run a war," the ranch's owner mumbled.

"I can't argue that, Mr. Culpepper," Whitey responded, the foreman's eyes studying the same lame steed. "But sometimes you go to the war, and sometimes the war comes to you. We're holding our own, sir."

Maybe, thought Culpepper. Maybe not. We sure have buried our share of good men.

Their conversation was interrupted by the lookout on top of a nearby outbuilding. "Men coming in... at a gallop," the shouted communication warned.

All around the area, the hired hands scrambled, dropping bales of straw, bags of feed, and other common items associated with a working ranch. In a few moments, wire cutters, shovels, and hand tools were replaced with rifles and shotguns.

"Two men," informed the lookout, now scanning the approaching riders with large binoculars. "It's Reed and Hutch! Stand down! Everybody stand down!"

"What the hell are they doing coming in from that direction?" asked Mr. Culpepper, not really expecting Whitey to know. "How come they didn't give the signal?"

"No idea," the over watch replied. "Given the wear and tear they're putting on those horses, something has to be wrong."

A few minutes later, the riders were careened inside the compound, pulling back hard on the reins to stop their animals in front of the boss.

Reed started talking as he dismounted, "We were bushwhacked by a stranger," the man began reporting in a rushed voice. "Those shots we heard earlier this morning... it was some guy and his wife and kid. He claimed the Tejanos ambushed their truck."

"Whoa, whoa, slow down, son," Mr. Culpepper said. "What the hell are you talking about?"

At a more manageable speed this time, Lefty and Hutch relayed the story of Bishop getting the drop as they rode past, followed by a recounting of what the outsider had told them.

The old rancher rubbed his chin, pondering at his own pace. "What did you say this man's name was?"

"Bishop," Hutch replied. "His wife's name was Terri. Do you know them, sir?"

Mr. Culpepper turned to Whitey, "Last time you went to the market at Meraton, wasn't there some guy there who had just killed a bunch of outlaws? Wasn't his name Bishop?"

"Yes, sir, sure was. He was a very capable hombre according to the local gossip."

"Must be the same man, Mr. Culpepper. This fella got the better of us easy as pie. His rifle barrel wasn't wavering none, either. Cold, cold eyes on that fella," Hutch added.

"He looked like one of those soldier pictures I saw once up at the Alpha recruiting station," added Reed. "He had stuff all over his chest and fancy accessories on his rifle."

Culpepper chuckled, "So how did you manage to get away from this superhero?"

"He took us back to the encampment where his wife and kid were holed up. They turned their backs on us, and we high-tailed it out of there. He had them sheltering inside one of those cuts in Windy Ridge."

Whitey stepped forward, leaning in close to the boss and speaking in a hushed tone, "We could use a man like that about now, Mr. Culpepper. He probably has some friends in Meraton that might further our cause. Sounds like he's good and pissed at the Tejanos."

The old rancher hooked his thumbs in his pants pocket, his regard far away in thought. "Whitey, take a few of the boys and go bring them in. Maybe this bad ass named Bishop will appreciate his wife and child having a roof over their heads tonight."

"Shit!" Terri hissed, pausing to massage her stubbed foot. "I can't do this at night, Bishop. We have to find someplace soon, or I'm going to break my neck."

Her husband was obviously frustrated, the couple having wandered through the darkness for the last hour. Even with his night vision, their chances of finding suitable shelter in lowlight conditions were slim.

"I knew better than to try and find a hide in the dark," he whispered back. "But we didn't have any choice. Here, let me show you how to do this again. It helps."

Throwing the small lever that detached the NVD monocle from his rifle, Bishop passed the device to his wife. "You look through it and map out 10 steps. Visualize it your mind... memorize each footfall. Then repeat after you've walked that short distance. Try it."

Terri did as instructed, lifting the small optic to her eye and peering through. The world surrounding her suddenly became brighter, the landscape painted in glowing hues of black and green. "Why can't I just walk using this?" she asked in a quiet voice. "That would make it much easier."

"Because I need to use it to scout around. If we take turns and use our memories, we can move at a good pace and…"

Bishop stopped, the whinny and snort of a horse causing him to go on full alert. Terri heard it, too. After scanning their surroundings with the scope, he motioned Terri to a small space between two rocks. He was pleased that her rifle was already in her hands.

Putting his mouth right next to Terri's ear, Bishop whispered, "Stay here. Don't move. I'm going to see what's out there. Don't shoot me when I come back."

Terri wanted to protest, a hundred questions racing through her mind. How would she know it was him? What if Hunter cried out?

But he was gone, vanishing like a ghost into the blackness. "I hate it when he does that," she mouthed to a sleeping Hunter.

Rocco heard the horse too, the raiding party and he working their way through towards the Culpepper ranch. Their hastily formed plan was simple enough. They were hoping to catch a sleeping sentry or unaware guard. If they could get close enough, with the element of surprise, they could inflict some real damage onto their foe. If nothing else, they would cause the Salineros to lose some sleep.

The thought of riders being out at night was worrisome. It was particularly rare to skirmish after sunset, the majority of the war being conducted during daylight hours. Had his enemies come to the same conclusion – deciding to escalate as well? Were they upping the ante?

With a few hushed commands and vivid hand motions, he scattered his men to the rocks. He watched as best he could, the slender moon providing little light. Taking one last glance around, he was pleased – this was as good a place to set a trap as any. Rocco moved off to join his men and wait for the fly to enter the spider's web.

Whitey wasn't worried about an ambush, at least not from the Tejanos. His adversary never operated at night, and his own posse was venturing only a few miles from the ranch. While the enemy had gotten bolder over the last few weeks, his own men were still deep in Culpepper territory. Given the vast expanses of the desert and the hazy moon, the chances of two parties bumping into each other were next to nil.

This Bishop fellow… he might be another story.

Hutch and Reed were leading the way, fresh animals and a quick meal improving the two riders' resolve. The foreman hoped the cowpokes could remember the way back to the newcomers' hiding place, prayed this Bishop character wasn't trigger happy when it came to noises in the night. He planned to shout a greeting when they got close – approach under a white flag. It was risky… but the best he could manage.

As they wound their way up Windy Ridge, the boulder field grew denser. With every step, Whitey grew more apprehensive; the route was making him uncomfortable. The high rock formations provided a million hiding places, the rough terrain difficult on the horses. It just wasn't a good place to operate after sunset.

He reined in his mount, pulling to the side of the trail and listening while the remainder of his men and the pack animals passed. We're making too much noise, he determined. That's the problem with horses; it's almost impossible to keep them still.

Glancing toward the front of his column, Whitey could barely make out the lead rider in the distance. Not a good night to be out hunting for man nor beast, he mused.

Despite the lack of vision, he knew the territory well enough to determine they were going to have to dismount and walk the animals in a few minutes. That would slow them down even more.

Rocco watched the shadowy forms of the riders pass below him, his heart filled with both fear and excitement. For once, they were in the right place at the right time, his men on both sides of the trail being followed by the Salineros. It took all of his discipline to remain still, his adrenaline-charged system demanding oxygen, the fear of impending combat forcing his body to be absolutely silent, not even chancing a breath. Wait, he kept thinking. Wait until the last rider is in our midst - then we can kill them all.

And then there weren't any more men passing beneath the Tejanos leader. He could still see the outline of one man, the cowboy idling beside the trail. Slowly, ever so cautiously, Rocco raised his rifle, centering the front post of his sights on the target. He flipped off the safety, his tingling body jerking at the seemingly thunder-like click.

Bishop knew someone was very, very close. He just didn't

know where. A muted sound that suggested the slightest brush of cloth against rock, a hint of human movement in the night betrayed the attacker. It was more instinct than fact.

With his muscles charged to react, ears searching the night, the Texan slowly placed one boot in front of the other, rolling each step from toe to heel so as not to make a sound. His rifle was high against his shoulder, sweeping all around as he scanned with the night vision.

The metallic click of Rocco's safety told Bishop to duck. The Texan recognized the sound immediately, his body tensing for the impact of a bullet. After a few moments, when no pain tore through him, he began to consider that perhaps he wasn't the target.

Replaying the sound in his mind, Bishop thought the rifle's owner was right around the edge of the truck-sized slab of rock he'd been negotiating. Recovering, he continued to circle the formation, now more vigilant than ever.

Rocco's finger applied pressure to the trigger just as the barrel of his weapon came into the view of Bishop's night vision, less than ten feet away. The Texan's thumb flipped off his own safety a moment before the black night erupted into complete bedlam.

In reality, the clicking noise of Bishop's carbine saved Whitey's life. The ranch foreman hadn't survived the numerous firefights with the Tejanos without developing cat-like reactions; allowing him to duck low in the saddle the moment the metallic noise reached his ears.

Bishop's NVD shut down, the billowing ball of white light spewing from Rocco's shot overrode the device's safety circuit. He found himself blinded and utterly confused. He wasn't the only one.

Rocco's shot was the signal to his men, gunfire erupting up and down the trail. Hutch was hit instantly, a 12-gauge blast tearing the unaware cowboy completely out of the saddle.

The calm, quiet Texas night exploded in complete mayhem as the ambush was unleashed, men on both sides wondering if the doors of hell had suddenly opened in the middle of the desert.

Horses shrieked and bolted, bright flashes of gunfire strobing up and down the darkened trail like the sheet lightning of a desert thunderstorm. Hot lead filled the air, a nearly constant roar of shouting men, firing weapons, and the screaming of the wounded governing the night.

The Culpepper men weren't trained soldiers, but they were all combat veterans. Caught in the middle of the Tejanos' kill-zone, they should have withered and died in a few moments.

Darkness, poor marksmanship, and the confusion of their opponent increased their chances of survival.

The riders dismounted, some on purpose, others having no choice as their horses were shot out from underneath them. They scrambled for the nearest cover, returning fire as best they could.

Initially, the Tejanos sensed victory, many of them exposing themselves to gain a better angle on the fleeing men below. Their overconfidence was an error, and the battlefield punished missteps.

Desperate, bewildered, and expecting to meet their maker, the cowboys along the trail had no target except for the muzzle flashes surrounding them in the rocks. It was enough, their return fire wreaking havoc on the Tejano shooters.

In less than a minute, the ambushed Salineros were climbing, scaling, and rushing into their enemy, the pitched battle breaking down into a dozen small skirmishes of close-quarters fighting. It was brutal.

Night fighting, even amongst professionals, is a soldier's worst nightmare. To accomplish coordination, communication, and effective maneuver without the benefit of daylight requires countless hours of drills, state of the art equipment, and competent commanders. Neither side possessed such assets.

Despite being hardened by the months of conflict and extreme individual bravery, the battle devolved into a swirling fur ball of small, man-to-man clashes.

Bishop wanted none of it. After the initial shock and awe, it had taken the Texan a few moments to ascertain what was happening around him. When he realized none of the gunfire was aimed specifically at him, his only thoughts were of Terri and Hunter.

But retracing his steps proved impossible.

Men were darting in all directions, shouting, shooting, and sometimes dying. Twice Bishop had to innovate his route back to Terri's hide, the boiling conflict rambling across the desert floor and blocking his path.

After a few minutes, he approached what he believed to be Terri's nook, only to find the indentation empty. Cursing their bad luck, he began to circle cautiously, desperately wanting to avoid the fight raging around him.

Having the only NVD on the battlefield gave the Texan an advantage, the device now rebooted and functional. More than once he cut away from gunfire, snaking his away around the roving combatants. But he couldn't find Terri and his son. The rocks were beginning to look the same, dodging the rolling skirmish interfering with his sense of direction.

Anger and regret started to well up deep inside Bishop's

gut. His mind flashed images of a frightened, huddling Terri, clutching Hunter close as the battle raged around her. He should have never left her side. What the hell had he been thinking?

Bishop paused, keeping close to a flat stone formation and trying to reorient his position. He noticed the two men stalking him, both moving forward as if they believed he was an enemy. Splinters and chips of stone stung the Texan's skin as the two shadowy outlines began firing, Bishop diving to put cover between his body and the shooters. He found he was trapped in a dead end, completely surrounded by solid walls of rock.

"I've got no dog in this fight," he whispered, praying the two attackers would move on. Chancing a glance around the corner, he saw they were still advancing in his direction, weapons high and ready.

"Fuck!" he snapped, the red dot of his aiming optic showing bright against the NVD's darker display. He centered on the green and black image of the nearest man. Bishop squeezed, the carbine pushing gently against his shoulder. Two shots - realign on the second man, two shots. Both attackers went down instantly.

The act made his stomach hurt, that pain quickly morphing into a simmering anger. "What choice did I have?" he kept asking himself. "They probably aren't taking any prisoners." Still, it sickened him. Bishop had no quarrel with either side. Killing was difficult enough when an undeniable threat existed, taking human life because of bad timing didn't settle well in his gut. Memories of the Brighton bloodbath surfaced, vivid images and the smell of death filling his senses.

He retreated into the miniature box canyon, hoping to avoid any more killing by staying out of sight. Fighting back the urge to wretch, Bishop pulled a quick drink from his water tube, his mind struggling between the need to stay put, and the unrelenting anxiety to find his wife and child.

A barely audible moaning at his feet nearly caused him to kill again.

His weapon snapped to the source of the noise, his finger automatically applying pressure to the trigger. It was a microsecond of hesitation that stopped him from ending another life. He hadn't seen the wounded man the first time, all of his attention focused on the two gentlemen chasing him through the rocks.

The guy at his feet was bleeding and obviously in some pain. After checking that no one was sneaking up on his hiding spot, Bishop bent and began examining the wounded fighter.

There was a single bullet wound in the fleshy part of the upper arm, another in his calf. Neither appeared to be life threatening. Bishop found more bleeding on the back of the guy's head, but there wasn't any apparent lead damage there. After glancing up at the surrounding rock, the Texan decided the gent had been hit and then had fallen from above.

Bishop rose, checking to make sure he was still undetected. The sounds of gunfire continued to rage throughout the area, the occasional shout of a human voice echoing over the rocks. The din wasn't constant like it had had been, but it was clear there were still plenty of men fighting for their lives.

Pulling the blow-out bag from his vest, Bishop did some quick work on the injured man, spraying both bullet wounds with an antibiotic aerosol and then wrapping each with a bandage.

"Aqua," the fellow croaked in a weak voice. "Aqua."

Despite the guilt of having killed that night, Bishop's kindness only extended so far. He had no desire to allow some stranger drink from his limited supply, didn't know the guy well enough to swap oral germs. But, the injured man wouldn't shut up.   There was still combat raging all around the Texan's position. Bishop wanted nothing more than to remain out of sight and wait for the conflict to die down. The wounded, still-dazed man knew none of this. Every few seconds, he repeated his plea for water, his voice gradually becoming stronger as the time passed, sure to draw attention from the roving skirmishers still engaged throughout the area.

The Texan knew what the man was experiencing. Fighting was damn thirsty work. Any loss of blood made things more desperate. The body would be working hard to replace its fluid, and that meant water. Bishop had been there – far too many times.

Again, the raspy voice begged for a drink. Frustrated, almost crazy with worry about Terri and his son, Bishop stepped to the prone man and took a knee. His hand reached for the fighting knife strapped to his chest rig, palm closing around the weapon's familiar tang.

But he couldn't do it. It just wasn't right.

"Open your mouth," he whispered, changing his grip from the knife to his water-tube. The wounded fellow's eyes opened, but his lips remained tightly pursed. "Open your mouth," Bishop repeated, his voice louder than intended.

Finally realizing what was happening, the guy did as Bishop instructed. After squeezing the bite-valve, the Texan watched as a small stream of clear liquid dripped into the fellow's mouth.

Bishop let him have three mouthfuls before turning off the supply. The man managed a half-smile and then closed his eyes again. Bishop moved back to watch the entrance.

While she had no way of knowing, Terri was less than 50 feet away from her husband. When the fighting had erupted, she'd pushed Hunter as far back into the shallow crevice as possible, placing her own body between her infant and the battle that raged nearby.

Fighting off muscle cramps and thirst, she refused to move for over an hour, terrified that a stray bullet would end her son's life.

A half dozen times she thought Bishop was coming back, each instance allowing momentary relief, but then resulting in disappointment. The footfalls of someone running nearby offered her hope, until the sound scampered right past the entrance to her nook. Another time she heard whispering, only to realize a few moments later that the dialogue was in Spanish. The anticipated joy of her husband's return quickly morphed into sheer terror as she realized how close the battle seethed.

She had to do something... anything. Hunter, snuggly wrapped in his father's shirt, was awake and wide-eyed, but didn't cry. Terri was thankful for that small miracle. She opened the last bottle of water, drinking a portion herself, holding the opening to her son's lips and offering him little tastes. More dribbled down his chin than was swallowed, but she was convinced he had managed to consume a little.

Almost two hours had passed since the shooting began, the ebb and flow of the battle swirling all around her. Terri experienced a rollercoaster of emotions, one minute convinced Bishop had been killed or wounded, the next believing her husband was probably nearby, dispatching evil men who ventured too close to his family. The not knowing was the worst.

At three hours, she decided the pitch of the firefight had definitely lessened. More than once she considered gathering up Hunter and making a run for it. But where would you go, she reasoned. You have almost no water, food, or ammo.

Staying put was the only choice.

Again, the sound of someone running came to Terri's ears. Please be Bishop, she thought, just as a man flew into the crevice, almost crushing her against the stone face. It wasn't her husband.

The intruder was soon joined by a second man, the space much too small for two adults, let along three and a baby. It was obvious the two new arrivals were taking cover, both of them looking back toward the opening as if being pursued. It took an entire second before they realized they weren't alone. "What the hell?" a male voice hissed. "Who is…. What? It's a woman."

Terri was desperately struggling to reach for her pistol at the same time as shielding Hunter from the crush of human flesh.

Reed realized what the woman was reaching for, his arm moving to block her draw. She started to cuss, "Get your fucking hands off of me you son of a bitch or I'll…."

"Shhhhh," he pleaded, moving his dirty, sweaty palm to cover her mouth. "You'll get us all killed. Now hush," he barked.

Outmatched and trying to protect Hunter, Terri didn't have much choice. She nodded, badly wanting the intruder's filthy hand out of her face.

Just as he removed the gag, the commotion of several running men came echoing into the hole. Terri could sense her two roommates tense, the fellow closest to the opening trying to push further back and out of sight.

Terri couldn't see a damn thing outside the nook, two large bodies between her and the open spaces beyond. But she could hear and realized that at least three other people rushed by, hustling at a rapid pace as if they were chasing someone. Or being chased.

A minute later, her two guests relaxed. Shortly after that, the outside man chanced a glance right and left around the opening. He ventured out, finally allowing Terri enough space to breathe freely.

"Whitey," the man next to Terri said just above a whisper. "This is Bishop's wife. The woman with the baby."

"Where's your husband?" came the soft response.

"I don't know. He left to scout ahead right before all the shooting started. He told me to stay put."

"Lady," began Reed, "You can't stay here. The Tejanos have gotten the better of us tonight. If they catch you and that infant, they'll kill both of you right on the spot. Come with us back to the ranch. We can get more men and search for your husband after it gets light. Mr. Culpepper sent us back here to retrieve your family. You'll be safe there; I promise."

Terri didn't want to go. She expected Bishop to come back any minute, and the thought of leaving him behind was simply unworkable. But then she thought about Hunter. The child wouldn't be quiet forever, and what if Bishop didn't come back for a long time? How would she care for Hunter alone in the desert? And besides, wouldn't her capable mate know to come looking for her at the ranch?

She also realized that even if her husband was injured in the battle, there was little hope of finding him until daylight. How would she mount a search in the dark and still keep Hunter safe?

No, she told herself, the odds would be better with a large group of armed men after sunrise.

"Okay," she finally conceded, hefting Hunter in one arm, her rifle in the other. "Lead the way."

Chapter 4

Gradually, Bishop noticed he could see further into the boulders as dawn approached. There hadn't been any gunfire for over an hour, and he was eager to reunite with his wife and child. It had been an exhausting, brutal night, the need to remain diligent while worrying about his family taking a toll on the Texan.

His patient was now sitting upright, slowly recovering from what proved to be an egg-sized knot on the back of his head. The two minor gunshot wounds weren't contributing to the man's recovery. Twice throughout the night, Bishop had provided the fellow water. On the last occasion, he'd handed the silent man two anti-pain tablets. It was the best he could do, given his limited kit.

Deciding it was light enough to move out, Bishop turned to his unspeaking canyon-mate and bid his farewells, "Good luck," he offered, before turning to leave.

"Wait," came the reply, "If you help me, I will help you."

"So you can speak," Bishop answered. "And exactly how do you propose to help me?"

"You are the man from the pickup truck yesterday – right? You are going to retrieve your wife and child – right?"

Bishop nodded, wondering how this fellow could possibly know those details.

"My name is Rocco. I am the leader of the Tejanos. If you help me back to my people, I will guarantee your safe passage out of this valley. We will try to repair your truck and return it to you, but I can't promise that our attempt will be successful - it was significantly damaged."

Bishop, nodding his head, acted like he was considering the offer. He stepped closer to the man, taking a knee beside him. Like a diamondback striking prey, his knife was out and against Rocco's throat.

"You low-life piece of shit," Bishop growled, "You almost killed my wife and son. You shot up my pickup for no good reason. Why shouldn't I shove this blade through your neck and watch you choke on your own blood?"

Rocco stared into Bishop's eyes, knowing instantly that this man would indeed kill him without remorse or hesitation. He'd never seen any creature's stare so cold and uncaring.

"We didn't know, Señor. I swear this. We thought you were mercenaries and hired guns driving to join the Salineros. They have been butchering our people for months. That is why we attacked you."

"And so now we're comrades? Now you're going to promise

my safety? I'm having a little problem with trust, my friend."

Rocco nodded, the motion causing him to grimace in pain. "My forces won the fight last night. I know this because the Salineros only ride horses, and I've not heard any hooves for hours. My men may have already found your wife and son. Perhaps they will catch you looking for them, and more people will perish due to misidentification. I think you need me, Señor. I am convinced we need each other."

Bishop pulled the knife away, but didn't return it to the sheath. He had to admit, the man had a point. "Okay, friend. I'll help you back to your people. But know this – if you betray me, you will die first. Do we have an understanding?"

"I know you're not my enemy. You gave me water and tended to my wounds. If you were truly working for Mr. Culpepper, you would have shot or stabbed me many hours ago. I have no reason to betray you."

Bishop helped the man to his feet, the wound in his calf the most limiting factor to mobility. With one arm draped over Bishop's shoulder, they proceeded out of the mini-canyon and into the valley of boulders.

Given Rocco's hobbling pace, their progress was slow. After traveling for only a few minutes, a voice called out in Spanish, "Look! Look! It's the jefe; he survived!"

Two men approached at breakneck speed. "Ask them if they've spotted my wife and son," Bishop said.

Both men indicated they had not found anyone matching the general descriptions of Terri or Hunter. Nor had they found the bodies of a woman or child.

Bishop listened to the excited exchange between Rocco and his men. After it became clear that they were no longer discussing Terri and Hunter, he turned away to begin his search alone.

"Where are you going?" Rocco asked, switching to English.

"I've got to find my family," Bishop replied over his shoulder, continuing to walk away.

"There will be 50 men from my village here within the hour," Rocco reported. "They are coming to recover our dead and wounded and to make sure the Salineros don't retrieve theirs. Stay here with me, and I'll have my men search for your loved ones."

Bishop shook his head, "No, thanks. I don't want to wait. I need to know my family is okay."

"But, Señor, I'm afraid my comrades will shoot you on sight. It could happen."

Bishop was about to deny the offer a second time when a whistle sounded. Turning to ascertain the source, the Texan spotted a long column of armed men approaching, the point-man waving to Rocco.

"And there they are now," announced the Tejanos commander.

It was a boy of no more than 13 who darted toward Bishop. He carried a rifle, secured across his back via a timeworn rope, the ancient, bolt-action Lee Enfield almost as tall as the lad.

The kid didn't say a word, instead holding an empty water bottle out for Bishop to see. The Texan recognized it immediately as the one he'd given to Terri. "Where did you find this?" he asked.

The young fighter pointed and then motioned for Bishop to follow. It was only a short distance away, the site looking completely different in the light of day. Still, the Texan was pretty sure it was the same nook where he'd left his wife and son during the night.

"We also found this," offered a nearby man, holding up Bishop's spare shirt.

After checking the cloth for blood, Bishop examined the sand in the bottom of the crevice. No crimson there either. The area was far too trampled to detect any footprints.

"Where would you go?" Bishop whispered, trying to put himself in Terri's shoes. Which direction would his wife travel to locate a safe haven from the skirmish? Would she have been able to choose her own route in the post-battle quiet? Or had she fled in the heat of the mêlée, choosing the path of least resistance available to her?

A nearby commotion interrupted his thoughts, two men exchanging words with Rocco, their excited voices and exaggerated hand gestures announcing the exchange was something important.

Turning to face Bishop, Rocco rambled to him. "Your wife is with the Salineros," he said without fanfare. "Two of my men were chasing the cowboys when they spotted some unusual activity. They identified your wife, holding the baby, riding off with them just a few hours ago."

"Are your men sure?" Bishop asked. "How could they tell in the dark?"

"Apparently, your son's strong lungs are what initiated the ceasefire, Señor Bishop. My men tell me they were certain one of the riders was a woman, and the infant with her was crying."

"Shit!" Bishop snapped, his frustration coming to the surface. "How far away is the ranch?"

Rocco stuck out his arm, placing a gentle hand on Bishop's shoulder. "It is but a few miles, my friend. But even if you could find your way there, the Salineros would shoot you on sight. Even now, we are getting ready to retreat to the safety of our village. My scouts indicate the Culpepper militia is heading this way with almost 100 men."

"So?" Bishop offered, "I've got no quarrel with them."

Shaking his head, Rocco tried to explain. "That won't matter. Consider the situation from their perspective, Señor. They are no doubt enraged by how badly we Tejanos injured their forces last night. They don't know you. Even if you are very lucky, and they don't shoot you on sight, they will ask many difficult questions of you. How will you explain avoiding capture? How will you describe surviving the night? They are not likely to believe you accomplished these feats without our help. In their minds, you are guilty by association."

Again, Bishop had to admit the man had a point. It was easy to visualize the gathering army of angry cowhands, howling for revenge over friends lost in last night's conflict. They wouldn't be a friendly bunch, which typically resulted in few questions and quick trigger fingers.

"Come back to the village with me, Señor. There's nothing you can do for your wife and child at the moment. While I cannot say for sure how the Salineros will treat her, I doubt Mr. Culpepper will view a woman as a credible threat. For now, I can't see where you have any choice but to return with us. To approach the ranch without a plan would be certain suicide. Where would your little family be then?"

Bishop stared toward the direction of the ranch, his heart resistant to the cruel reality of Rocco's words. A swirling storm of thoughts flooded his consciousness, pitting logic against pure emotion. How can I even consider walking away from my soul mate and my son? He replayed the encounter with the two cowboys of the previous evening, some reassurance coming from the fact that he'd been ready to take Terri and Hunter to Culpepper's ranch at that time. Now, they were there, albeit under completely different circumstances. Was that really such a bad thing?

Yet, he was out of water, dead tired and had next to zero food. The sun would be at its zenith soon, the day promising to be a scorcher. He truly didn't have any options.

"Okay," he answered, turning to Rocco. "Lead the way."

Nick hit the trail at a dead run, his ears struggling to separate the pounding of his own boots from any possible pursuit. They were back there; he just didn't know how far.

He'd been after water, kneeling beside a small stream to fill his "dirty" canteen. Later, when time and location allowed, he'd boil the liquid and refill his Camelbak for drinking. Evidently, the watering hole had been a popular destination, several men appearing along the opposite bank less than a stone's throw away from his position.

Tucking his carbine in the crook of his elbow, the big man lowered his chin and focused every fiber of his being on pumping his legs. Distance was life.

For a man with a pack, weapon, load vest, armor, and boots, his first hundred yards would have impressed a professional football scout. It's amazing how the fear of capture and torture will motivate a man, he mused.

Reassured by the absence of bullets zipping past his fleeing body, he slowed the pace. This was going to be a marathon, not a sprint – he needed to conserve.

The foliage of the surrounding pine forest grew denser, low branches and the occasional bush prompting him to duck, cut, and leap. Nick didn't mind; the concealment was more of an ally to the pursued than the pursuers. He knew where he was going; the men chasing him did not.

Settling into a fast jog, the big man kept his pace measured and steady. The fact that he was running away from the only source of water in the area meant little at the moment – he just needed distance. If he survived the next 20 minutes, there would be time enough to stop, regroup, and make a plan.

Of all the times for Bishop to decide he needs a vacation, he thought. He would have handled this contact differently. He wouldn't be running for his life right now.

For the third time he adjusted his angle of regress. His training from so many years ago kicked in, hammered into the brain of a younger, less-experienced soldier by hard-core instructors at Fort Bragg – when being pursued, never travel at 90-degree angles.

The time and distance passed, Nick's knees now sending a message, the level of pain from those joints competing with his lung's unhappiness from a lack of oxygen. He started looking for a hide.

It was almost two minutes before suitable terrain came into

view. There was a cluster of trees ahead; four or five good-sized pines huddled together at the top of a slight ridge. He'd have cover, concealment, and the high ground. Another quick glance over his shoulder told the ex-Green Beret that no one was right on his heels.

His body celebrated the end of the run, tingling zips of recovery expanding through his limbs as he dove prone into a nest of trunks, pine needles, and low vegetation.

His M4 was equipped with a magnifying optic. He quickly dialed in the highest zoom level and began scanning for pursuit. He didn't have to wait long.

A flush of disappointment blew through the big man's mind, a tinge of embarrassment that the three men emerging from the forest didn't seem to be struggling to keep up with his pace. "I'm spending too much time in a chair," he thought, noting that his antagonists weren't even breathing hard.

As the trio approached, Nick experienced a minor ego boost – they were young. The oldest of the trio was probably 20 years old… tops. Old age sucks, he thought. Just my luck I'd run into the local track team.

And they weren't unskilled.

Nick watched as the three entered a less-dense section of the forest, either instinct, training, or leadership making them spread apart and maintain a respectable amount of spacing. The lead man held his rifle high and ready, the following duo moving off to shore-up his flank. This isn't going to be easy, he considered.

Their body language indicated they were listening, standing stock-still with heads tilted, probing the woods for audible sign of their prey's scurrying footfalls. "I'm not running anymore," Nick grinned, watching his pursuers exchange puzzled glances. "Where did I go?"

Acknowledging that he wasn't going to outrun the three sets of younger legs left only one option. He'd have to discourage their pursuit.

There was a checklist engrained in Nick's mind – a sequence of steps to be executed before engaging any foe. He scanned the circle of his perimeter, verifying he wasn't being cut off or flanked. Next, he plotted his egress, making sure he knew exactly where to run. When he opened up with the carbine, it was going to send a loud, definite invitation to anyone in the area, and he didn't want to hang around to see how many showed up for the party.

For a moment, he pined for a noise-canceled weapon. He'd used what most people called a "silencer" on multiple continents, but the application of such technology was limited. Canned rifles required sub-sonic ammunition to optimize the sound reduction, and that meant far less range and stopping power – a great option for close quarters black ops, but not the best for fighting on open ground.

Next came the most critical decision, a choice he wanted to finalize now, rather than trying to make up his mind when the lead was flying. How long would he engage before breaking contact and heading off?

The list of prerequisites was processed in mere moments, a lifetime of training, discipline, and experience allowing cool calculations and mechanical execution. His analysis became robotic.

Distance to target? 210 meters.

Wind? Calm.

Bullet drop? Two inches.

First target? The leader, of course.

He centered the red circle of his optic on the man's thigh, applied a fingernail's worth of digit to the trigger... and gently increased the pressure.

The 5.56 NATO carbine barked, a gentle, familiar shove against Nick's shoulder. He knew the rifle's muzzle would be pushed high and right by the recoil – naturally moving into the next target.

As anticipated, the men on his tail hesitated for just a second, the human startle reflex overriding conscious mental thought. It didn't last long, but it was enough.

Nick's second shot was on the way just as his foes began to recover from the surprise. The man's head started to turn, but his body hadn't moved. The 64-grain bullet slammed into his leg at over 3,000 feet per second.

Striking bone, the soft-nosed projectile fragmented into a dozen pieces, each tearing flesh and sinew as it tore through the victim's limb. Two of the larger hunks of burning lead headed higher, shredding tissue before exiting the buttock.

The third target reacted quickly, diving for the ground as he watched both of his comrades fall. Luck was with the young hunter, a clump of grass and dead wood blocking Nick's line of sight. By the time the lone survivor had recovered enough of his wits to check on his friends, Nick was moving.

He could have easily killed with the first two shots, but sending dead young men back to their mothers wasn't what the Alliance was all about. That aside, Nick's mercy wasn't primarily due to the tracker's youth. While he judged them to be only 17-20ish, that was obviously old enough to carry a rifle and hunt men. I've had much younger combatants try to kill me on battlefields all over the planet, he thought.

No, Nick intentionally sought merely to disable for tactical reasons. A wounded man drained resources from the enemy. Injuries required assets for care and transportation, and ultimately, they result in almost as much discord and grief as a death. For weeks, healthcare would have to be administrated, including feeding, bathing, changing bandages, and checking for infection. Over time, the adversary would pay a much higher price for a hospital bed than a grave.

Most men would have broken contact and moved off, content with removing two out of three complications from their lives. Not Nick. Not today. Not on this mission.

While his friends withered and moaned in pain, the unharmed pursuer belly crawled toward his leader, calling out his friend's name. The downed body of a comrade was within reach just as Nick's charging bulk enveloped the kid's line of sight.

Already near panic, the young man's eyes opened wide with terror as he realized the hunter was now the hunted. His brain was firing commands for his arm to raise his weapon, but the limb was frozen stiff with fear. When he spotted the muzzle of Nick's carbine center near his nose, the hapless fellow squinted shut his eyes and lowered his head to accept certain death.

But the bullet never came.

Instead, the slightly built, young man felt a vice-like grip clutch his hair. The force that jerked him from the ground was more powerful than any sensation he ever experienced from contact with another human being. He struggled to gather his legs, desperately scampering to take his weight off the screaming follicles in his scalp and put it on his feet where it belonged. When he finally managed to stand, he was staring into Nick's glaring eyes. He was reminded of a great wolf he'd once seen in a zoo.

"How many are chasing me?" growled the huge man.

"I... I... I don't know," came the choking, high-pitched response.

Nick, still holding a handful of the kid's locks, lifted his victim off the ground and shook him like he was trying to shake crumbs out of a napkin.

After a whimpering, tear-filled session of sniffling had passed, Nick asked again. "How many are chasing me?"

"Seriously, I don't know. A lot... they're calling everybody in... more than a hundred, I guess."

Nick realized the kid probably didn't know much more than that. "Look at me!" he ordered.

The prisoner did as he was told, raising his bowed head to make eye contact. Nick's fist snapped the young fellow's head back, the blow lifting his heels completely off the ground. He was out cold before his body bounced across the soil. "Sorry, kid, but that beats getting shot like your buddies."

Nick took their weapons, slinging two hunting rifles and an AR15 across his already burdened shoulders. He'd find a good spot to stash them later.

One of the wounded men reached for a pistol, the effort rewarded with a broken wrist as Nick's boot crunched the bone before it launched the sidearm nearly 20 yards away.

He patted them down, taking anything of value. The now unconscious leader had prepared for the mission, carrying AR ammo, some homemade bread, and a two-way radio. "Plunder," Nick remarked, stuffing his pockets with the bounty.

Pivoting to disappear into the woods, he stared down at the first man he'd dropped. The guy was bleeding out, probably due to the bullet striking a main artery. "Fuck," he grunted, scanning the surrounding underbrush for any threat.

In less than a minute, he pulled off the injured hunter's belt and applied a tourniquet.

Then like a ghost, he melted away into the forest.

Terri relaxed somewhat, relieved no one had tried to take away her firearms. The sleepless night, combined with the stress of worrying about Bishop, had fouled her mood. But she couldn't show it, Hunter at an age where he mirrored his parents' moods.

On the ride to the Culpepper ranch, Terri learned that one of the men with her was the second in command. After they had ridden down into the flatlands, her two escorts loosened up and began talking.

"I was in Meraton over a year ago," announced the one named Whitey. "I was passing through, trying to make my way down here to the ranch. Mr. Culpepper was a friend of my father's, and I thought he'd take me in. I was living in Amarillo at the time, and the entire town went nuts when everything fell apart. I didn't have any place else to go."

"A lot of people found themselves in a similar spot," Terri replied. "Bishop and I lived in Houston back then. I lost count of the number of times we were almost killed while traveling across Texas. Those were bad times, for sure."

"I remember people talking about your husband when I was in town. As I recall, he'd shot it out with a bunch of bank robbers."

Terri grunted, the rush of memories transporting her back to a time when life was so uncertain... the future so unknown.

"Yup," she replied. "That's my Bishop. Winning friends and influencing people wherever he goes."

The next question from the cowboy took her completely by surprise. "Have things gotten any better... back in the world?"

They have no idea about the Alliance, she realized. They don't know who I am, or that people have regrouped.

Terri thought to bring her co-riders up to speed with current events, but then stopped. She was a woman alone with a child, keeping company with people she didn't know and right in the middle of a war zone. She decided to keep her mouth shut for the time being. "Maybe a little," she replied with a neutral tone. "Bishop and I have spent quite a bit of time at his small ranch. It's very isolated, kind of like this area around here."

Her answer seemed to satisfy the two men. Before long, they were approaching a group of structures – the Culpepper ranch.

There was a main house, a single-story affair that wouldn't have been anything special in most big city neighborhoods. Two dominant pole barns, several corrals, a handful of outbuildings, and a long row of house trailers met her eye. It was obviously a less prosperous outfit than Mr. Beltran's massive operation, but an impressive spread nonetheless.

After signaling the lookouts, Whitey had ordered Reed to escort Terri to the main house. The foreman had ridden off, obviously in dread of delivering his boss the bad news about the ambush. As far as the two men knew, they were the only survivors.

Reed escorted Terri around to the back door where an older Latino woman was hanging clothes on a line to dry. "Chita," Reed greeted, tipping his hat. "This is Terri and Hunter. They are Mr. Culpepper's guests."

The woman nodded, smiling sweetly as she moved to hold Hunter while his mother dismounted. Unaccustomed to spending much time in the saddle, Terri's legs and butt were stiff from the rocky ride.

A series of stretches and bends followed, Terri mumbling, "How do they do that all day long? They should do a 'Buns of Steel' infomercial." Finally getting comfortable with the concept of using her limbs, her next priorities were related to having spent the night in the desert without facilities. Hunter was fussing, no doubt wondering where his breakfast was.

Chita appeared friendly enough, inviting Terri into the ranch house and showing her to a spare bedroom. The lingering aroma of scented candles permeated the structure, several half-burned examples grouped here and there. The home was neat and tidy. There was running water, courtesy of a windmill driven pump she had noticed on the ride in.

"Beats the heck out of sleeping on a rock," Terri announced to her son, running a sink full of water with the intent of rinsing the desert grit off both their bodies.

A few moments later, a naked Hunter was enjoying a rather enthusiastic splashing session in the basin. A knock on the door signaled Chita was back, the woman's arms full of clothing, including a cute, little outfit for the baby. Terri thanked her with a smile, happy at the prospect of clean duds.

"Are you hungry?" Chita asked in heavily accented English. "Does your son need food as well?"

"Yes, if it's not too much trouble," Terri responded. "That and sleep. Neither of us has slept much lately."

"Mr. Culpepper wishes to speak with you after you've freshened up and had a chance to eat. I'm sure you'll have an opportunity to rest after that. I'll bring you both some food."

Terri eyed the bathroom's shower, but was unsure of what to do with the currently occupied and thoroughly delighted Hunter. As nice as the accommodations were, the ranch was not equipped with a playpen for the wriggling infant. She decided to take him into the water with her. There was even soap.

Twenty minutes later, Terri was escorted outside to the front porch where a man rested on a lawn chair, observing a long line of riders exit the main compound. Complete with western plaid shirt and faded blue jeans, his dress was that of a man who spent most of his life in the saddle. Only the snakeskin boots set the man apart as a gentleman of means. A timeworn Stetson shaded a face lined with worry and fatigue, but Terri was most uneasy about the melancholy look in his eyes.

Upon sensing Terri's presence, the leather-skinned man stood and removed his hat. "My name is Sam Culpepper," he began. "I'm the ramrod of this outfit. Have been for 46 years."

"I'm Terri," came the reply, "and this is my son, Hunter."

Indicating Terri should sit in a nearby chair, Mr. Culpepper returned to his own perch. Chita appeared with a tray, conspicuously empty but for two glasses of water.

"I'm sorry I can't offer you anything else," the old man stated. "Times are difficult, to say the least."

"I want to thank you for the kindness you've shown my son and me already, Mr. Culpepper. You've been a most gracious host."

He nodded, his eyes never leaving the seemingly endless line of riders now stretching toward the horizon.

"Where are they going, if I may ask?" Terri ventured.

"They're going back to Windy Ridge and the valley beyond. I hope they find your husband alive and well, but I'm not optimistic about that. According to my men... at least the ones who made it out alive... the Tejanos had many rifles in that valley last night." He returned to the seat, folded his arms, and sighed heavily while considering his next words. "This war is escalating. I guess we're going to have to fight at night now. I should have seen that coming."

Terri let his statement settle, hoping he would continue without her prompting or prying. He didn't.

"Can you tell me about this conflict?" she asked gently. "My husband and I seem to have become involved somehow."

He grunted, nodding his head. "Yes, you have. There's not much to tell really. On the north side of my property lies a large salt bed. It is quite the anomaly out here in the desert. Some years ago, a geologist from A&M was out this way and asked to take a look at it. We rode out there, and he told me how it was formed. He explained that a prehistoric lake had existed below the surface, and as the saltwater evaporated, it pushed the mineral to the surface. The salt is nearly pure and finely granulated – a rare occurrence in nature."

"I think I've seen it," Terri responded, remembering an escape from Fort Bliss and a stolen ATV. "My husband was raised around here, and he pointed it out to me a long time ago."

"It was really an eyesore for years," Sam continued. "Over a thousand acres of basically useless land. Nothing grows there, and cattle don't require all that much salt. Back during normal times, nobody paid much attention to it. It was cheaper and easier to go to the grocery store or have a truck deliver packaged salt."

"We found out the hard way how important salt is," Terri said. "After we got here from Houston, it seemed like we were always short on salt."

"Back in the Old West, that salt bed was an important resource," Sam noted. "Silver was minded in this area for years, and the miners would haul off the salt by the wagon load and use it for the refining process. The settlers also used it to preserve meat, filter water, and make everything from soap to laundry detergent. The war we're fighting now isn't the first scuffle over that damned mineral. About 150 years ago, there was another conflict people called the 'El Paso Salt War.' A lot of men died then, too."

Terri tilted her head, never having heard that part of Texas's history before. Again, Mr. Culpepper fell silent.

She was just about to ask him about the current dispute when a rider approached the house. Terri recognized Whitey from last night. "We're leaving you short-handed here, Mr. Culpepper. There are only twenty men left hereabouts. We'll be watching for a flare if they hit the ranch."

Sam nodded his understanding. "You be careful, Whitey. We've already lost enough men to those animals. Bring everybody back, including this lady's husband if you find him."

Whitey tipped his hat and said, "Will do, sir," and then rode off, spurring his horse to catch up with the long column of riders.

"Are you expecting a major battle?" Terri asked, impressed at the show of force.

"No. They'll fade away, back across the river and into the hills. I fought in 'Nam... battled the Viet Cong. They used the same tactics against us for years. The Tejanos won't make a stand unless they have superior numbers. It's a classic guerrilla warfare tactic. If I don't send out a large party, they'll ambush us. If I do respond with a large force, I waste valuable resources chasing ghosts."

Terri could hear the frustration in the man's voice and now understood his sadness. Before she could say anything else, he stood and looked her in the eye. "That's why I sent my men back last night... sent them to retrieve you and your husband. I hear he's a fighting man, and I'm about at my wit's end. I was hoping he could come up with a solution, but instead I lost eight good men and now have you and your son to feed and shelter. You and I both are praying we find him this morning."

Mr. Culpepper's words took Terri by surprise. Before she could react, he stepped off the porch and moved with purposeful stride toward the barn.

The village of San Ignacio was a timeless settlement. Nestled along the winding Rio Grande, it was a quaint community of stucco, adobe, and mud-straw structures.

They had crossed the great river via one of the half-dozen foot bridges that connected Chihuahua, Mexico with the Lone Star state. The river was narrow here, dipping into sandstone canyons sometimes less than 50 feet in width.

Were it not for the waterway, it would be difficult to detect any international boundary. The long line of Tejanos had passed through nearly identical bergs on the Texas side, unincorporated places with names like Fort Hammond and McLeay.

To Bishop's eye, the only difference between the settlements on either side of the waterway had been which pre-collapse flag had flown over the local post office. The people looked the same, as did the architecture, menus, customs, and churches.

Like every community in the world, San Ignacio had suffered during the fall of society. Empty homes, closed businesses, and thin residents were all in plain view.

"Our village hasn't grown in over 50 years," Rocco informed Bishop. "El Paso and Juarez to the north were like bright lights to the moth-eyes of our young. They saw opportunity there that didn't exist here. Some of them eventually drifted back, longing for the slower pace of life - but just a few. The only ones who never ventured to the metro areas were those too poor to even chance life in the big city."

Bishop nodded, "Our agricultural towns suffered the same problems. There used to be a saying, 'How do we keep 'em down on the farm?'"

Rocco smiled knowingly, "When everything went to hell, many of our young people came back. The cities became even more dangerous – hostile, violent municipalities where there wasn't any food. For a while, our village was actually indebted to the apocalypse... so many of the children and grandchildren returning to their families."

It was understandable. In times of crisis, it was human nature to long for the security of home and family. He'd done exactly the same thing, leaving Houston to return to the land of his youth.

Bishop spied small patches of gardens and the occasional milk cow chewing slowly in the mid-day sunshine. There seemed to be chickens everywhere.

"I don't get it, Rocco," the Texan said. "You say you are fighting and dying for salt, but I see plenty of other food sources here. I know salt is important for storing meat and other preservation tasks – but do you really need it badly enough to die for?"

The Mexican laughed, slapping Bishop on the shoulder with an affable swat. "Come along, Señor, let me show you something," he said, tugging Bishop's arm toward a side street.

The two men walked less than a block, Rocco glancing at the small adobe homes dotting the dirt lane. Finally spotting what he was looking for, the big man stopped and shouted a greeting in Spanish, "Marco? Marco are you home?"

A small tangle of black hair appeared in the glassless window, nudging aside the wispy material that served as a curtain. Bishop could barely detect the eyes peering over the sill.

"Marco, come on out here. I have a friend I want you to meet," Rocco continued.

A minute or so later, a reluctant figure showed through the doorway, clinging to the shadows as if he were scared of the rifle-toting gringo standing with the village's leader.

"Come on now, boy. No need to be reserved. This is my new friend, Bishop. He is a great warrior from Texas... but a friend to the Tejanos."

Finally, the lad appeared, Bishop estimating his age around 11, give or take. When the kid stepped through the threshold and into the light, Bishop couldn't help but inhale sharply.

The child's skin was blue. Not painted blue, or tattooed blue, but pigment deep, royal sky blue.

Throwing Rocco a questioning look, the Texan inquired, "Is this for some ceremony? A tattoo custom? I don't get it."

"It's a side effect. Marco had tuberculosis, almost died from it. So did hundreds of others here and in the nearby villages. We treated it the only way we knew how – administering colloidal silver. For some people, the protocol turns them blue."

Rocco tousled the boy's locks and then urged him back into the home. The two men pivoted, returning to the main street and joining the still passing line of Tejano soldiers.

"Sorry to be so dense," Bishop finally said, "but I still don't get it. What does salt have to do with tuberculosis?"

"When the TB started spreading like wildfire and there was no help from Mexico City, we sought the only natural cure the elders could remember being effective. We sent men to reopen the old silver mines so we could extract small amounts of ore. But you need salt to refine silver, Bishop. Lots of salt. And that is why we have no choice but to fight."

"Everyone looks pretty healthy to me," Bishop noted, looking around. "I've not noticed any coughing or feverish looking folks. Have you turned the tide against the bacteria?"

The village leader nodded, "Drinking the colloidal silver doesn't cure the bug. It only seems to put it into remission. We have over a thousand infected souls that will grow sick and surely die if we don't keep supplying them the medicine. We have no alternative."

Bishop stopped cold, his complexion going cold white with fear. "Are the people contagious while they're drinking the silver water?"

Again, Rocco busted out laughing at his new friend. "No, Señor. We don't believe they are."

"What's so funny?" Bishop asked, thinking his inquiry was completely legitimate.

"I'm sorry," Rocco said, trying to keep a straight face. "The man who held a knife to my throat just a short time ago and looked at me with the devil's own eyes. The same man shot his way out of my best ambush on the road. I just find it funny that a slayer such as you would be frightened of tiny, little bug-germs."

Bishop got it, just a little embarrassed over his reaction. "Damn right I'm scared of tiny, little bug-germs. I'll let you in on another secret – I'm scared shitless of my wife, too."

Chapter 5

Sleep came easy on the bed covered with pima cotton sheets and a real comforter. Once Hunter had filled his belly full of rice and carrots, he had easily succumbed to deep slumber. With her tummy full and her son safely snuggled on a thick patchwork quilt, mother hadn't taken long to join son.

She estimated it was late afternoon when the thunder of horses' hooves awakened her. Hunter was sprawled on the floor beside her, wide-eyed and content with new surroundings. After a quick diaper change and splashing a handful of water across her face, Terri hurriedly pulled a brush through her hair and made for the back door. She was curious, bored, and wondering if the ranch's men had found Bishop.

One look from Whitey told her they hadn't. That was the bad news. "We didn't find his body either," the foreman advised, trying to emphasize the positive. "And as usual, the Tejanos only left with their own dead," he said, pointing at several bodies draped over the horses' backs.

Terri sighed, nodding her understanding of what the man was trying to tell her. "So you think the Tejanos have captured my husband – right?"

Whitey looked down, shuffling his boots in the dirt. "Yes, ma'am, I'm reasonably sure they did."

"What does that mean?" Terri asked, not one single bit happy with the cowboy's reaction.

"It means they'll most likely kill him," came Mr. Culpepper's voice as he joined them. "Any of our men that have fallen into their hands have been executed. And I'm not going to lie to you, they didn't die quickly."

Terri's face flushed with anger. "I need to get to Alpha... and I need to get there right fucking now. I will have 10,000 men with battle tanks and Apache helicopters hit that village in less than two hours."

Both of the cattlemen simply stared at the irate woman next to them, her reaction predictable, but her words not making any sense. "Ma'am... Miss Terri... I know you're upset, but..."

"Seriously, gentlemen. I must get to Alpha or Meraton or Fort Bliss... it doesn't matter. I will bring down the wrath of hell on those people if they don't let my husband go."

Whitey was visibly shocked by the words coming from the polite, demure, young mother he'd rescued from the valley. Mr. Culpepper, on the other hand, tilted his head, intently studying his guest.

"It's five days ride to Alpha from here," the older rancher stated calmly. "Almost as far to Meraton. Even with my best horses, you'd never make it before your husband's fate is sealed - one way or the other."

"You don't have any cars or trucks?"

Whitey snorted, shaking his head at what was apparently a naïve question. "We haven't had any gasoline in six months."

"Our truck…" Terri started.

"The Tejanos have your truck. And from what you've told me, even if they haven't used the gasoline already, there's no way we can go and bring the vehicle back here."

"Is there a radio? A shortwave radio anywhere nearby?"

Mr. Culpepper was patient with his response. "I have CBs. We used them to communicate with the hands as they worked around the spread, but the last of the gas was used in our generator a long time ago. There's no electricity, Miss Terri, and even if there were, the range of my equipment is very limited."

Terri began pacing like a caged cat, the helplessness surging through her core something the leader of the Alliance hadn't experienced in quite some time.

The whole predicament was all so stupid and meaningless. Less than two hours' drive away, there were ample resources to resolve this dilemma, and she couldn't access them because of a simple lack of communication.

It dawned on her that the entire range war at the root of this situation was just as senseless. People back in her world had access to salt. She didn't know exactly where it was coming from, but one thing was for certain – no one in the Alliance was fighting and dying over the crystalline substance.

Culpepper and Whitey watched her pace, both men still digesting her response and words. Whitey came to the conclusion that she was just a loyal, loving wife having an exaggerated reaction. Mr. Culpepper wasn't so sure.

After giving her a few minutes to walk off her surge of anger, the older man spoke. "Even if we could figure out a way to get a message through, what makes you so sure you could summon enough help to rescue your husband?"

Terri stopped mid-step, throwing her host a look that implied he'd just asked an incredibly dumb question. But then she caught herself, remembering where she was.

"I need to tell you a story, Mr. Culpepper. It's going to be a little hard to believe, but true nonetheless," she said sweetly.

Bishop chewed the last of the flatbread tortilla, the fried wrapper encircling a mixture of meat and cheese that was quite filling. He started to ask about the meat, but changed his mind. Some things were just better left to the imagination.

A deep yawn followed, the combination of a full stomach and lack of sleep taking their toll. Rising with the thought of finding a horizontal surface, he wandered outside of Rocco's modest home hoping to find the village leader and discuss the matter of a cot or bed.

He was a stranger in the village, that fact made obvious by the short glances and occasional frowns from the locals. As he strolled along, Bishop couldn't help but wonder if his race had anything to do with the unfriendly atmosphere. He'd seen a few other whites among the local Latinos, one of the soldiers mentioning that some of the local ranchers had sided with the villages on this side of the border.

A few of the men stared at his rifle and kit, probably wondering why Rocco was letting a strange gringo wander around their town armed. Others merely ignored Bishop, directing their eyes straight ahead.

After inquiring about Rocco's whereabouts and being answered only with pointing fingers, Bishop soon discovered his host leaning against the bullet-ridden pickup.

There were several men gathered around, a few of them actually working on repairs. The entire picture further soured the Texan's mood.

Trying to sound friendly, Bishop asked, "What's the prognosis? Will she run again?"

Rocco shook his head. "Unknown at this time, Señor. If it is possible, I will keep my word."

Another man approached, stepping from the back of the truck and rambling on in Spanish. Bishop could tell the conversation was about him, picking up a few words here and there.

Rocco and the new man verbally volleyed back and forth, quick bursts of conversation that sounded emotional, but not angry. Finally, the village's leader turned to Bishop in an effort to explain. "He thinks I should just shoot you and take your equipment. He doesn't understand why I'm helping you at all."

Before Bishop could reply, several locals started to gather, the sheer numbers making the Texan uncomfortable. He decided to suppress the smart ass remark cued up in his throat. "And you said?"

Rocco grunted, then waved a dismissive hand through the air. "I informed my hot-headed friend that you had saved my life," he said, pointing to the bandages and wounds. "I told them that I appreciated that fact and wouldn't go back on my word."

Bishop's eyes darted from Rocco to the boisterous local, finding the Latino staring in a most unfriendly manner. The Texan swept the crowd, spotting several others who seemed to echo the threatening perspective. For what seemed like the hundredth time since embarking on the vacation, the Texan was having second thoughts about his decisions.

That realization was immediately followed by Mr. Hard Ass producing a knife, followed by a sneering grin and a guttural outburst of Spanish dialogue. The surrounding men all snorted and cackled their support.

"He said that he regrets not capturing your wife, Señor. He remarked at how luscious her ass looked as it was scurrying away from our ambush, and how he was sure after a few evenings of his company, she would regret having spent her time with a queer like you."

Rocco started to move toward the challenging fellow, ready to quell the hostility. But Bishop's words interrupted the effort. "Is this man important to you, Rocco?" came the icy-cold question.

Short term memories of Bishop's knife being at his throat came back to Rocco, the leader's eyes going to the fighting knife on Bishop's chest rig. "No, as a matter of fact, he's quite the pain in the ass. A second guesser of just about every decision."

"Want me to fix that?" Bishop asked, his eyes never leaving the man with the knife.

Trying to play out what would happen if a fight did occur, Rocco didn't answer immediately. Finally, scratching his chin, he said, "Well, I suppose it might help things in the long run. Do you have to kill him?"

"Probably."

"I would never deny a man a chance to protect his honor, especially against another who speaks of a wife in this way."

Bishop flipped the carbine around to his back and drew his own knife.

The move seemed to surprise Mr. Hard Ass, his gawking eyes dancing between Rocco and his friends. Much to the fellow's chagrin, Rocco swept the ground between the two potential combatants as if to say, "Be my guest."

Bishop sensed the man's hesitation as well. "Tell him I won't kill him if he drops the knife and admits that he's only mad because his dick won't get hard."

After Bishop's taunt was repeated in Spanish, several of the men laughed, which only seemed to enrage the antagonist. He charged.

There were only three steps between the two combatants,

but the villager's lowered head and Indian-like battle cry gave Bishop plenty of notice. The Texan side-stepped his attacker, having plenty of time to put a boot on the man's ass as he passed. Laughter erupted from the growing throng.

That small flash of engagement made Bishop realize the foe he faced was an amateur. While there wasn't any doubt of the fellow's willingness to fight, it was clear he wasn't professionally trained or all that experienced.

"Tell him to knock off this bullshit before he gets killed," Bishop said to Rocco, never taking his eyes away from the now-circling villager. "Tell him he's completely out of his league, and I don't like one-sided fights."

Again, Rocco's voice sounded in the local dialect. Again, the local charged, this time slashing back and forth through the air with his blade.

But his arm was trying to sweep too wide, the arch of the swings taking too long to recover. Effortlessly timing the move, Bishop stepped into the man's wheelhouse just after the blade had whooshed by. He could have easily driven his knife-edge into the man's chest but didn't. Three brutal rabbit punches slammed into the fellow's face, each landing with head-snapping force.

The villager went down, and in a blink, Bishop was on him.

The Texan's blade pressed hard on the beaten man's throat, his knee pinning the shocked fellow's knife-wrist to the dirt. "Ask him to repeat his words about my wife."

Rocco did, but there wasn't any response from the wide-eyed fellow at the tip of Bishop's knife. "I don't think he heard you," the Texan growled.

Again, the village's leader repeated the demand, the mandate accented by Bishop's moving his blade just enough to draw blood and pain.

A torrent of frenzied Spanish erupted from the gentleman under Bishop; the tone of his voice made it clear the fellow was pleading.

Rocco laughed after the antagonist had finished his little spiel of retreat, as did several of the bystanders. "In summary, Señor Bishop, he says you must have completely misunderstood his meaning. He was trying to compliment your wife's fine figure, and meant to imply that you and she were a perfectly matched couple."

Bishop looked down into the now smiling man's eyes, his foe trying to nod in friendliness - despite the cold steel at his jugular.

"What should I do, Rocco?" Bishop asked. "Will they think I'm soft if I let him live?"

The local leader scratched his chin, moving just a step closer and lowering his voice. "I'd kick his ass a bit more, and then let him go if it were me."

Bishop nodded, rising slowly, never taking his eye from the now humiliated hombre.

After a few of his friends had helped their bleeding comrade to his feet, he was quickly hustled around the corner. "I suppose a couple of his buddies will help him come back in a bit," Bishop said to his host. "I bet they'll bring rifles with them the next time."

"No, I don't think so. I know these men, have lived around them all my life. You showed honor and mercy. They'll respect that."

Bishop wasn't so sure but accepted Rocco's words with a nod. "Now, about my truck...."

There were at least 20 of them, spread across a skirmish line and making more noise than a herd of elephants on crutches. Nick was perched on a limb about five feet from the ground, using the elevation to scout the area ahead, making sure no one was catching up from behind.

Using his optic, he studied their spacing, speed, and alertness. A grunt escaped his throat, "Training, gentlemen," he whispered, "it's all about the training." Exhaling in a deep sigh, he continued to observe what the ex-military operative considered a "Three Stooges" level of execution. "The semester is about to start – class will soon be in session. I'm your professor today, and our subject is how not to conduct a manhunt. There will be a quiz."

The men hunting Nick were spread too far apart, 25-30 paces separating each member of the group. That formation left wide gaps – an abundance of opportunities to bypass their prey. Nick resolved to make them pay for the poor tactics.

For the last 24 hours, they'd been trying to close the umbrella, gradually tightening their patterns, slowly closing in from all points of the compass. The retired Special Forces Sergeant had played along, intentionally exposing himself now and then, teasing his pursuers.

He estimated there were at least 300 men tromping and stomping through this section of northeast Texas, all of them seeking to kill or capture his carcass. Now it was time to go on the offensive and really piss them off.

It didn't take long to identify the perfect spot. Nick had

watched the pursuers long enough to know they were neither professional, nor motivated. Just a few minutes of observation convinced him that they were definitely leaving stones unturned. There wasn't any need to expend a lot of energy creating an expert hide.

Ten years ago, the Rocky Mountain juniper would have made an excellent Christmas tree. Thick, full branches of bushy, dark green needles indicated a healthy specimen, the evergreen foliage draping gracefully to the forest floor. Its abundant height now far exceeded the clearances of most household ceilings, the crown nearly 20 feet high, and excusing the specimen from holiday duties.

Nick found the tree's younger sibling a short distance away. Being careful to twist and not snap, he removed three thin branches from the smaller example, each about as long as his arm.

Carrying his small bundle of kindling, the big man returned to the mature juniper and went prone. Lifting the ring of foliage, he backed in feet first, careful not to disturb the layer of old needles and leaves littering the ground.

Twice he had to risk making a noise, his way hindered by an offshoot bough or twig that required a hardy kick. As he backed in closer to the trunk, he pulled the kindling and his rifle along. He had to maintain a low profile to the ground, the tree's lower branches scraping across his back and legs as he wiggled, pushed, and wedged his way underneath the canopy of green.

After a few minutes, it was clear he couldn't move any further. Still, the big man was pleased with his hide. He was on the pine's far side, away from the approaching hunters. This positioning was intentional, as he knew most searchers spent far more time looking ahead than behind. They would pass by him, probably without glancing over their shoulders.

And even if they did, he was nearly invisible. While it was impossible to be sure without a comrade verifying his cover, Nick believed a man could stand less than a foot away from the juniper and not be able to·see him. It would take the most bizarre, unlikely set of circumstances for anyone to discover his position. The carbine would sing its song if things played badly.

Voices were the first indication that the pursuers were close. Nick grimaced, almost insulted at the lack of discipline his hunters were maintaining. As he lay listening intently, the big man heard everything from a prediction of cold temperatures that night, to a detailed observation of how short Dottie Mae's skirt was yesterday. If he'd been leading these men through the pine forests of Fort Bragg, they would all have been doing pushups in the mud until their arms fell off.

Footfalls began to intermix with the weather and fashion reports, the occasional scrape of a boot or the snapping of a twig announcing their proximity. A few moments later, Nick spied a pair of blue jeans standing not more than four feet from his juniper fortress.

"Psst... hey dickweed... Steve... did you hear that?" whispered the blue jeans.

"What?" came a hushed, anxious voice from nearby.

"Did you hear that? I know I heard something.... Listen!" hissed the reply.

Nick's heart rate jumped, his mind certain he hadn't made a peep. What the hell could the man beside him have heard? His grip tightened on the M4, thumb poised on the safety.

"I don't hear a damn thing," came the eventual reply. "What is it?"

A loud, rumbling fart split the morning air, the flatulence immediately followed by belly-deep snickering.

"Asshole! What a fucking clown. C'mon, dude... this is some serious shit."

"Oh, fuck off, shithead," Mr. Blue Jeans replied. "That dude ain't within five miles of here. He's hightailed it back to West Texas or wherever the hell he's from. Chill out."

Nick's underbrush grin had nothing to do with the amateur status of his opponents, nor their schoolboy hijinks. He was smiling because of the intelligence he'd just gathered. Priceless, he thought.

It was 30 minutes before the operator chanced exiting his hide. While the skirmish line of armed men had long faded into the deep woods, he had to be certain there weren't any follow-on forces behind the initial formation. Again, his adversaries displayed their lack of experience.

He headed out in the direction opposite of his pursuers' route, but his logic had nothing to do with putting distance between himself and a sizeable, armed foe. Nick understood that his enemy was losing interest in catching him, some of them even doubting he was still in the area. He had to correct their perspective.

It was two miles before he came upon their transports, three ATVs and four pickup trucks parked along what had been a muddy logging road. Shaking his head, Nick questioned his antagonist's seriousness – not a single sentry had been posted. "Damn! Not even a welcoming party. A guy could take this personally."

Pulling his fighting knife, he ducked underneath the first truck and rammed the thick steel blade into the gas tank. Within two minutes, the three remaining vehicles were all leaking petrol.

He pushed the ATVs close to the pickups, allowing plenty of time for the flammable vapors to inundate the area. Satisfied with his handiwork, Nick then surveyed the terrain for a suitable path of escape.

Next, he retrieved a small limb lying on the ground, offering just enough dry foliage to feed the flame for a few moments. He held it under the still-flowing stream of fuel for a quick douse, and then stepped back to a safe distance.

His kit contained a book of waterproof matches for just such occasions. A second later, he lit the torch and tossed it under the nearest truck. There was a significant whoosh, and then a ball of fire that would have impressed even the most persnickety pyromaniac. Nick watched as the blaze leapt to the surrounding pools of gas, the inferno growing as it spread. Then he wistfully sighed and remarked, "Dang it! Left the marshmallows at home."

Nick trotted away, heading off to find a hiding spot for the night.

When the remaining fumes inside one of the punctured tanks reached a critical temperature, the container exploded with noteworthy force. A huge, black cloud of ominous smoke and flame soared skyward as the detonation's thunder rolled through the forest. Three more nearly-identical blasts soon followed.

The ex-Green Beret paused his stride, turning to watch the columns of fire and ash rising above the forest canopy. "That's really going to piss someone off," he smiled.

The massive bonfire was raging in full glory by the time the owners came rushing back. A long string of breathless men and boys appeared, hustling through the trees to see what was burning. The once-formed skirmish line was now a ragtag, undisciplined parade of markedly angry, cursing individuals.

Many of the former hunters began swearing about their bad luck, extended streams of foul language competing with the roar of the inferno. Others only shrugged their shoulders and started walking home.

Mr. Gospel wasn't happy with being called out so late at night. He had just settled in, removing his boots for a quiet evening at home.

When the chief banged loudly at the front door, Standowski had answered with a shotgun. Despite the law and order his men maintained in Cartersville, in this day and age, prudent fellows said, "Hello," while chambering a round.

"Stan, put that damn thing away," the ex-city cop and longtime friend chided. "One of these days, you're going to shoot me or one of my men."

"With that stranger on the loose, I'm keeping it close at hand," the town's leader replied. "That son of a bitch is dangerous as hell."

The silver-haired cop chuckled. "If I had been that drifter and wanted to murder your sorry ass, do you think I would've knocked?"

Standowski ignored the rebuttal, motioning his old friend inside. "What's up?"

The head of Cartersville's security forces delivered the bad news, informing the de-facto mayor of the destroyed vehicles and failure to capture the fugitive. Stan took it all in, only occasionally grunting or shaking his head.

"We have to catch that bastard, and we need to do it quick. I don't care how many men we need to send out into those woods; I want that asshole standing trial, and then I want his head on a pike, garnishing the courthouse lawn."

"Why, Stan? He's gone now... and probably will never show his face around here again. I've already been reassigning men who were guarding the gates and the trailers, pulling manpower from every one of our outposts. We have people murmuring about the three boys he shot, rumors circulating all over town. Let it fade, my old friend. Let it drift away, and a week from now, no one will even remember it happened."

But Mr. Gospel wouldn't hear of it. "That's how it starts! It's the little things that snowball out of control, and pretty soon we've got political unrest. From there, it's only a short distance to outright anarchy."

The old cop shook his head. "So you want to make an example out of this guy, regardless of the cost?"

"You're damned right I do. Look, my guys already hear gossip and whispered bullshit. People are talking about this Alliance and wondering if any of it's true. Word is all over the Exchange and spreading out to the farms. You need to catch this asshole, and then we'll have a little private persuasion session with him. Within a day, my boys will have him admitting he was lying about the whole ordeal."

The former chief was pensive. "You really think letting Nick go is going to cause us that much trouble? I don't know about that... I think you're overreacting. My advice is to let him wander off, and the whole affair will die down into nothing."

"But he's not wandering off, Chief. He has not gone back to wherever he came from. You said yourself just yesterday that he could have slipped away a dozen times. Yet, he hasn't chosen to do so. That man is up to something, stalking around out there in the woods and making us all look like fools. I don't know what he's got planned, but I'm sure we're not going to like it."

The chief couldn't argue with Mr. Gospel's logic. "I suppose you're right, as usual. Tomorrow morning, I'll put another hundred men on the hunt."

"What about Greyson and his boys?" asked Stan.

"I thought about that, but you know what an asshole that guy can be. I hate dealing with that prick. He doesn't give a shit about anybody but himself and that damn farm of his. The sons aren't much better."

Gospel nodded, "I know. I don't care for him much either, but they were the best hunters around here before the collapse. They've got all those fancy hog-tracking doodads... thermal imagers... night goggles and gawd knows what else."

The chief grunted, "Yeah, I know. Back in the day, they had better equipment than my department."

"Offer old man Greyson a reward if he brings in our fugitive. Let him and those boys he's always bragging about prove they're the best hunters in East Texas."

The sign at the end of the long driveway read, "Greyson Ranch: Safaris, Guided Hunts, Hunting Leases, and Equipment Rental."

The chief pulled his cruiser to the sturdy gate, noting the main house still boasted electric lights. Mr. Greyson hadn't been forthcoming when asked where he obtained the fuel for his generators.

The speakerphone buzzed, "What do you want, Chief?"

"I've got a proposition for you, Greyson. Stan sent me out to talk to you."

"You don't say," came the static-filled reply.

The gate swung open via a humming motor, making the old cop wonder just how much electrical power the ranch could produce... and how it managed to do so.

He continued through the threshold, driving slowly along the winding drive. An image appeared at the edge of his headlights, a sole figure holding a tactical shotgun of wicked-looking configuration.

The chief stopped the car, shaking his head at the old man's paranoia. "You won't need that scatter gun, Greyson," he announced as he exited the cruiser. "I'm here to hire you, not

69

arrest you."

"Hire me for what?"

The chief relayed the story of the fugitive troublemaker, highlighting that the man was a suspected thief, preying on the poor, nearly starving vendors at the Exchange. In addition, the wanted thug had blindsided a couple of the town's deputies, assaulting the unaware officers without cause.

Greyson was pessimistic. "More like a couple of your boys got a little forward with the wrong guy," the old coot grumbled. "No matter. What's the job pay?"

"What do you want?"

The chief's host scratched the salt and pepper stubble on his chin. "Well, for damn sure I ain't interested in any of the monopoly money Standowski prints up. We can always use more ammo though. We need .308 and .338, and of course, a man can never have enough 12-gauge shells."

"That might be arranged."

"We'll take 500 rounds, any mix if we bring him in alive. Our invoice will be 250 cartridges if he's dead."

The chief laughed, a pre-rehearsed reaction, no matter what the old man asked for. "Come on, Greyson. You know ammo is in short supply everywhere - they ain't making it no more. The town will pay 300 rounds alive, 150 dead."

Back and forth the negotiations went, the two men haggling more for the sake of victory than the actual terms of reward or cost.

When they finally came to an agreement, the chief extracted a map from his front seat. "We think he's in this area here," he explained, drawing an outline with his finger. "I don't have anyone out there at night, so anybody you see is fair game. I'll hold my boys back until 9 a.m., and then we're coming in with 400 men."

Greyson laughed, shaking his head. "My old granny could outfox that plan. She could hear you coming with 400 noisy-ass rednecks a mile away. We'll get 'em, Chief. We'll go tonight. You head back into town and get our reward all counted out and wrapped up with a pretty, little bow."

Nodding, the old cop turned, strolling back to his car. As he reached the door, he heard Greyson call out, "Did you hear that, boys? We're going hunting. Get your shit in one bag."

Three outlines appeared, rising out of the darkness like ghouls in a horror flick. All of them sported high-powered rifles and were wearing various forms of camouflage. One of them, outfitted with a straw-colored ghillie suit, was less than 10 feet from the chief's cruiser.

The old officer had to smirk as he put the car in reverse. "At least he didn't call out all five of his boys for my welcoming committee."

The shallow canyon was really more of a wash than a formation. Shoulder-high from top to bottom, Nick surmised that drainage had sculpted the terrain.

Ridges of sandstone protruded from the north side, one of the flat, shelf-like rocks extending over three feet from the earthen wall of yellowish soil. It was shelter of a sort, large enough to keep dew or rain off his sleeping bag or hide the flames of a small fire.

Using his knife to dig, pick, and scrape, he cleared the soft dirt to excavate enough space to accommodate his oversized body. It wasn't the Waldorf, but he'd slept in worse places.

Next came the trip wires, barely over an inch above the ground and covered with dead foliage and pine needles. He spanned the primary approaches to his den, attaching the taunt ends to homemade noisemakers.

Standing back to inspect his labors, Nick surmised that only a well trained professional might avoid the web of early warning fishing line.

He gathered a small supply of the driest wood he could find, knowing the odor and smoke trail were risky. His desire for a hot meal and longing for steaming coffee overrode the odds of discovery. He'd keep the blaze small, the duration short. There was a slight breeze to disperse the aroma, and it was unlikely anyone would observe the smoke after dusk.

It was a tremendous relief to unshoulder the pack and remove his chest rig and armor. His endurance, strengthened by years of humping a heavy kit all over the planet, wasn't what it used to be. This is why men retire so young from the forces, he mused, stretching his stiff back and flexing a sore knee. We punish our bodies until they burn out, and then we're discarded, useless and old.

Unpacking a quick meal and making sure everything was ready to heat, Nick was soon gathering tinder. He didn't have to go far. In minutes, there was a slight pile under the ledge of his rock shelter. It was going to get chilly this evening, and the residual heat from his cooking fire would make the rock warm and cozy – at least for a short time. The sandstone overhang above the campfire would also help to disburse the smoke.

A few minutes later, the blaze was crackling, surrounded by

several baseball-sized stones. He wasn't worried about the fire spreading, but wanted to heat the rocks in case the air became cold later that night. Without weather forecasts, it was always better to be safe than shivering.

He let the water boil for 15 minutes, using the time to check both ends of his shallow draw. Survival, when being hunted, equated to diligence, caution, and discipline. His meal would be much more enjoyable if he wasn't worried about armed men stalking his camp.

He took a moment to hang his pack, suspending the ruck with a length of fishing line from a nearby pine. Texas was thick with fire ants and other assorted critters that always posed a concern. The last thing he needed was some nosey possum drawing the wrath of his carbine, an event which would help any nighttime hunters vector in on his locale.

The meal was crap, but then again, fine dining in the field wasn't often an option. Pulling his secret stash of Tabasco from his ruck, Nick sprinkled a few drops on the salted beef and onion stew concocted from his stores. He'd passed by a small lake a few hours ago, a thick patch of cattails growing on the water's edge. Taking just a moment, he'd pulled up a handful of the versatile plants. Now the tubers were steaming in the broth.

Even with the ultra-rare sauce, combined with liberal amounts of salt and pepper, it was a dismal meal. He downed a piece of goat cheese that wasn't moldy yet. No crackers. No bread.

Were it not for the game of cat and mouse he was playing with the locals, the campfire cuisine might have been greatly improved. Despite the lack of operational towers, Nick kept his cell phone in his kit as a small, portable library full of electronic books he'd downloaded over the years. He was sure there was a reference guide covering edible East Texas plants residing in the tiny computer's memory, but there just wasn't time to read, identify, and harvest the local foliage. Besides, he hadn't charged the unit lately and wasn't even sure it would turn on.

"Calories," he whispered, blowing to cool another spoonful. "It's all about calories and food energy. Just keep telling yourself that and choke it down. Diana will make you some of her world-class pasta when you get back to Alpha. That, and I'm going to make Bishop buy me... no, the whole team, a pizza. A thick one. With extra cheese. Hold the mold."

Nick judged his campsite sufficiently secluded to do a little housekeeping. His body and clothing were seasoned to the point where odor might give away his position. I feel like I've spent half of my life covered in a layer of dirt and filth, he thought. It's a wonder the muck ever washes off.

Picking up his carbine and an empty trash bag from his pack, Nick made the call to chance movement. A creek gurgled close to his location, the route blocked only by his web of tripwires. He had hurt those hunting him pretty badly, and doubted they'd regroup and risk a nighttime endeavor. Besides, he'd sleep better if he were a little cleaner.

The plastic bag was soon swinging against his leg, the bulging vessel full of water for laundry – no need to boil.

But it would be nice to scrub off the grime with warm water.

After a few moments of consideration, he decided to throw another wrist-sized piece of dried timber on the fire, just enough fuel to heat another container of water. His clothing would have to do with a cold wash.

He stripped down, tossing his threads into the bag. No detergent. No spin cycle.

After sloshing around the bag of garments, he extracted his field wardrobe, wringing out each piece and then attaching it to a line above the smoldering column that was rising from the overhang. The smoke would kill odor-causing bacteria as well as help to dry the duds.

By the time he'd finished with his laundry duties, his bath water was nice and hot.

Just like washing a car, he started from the top down, wishing for a small bottle of shampoo or soap. With a corner of the always-present Shemagh serving as washcloth, he scrubbed and rubbed. The hot water refreshed him, and while the rag-bath was better than nothing, he still longed for a nice, hot, shower.

Rinsing and wringing the Shemagh, he hung the towel-sized cotton cloth to dry with his outerwear. He took a moment to examine the well-worn piece of kit, the number of uses for such a simple item never ceasing to amaze the ex-soldier.

Most people, when visualizing Arab-style head wraps, thought they were purpose built articles like Western hats. That assumption was incorrect.

While the big man didn't know the full ancestral linage of the Shemagh, he know that people all over the globe used one form or the other of the multi-purpose cloth.

Nick had first been exposed to the article of clothing when cross-training with the British Special Air Services, or SAS. He'd noticed all of UK operators using what he thought were some sort of military issue wraps, or ascots.

"You can use it as a scarf," replied one burly Scotsman, "It will keep your pack straps and weapon sling from eating into your neck on a long trek. I've also used it like a bandit's mask during sand storms, or to keep road dust out of my lungs."

"See these little cotton twirlers," added another SAS

trooper, holding up one of the bundles of thread dangling from the fringe. "These are great for starting a fire. I've used my 'Smog' for filtering water, as a sunshade, for camo or a disguise, and as a field dressing. I keep two of them in my kit at all times."

Nick had been sold, acquiring his first example in a Baghdad open market for a dollar. Like so many local items, the handy square of cotton caught on with the invading armies of NATO, soon a common sight on foreign troops.

Dressing in the spare fatigues from his pack, Nick spread the now empty plastic bag across the ground and then unrolled his GI-issued sleeping system. It was time to hit the hay.

As he began his climb under the rock roof, he considered repacking his still damp clothing. Years of experience taught him that unexpected guests might mean breaking camp in a hurry, and leaving any of his precious supplies behind would hamper the mission.

Again, optimism reigned in the ex-soldier's mind. He'd let the clothing dry in the dying fire and repack in the morning.

Ten minutes later, the only sound in the shallow grotto was the slow and steady breathing of a sleeping man.

Chapter 6

Greyson surveyed the two hounds, nearly as proud of the canines as he was of his own sons. They were special dogs.

They were Dogo Argentinos, a breed especially developed for hunting feral hogs in South America. Larger and more powerful than pit bulls, they were built to handle even the surliest boar.

Greyson had taken the animals' training seriously, schooling his beloved stalkers to track men. More than once a tourist-hunter had gotten lost on his sizable ranch, and the dogos had been used to locate the wandering greenhorn.

"Find me a man," he whispered to the two eager canines. "Go on; find me a man."

Releasing their collars, the beasts' master smiled as both bounded away, their noses scanning the earth in search of quarry.

Turning to his sons, he announced, "The chief tells me this fugitive is one dangerous SOB. Bring the thermal images, the AR10s, and plenty of ammo. I'll watch the dogs' locator beacons. And whatever you three dumbshits do, please don't get spooked and shoot each other. Your mother is already pissed enough because I agreed to take this job. I don't want to sleep on the couch for a week."

Two of the boys grunted, not chancing a proper laugh because they were unsure if their father was teasing or not.

Greyson pulled a small device from his truck and switched on the power control. The surrounding woods were illuminated with the soft glow from the small unit's screen.

About the size and shape of a handheld radio, Greyson watched two red dots slowly progress across the image of a map. Two sets of GPS coordinates appeared in the lower left-hand corner, the exact location being broadcasted from the dogs' collars.

"Let's get going," the father announced. "Those devices only have a range of seven miles, and the dogs are moving fast tonight."

Forty minutes later, the display showed both animals were now following each other, their progress slowing considerably. From years of experience, Greyson knew they had picked up a trail.

Motioning for his sons to keep up with him, he changed course, guiding his party through the moonlit forest on a heading that anticipated where the two dogos would stop.

"I know where you're hiding," Greyson whispered, smiling at

the tracker in his hands. "You're just south of the creek in one of those washes. That's where I'd hole up, too."

Motioning for his boys to gather around, Greyson held up the GPS display. "He's going to be right here. There's a whole series of small undulations and crevices to hide in. Let's head up here to this high ground, find a couple of good trees to climb, and use the thermal to find him."

Nods and sly grins were the only responses, the hunting party slightly altering its direction. "Piece of cake," Greyson muttered, thinking about the town's inept attempt at a manhunt. "Never send boys to do a man's job."

The dogs stopped a few minutes later, their training requiring them to sit perfectly still once they had located the prey. If it moved, they would follow. If it didn't, they would hold their position until their master arrived. While Greyson couldn't be sure they'd found the right man, he was confident they had sited a human in the woods. According to the chief, the only person who should be out in the forest was the target.

Again, he showed the boys his display, each nodding knowingly, then proceeding toward the objective. Greyson could hear rounds being chambered as his sons moved off. A few minutes later, the oldest pointed upward, his two brothers pushing him up into the low branches of a tree. Dad watched the dim outline of his son disappear into the intertwined, overhead foliage.

It took a slow sweep before the climber spotted the first heat signature through the thermal optic. While the high-tech scope couldn't "see through" trees or underbrush, it could detect body heat at over 400 meters. The target could be positively identified at 250.

Frowning, the younger Greyson whispered down, "I see heat... and maybe part of a body, but I don't have a shot from here. The canopy is just too thick."

"Come on down then; we'll move in on him."

They were 150 meters from Nick's camp when the older son held up his hand for everyone to stop. "Got him," he whispered to his comrades. "I can see him plain as day."

"Kill him," Greyson ordered without emotion. "Let's get this over with."

Nick thought he was dreaming. Two loud "thwacks" sounded nearby, followed by thunder... no... wait... those were gunshots.

A surge of energy bolted though his body, the large man rolling out of his rock-roofed shelter to bring his weapon to bear.

With a hundred questions racing through his mind, Nick swept left and right, trying to find the threat. But there was nothing.

How did they get so close without tripping his wires? How did they find him? How many... and more importantly, where are they?

The impact of two more rounds rendered the answers unimportant, both bullets striking his hanging fatigue shirt and then smacking the sandy soil behind.

For a moment, Nick thought the attackers were simply bad shots. A quick glance at his garment made him reconsider. Four neatly grouped bullet holes had landed dead-center between the breast pockets.

"They see the heat!" he realized. "Somebody's getting serious."

Evidently, the angle was bad for the hunters, as they didn't appear to be able to detect Nick's actual body, but only the heat from the flame dried, suspended shirt. That was just fine with him.

He started to reach for his pack, egress on his mind, but then reconsidered. They will be coming in, he thought. If I move, I might expose my signature... give them a better angle. Infrared. Thermal optics. How do I beat that?

An idea came to him, a decoy of sorts. He reached for the hot stones he'd been using to heat his bed and found them still quite warm to the touch. Taking the chance of exposure, he yanked out his sleeping bag and began stacking the baseball-sized rocks on top of the cloth.

A moment later, he was dragging the makeshift drag-bag to the spot where his pack was hanging. Quickly lowering the ruck, he began to fill it with the rocks.

That task completed, he raised the ruck again, tugging on the length of paracord used to elevate the pack. With his carbine in one hand, he gave the now heavy container of heat a good shove, sending it swinging across the narrow ravine.

Just over 120 meters away, Greyson's eldest son spied the pack's image in his optic, a man-sized blur of hot red and yellow colors appearing against the dark grey background. "There he is!" he hissed, losing another two-shot salvo.

"I got him, too!" added one of his brothers, his rifle joining the volley.

Nick was ready, scanning for the telltale twinkle of muzzle flashes. When the bright white strobe of his assailant's shots blinked through the foliage, his thumb flicked off the safety, and soon lead was flying both directions.

Every Greyson male was an expert shot. Since they had been strong enough to lift a rifle, all three of the boys had spent countless hours refining their skills. But they had never experienced anything shooting back.

Nick's first shot tore the AR10 from the older brother's hands, his second round striking the young man's chest.

The next brother was luckier, Nick's smaller 5.56 round merely shattering his hip bone. With a howl of pain, the 20-year-old went down, and bedlam erupted in the East Texas woods.

Greyson was hanging back to avoid being directly in the line of fire – wanting to stay out of the way when his boys tore into the stranger. At first, when he heard his son's scream of agony, his first thought was that one of his boys might have actually shot the other. The youngest of his clan began firing wildly, the thunderous reports of the haphazard spraying adding to the mayhem.

The old man had no idea where his other two sons were, no way could his shouts be heard over the constant blasting of the panicking boy's rifle. Knowing only the location of the active shooter and thinking his youngest might be in trouble, Greyson rushed into the fray to help. He wasn't the only one on the move.

Nick didn't have a good angle on the guy tearing up the pine trees with his blaster. The roar of gunfire and airborne lead made it obvious someone was shooting, but the rounds weren't anywhere close.

Nor did he know how many men were still out in the woods. He knew he'd hit one, probably two, but other than that, it was impossible to know the count of the remaining assailants.

Running half-bent at the waist, he zigzagged through the trees, hoping to flank his attackers. Some instinct told the Special Forces operator that it was a small party hunting his carcass, not dozens of men.

Using the sound of the still firing gunman as a reference point, the big man dashed 40 meters parallel, and then turned toward the source. He'd hit them from the left side.

Greyson busted unceremoniously through the underbrush, rushing up behind his scared shitless son. If the wild-eyed 16-year-old hadn't been shoving a third magazine into his weapon, he would have probably shot his dad. "Cease fire," the old man ordered. "You're wasting ammo! Cease fire!"

The boy's head was on a swivel, snapping right and left like he was expecting Satan and a host of demons to come flying out of the trees.

With the shooting now stopped, the next sound to fill the

Texas night was the moaning of the downed man. "Help me," grumbled the nearby voice. "I'm hit! Somebody help me.... Oh gawd, it hurts.... I'm bleeding!"

"Come on," Greyson ordered with a bark. "Let's go find your brothers. And safe that rifle before you blow my head off."

But the youngest wouldn't move, his short breaths and twisting head indicating a mental state of shock. Greyson slapped the boy across the cheek, the burning sting seeming to snap the lad out of it.

It wasn't difficult to find the wounded brother, his pleas clear in the night. As they approached the suffering young man, it finally occurred to the father that his third, and now silent son might already be dead.

Pulling a flashlight from his belt, Greyson surveyed his boy's wound. "Fuck!" he hissed, the light illuminating the crimson-soaked shirt and pants.

Without looking up, he said, "Come on! We've got to get him to town and a doctor right away."

When there wasn't a response, the now shaken father turned. His eyes grew wide when he saw the size and speed of the phantom-like outline, seeming to float across the ground and coming directly at him. His throat tried to form a warning just as Nick's rifle butt slammed into his temple. A second later, there were four members of the Greyson family lying in the pine needles.

After verifying there weren't any more hunters in the vicinity, Nick tended to his prisoners, at least the three that were still breathing.

He did his best on the injured man's wound, but without a very well-equipped field hospital, he knew the guy didn't have much chance. As Nick used his paracord to tie up what appeared to be the youngest and oldest of the hunting party, the gunshot man finally succumbed to blood loss and passed out. It was best, considering the pain he was enduring.

The older survivor had a nasty-looking, purple and blue egg on the side of his head, perhaps a concussion. The youngest had a broken nose, maybe a cracked jaw. Nick figured both of them would live. He didn't expect Christmas cards from either.

While he waited on the two uninjured men to regain their senses, Nick set about building two stretchers from sapling trunks and cross-members secured by the prisoners' belts and rifle slings.

By the time both of his bound detainees had gathered their wits, Nick was ready to put them to work.

"Despite my better judgment, I'm going to let you live," Nick stated, glaring down at Greyson and his youngest. "That's probably a mercy you wouldn't have shown to me."

Whether it was his throbbing head or a hurt pride, Mr. Greyson couldn't keep his mouth shut. "You son of a bitch, I'm going to..." but he never got a chance to finish.

Nick swooped low, his huge hand closing around Greyson's throat. With little effort, he lifted the prisoner into the air, pinning the struggling man against the trunk of a small pine.

With the older man's boots dangling helplessly in the air, Nick's voice was bone-chilling calm. "I don't have the time for this," the big man said, "I should probably snap your neck and gut the boy. Let the feral hogs have a high and mighty feast of your flesh."

Nick could tell his new friend didn't appreciate his plan. "Or you can shut your fucking mouth and perhaps live long enough to have breakfast. Your call."

Ten minutes later, two of the Greyson men were dragging their kin out of the forest on the makeshift stretchers. They led Nick to their truck, which sparked an idea.

"Drive to Cartersville's south gate," Nick ordered the father. "Stop a quarter mile outside of town."

Gospel and the chief were looking forward to breakfast as they walked through the Exchange. Both men knew instantly that the deputy running in their direction wasn't going to deliver good news.

"Sir, you better come to the south gate... right away," the breathless man stated.

"What's up?"

"It's the Greyson family, sir... or what's left of them."

After swapping troubled glances, both of the city leaders increased their pace toward the town's southern entrance.

They found a huge crowd of people gathered both inside and outside the wall, most of the onlookers surrounding a pickup truck sitting directly in the middle of the two-lane highway leading into town. Half a dozen deputies were trying to maintain order and keep everyone back. One of the berg's EMTs was helping two other men remove a body from the truck's hood.

The chief immediately sensed an air of apprehension circulating through the muttering onlookers, and the lawman didn't blame them. Greyson and his ilk were known as the best hunters and outdoorsmen in the area. They were tough, successful, and extremely well versed in taking prey. Now those men, well known for having taken dangerous game on every continent, were dead or bloodied. They had been deliberately left in front of the south gate, no doubt as a warning or message of ill intent.

By the time Mr. Gospel and the chief arrived, old man Greyson was sitting on the pavement, pressing a towel against his head while leaning against the front tire. Men were still cutting away his youngest boy, the kid pale with shock, like he'd seen a monster.

"We found them like this at dawn," remarked a senior deputy. "Somebody parked the truck right here, all four of them tied across the hood like trophy deer. Two of them were dead – gunshot wounds to the chest and gut. Doc says these two will make it, but the youngest is going to be eating broth for a while."

The chief digested his man's report, nodding an acknowledgement and then taking a knee beside a clearly hurting Greyson. "Sorry about your boys," he stated softly. "Was it the man we hired you to hunt down?"

Rage flashed behind the father's eyes, but he didn't say a word. Instead, Greyson threw down the blood saturated rag and struggled to his feet. "Man? Didn't you say he was just a fucking man, Chief?" he shouted, the anger in his voice causing a hush to fall over the crowd.

The lawman rested a hand on Greyson's shoulder, "Calm down… just calm down. You've had a rough night, and I…."

"Fuck you!" shouted an irate Greyson, poking his finger in the chief's chest. "That wasn't any gawddamn man! That was some sort of monster you hired us to kill, and you and Stan both knew it. How could you have sent anyone into those woods after a demon like that?"

A wave of astonishment rippled through the surrounding throng, hushed whispers and low murmurs exchanged among the onlookers. Some people were shocked by Greyson's description, others voicing surprise that anyone would dare speak to the chief in such way.

"Now just a damn minute, Greyson," Mr. Gospel said, stepping in. "We warned you he was dangerous, and you accepted the contract fair and square. You knew it was a risk up front. So I'd watch my mouth if I were you."

Something came over Greyson, a placid expression of

realization filling his face. His eyes changed their focus from Stan and the chief to the surrounding crowd. Nodding his head as if to indicate he agreed with Gospel's assessment, he held up his hands to show his temper was in check.

He casually stepped away, picking up the towel and returning it to his swollen head. He waited a few moments, pretending to watch two deputies cut his oldest son from the truck's hood. When he was sure Gospel and the chief weren't looking, he strolled to the bed of the truck and stepped up to tower above the crowd.

"Listen to me!" Greyson shouted. "Every mother's son, please listen to me! That man... that devil in the woods... he gave me a message... let me live so I could deliver it to all of you. He said he won't leave until the people of Cartersville are free to come and go as they please. He's staying in the forest, fighting for each and every one of you. And I believe hi...."

A single shot rang out, the onlookers startled back on their heels at the loud roar. Greyson clutched his chest in pain, staring down at the pistol in Gospel's hand.

Dropping to his knees, the old man managed a smile as he met Gospel's gaze head on. "He's going to skin you alive, Stan, and my only regret is I won't be here to listen to you scream."

Greyson fell over, his head making a sickening thud as it struck the tailgate. Gasps of astonishment rose from the masses, but Gospel didn't wait for any reaction to build. "Get these people back inside that gate," he screamed at the nearby deputies. "Somebody get these bodies out of here before they stink up my town."

Grim surveyed the security patrol, the obvious decline in their numbers causing the ex-contractor to smirk. Nick got it right, he thought. As usual.

He and the rest of the SAINT team had been observing the massive lots on the outskirts of Cartersville for the last two days. Each of the multi-acre sites was full of semi-trailers and patrolled by roving bands of armed sentries.

When Nick had first ordered them to circumvent the town and approach the oversized parking lots, Grim had been skeptical. "They must have used up all of the supplies in those semis by now," he'd commented. "What makes you think anything is left?"

"There must be goodies still in those trailers," Nick had

countered. "They wouldn't be wasting all of that manpower to guard empty boxes."

The plan had been simple enough. Nick would draw off resources from Cartersville, rampage around the huge forest that bordered the south side of town. He would do his best to give a merry chase and pull away as many of Gospel's men as possible. Once the heavily guarded yards were exposed, Grim and the boys were to execute the next phase of the plan.

And it appeared to be working, just as the big man had predicted.

Grim watched the two-man patrol trudge along the chain-link fence, their rifles appearing more of an annoying burden than a tool of the trade. Just a few days ago, there would have been six men working the same area, the additional manpower able to cover more of the perimeter.

Not only were the patrols smaller, they were far less frequent. Checking his watch, Grim noted the time of this latest passing, entering the data into a small notepad that held his log.

After the two sentries had passed the corner, he rose from his hide and trotted back to their main bivouac. A quick bark let Kevin and Cory know he was coming in.

"Your dad was right," Grim repeated to the other two. "Their perimeter is virtually unprotected now. Let's go ahead and execute phase two tonight."

It was good news for both men. This mission had seen them idling by throughout most of its duration, Nick handling the heavy lifting first in the town and now out in the woods. It would be good to finally take some action and see some progress.

"We'll eat at dusk so the smoke from the fire won't draw any attention. Cory, you enter the town. Remember what gear Nick said you'd need, and what is prohibited inside their wall. You'll have to leave all firearms and radio here with us. Don't forget ammo to barter with. Kevin and I will visit the trailers tonight, and uncover what the benevolent leaders of Cartersville are hoarding in their well-protected coffers."

After shooting Greyson, Gospel and the chief had returned through the south gate and continued about their business of the morning.

For lunch, the two men sent Gospel's assistant to the Exchange with money and food orders.

"I want to find that bastard, Chief," Stan began. "I want his purple body hanging by a rope, right on the courthouse square."

"Let him go, Stan," the elder lawman replied. "We've lost enough men. Besides, I think you're playing right into his hand."

"Huh? What makes you say that?"

"He could have eluded our people and been 100 miles away by now. Why is he taunting us? Why is he playing this stupid game of cat and mouse? I don't know the answer, but I can surely guess it's not going to be anything positive for us."

"He's trying to sow the seeds of dissent. He thinks by making us look weak, our citizens will give his Alliance a chance. I think his plan is pretty unsophisticated, actually."

The chief scratched his chin, contemplating his boss's statement. "Could be. Your instincts have been right most of the time, but some of his actions the last few days don't make any sense. He could have killed dozens of our guys by now. He could have easily killed all four of the Greysons. Why let them live?"

Gospel shook his head, looking at the chief as if he were a child that couldn't grasp the simplest of concepts. "I think you're overrating this guy - giving him too much credit. He's just some ex-soldier that was sent as an errand boy. Yeah, he fights pretty well, and he has been lucky. But I'm convinced that we can nip this thing in the bud by showing his dead carcass to the people. Besides, it will make anyone else think twice about challenging our authority."

"You are the boss," the chief nodded between bites of homemade bread and string cheese. "What do you want me to do?"

"I want to fill those damn woods with every rifle we can find. That's what I want you to do."

Shaking his head, the chief replied, "Volunteers are getting hard to come by, and the situation will get worse after word gets around that Greyson's clan was chopped to pieces. Our once proud and boisterous, southern men are now thinking twice about entering those woods."

Gospel grunted, nodding his understanding. "Offer a reward and pull more of our loyal men from the yards."

"That's dangerous, Stan. We're already stretched too damn thin out there. If a wandering gang of nomads finds those trailers, I don't have enough people up there to fight them off."

Waving his hand through the air, Mr. Gospel dismissed the concern. "When's the last time we had a sizable, hostile group wander into our little slice of heaven?"

Peering down at the floor, the chief's response was barely audible. "Six months... maybe seven since we've seen any kind of organized gangs."

"See? I've been thinking we're wasting too much manpower out there anyway. Reassign as many guards as you can and task them with eradicating this asshole. He is a real threat. It would be stupid to worry about something that might happen versus something we know is happening right now."

The chief nodded. "Yes, sir. I'll see to it right away."

Grim and the guys set about preparing the last hot meal they would have for a few days. A snared rabbit sizzled over the fire, the makeshift spit allowing the occasional drop of grease to crackle in the blaze. There was a helmet full of blueberries and three ears of corn they'd found growing in a legacy garden on the way to Cartersville. The lima beans, courtesy of the same plot, had been consumed at the previous evening's meal.

Cory was readying his pack, nervous about approaching the town without his weapon. Nick had warned them not to bring radios either. The team's least experienced member was to play the role of a random transient; poor, hungry, and bartering his way across the land. There would be no lifeline if things turned sour.

Kevin, as usual, was cleaning his sniper rifle. Nick's son had blossomed into a naturally talented marksman, his father's expert tutelage raising the young man's skill level to equal any shooter in the world. Every member of the team was glad that long range capability was in their inventory.

Grim took a moment, wondering if Bishop was enjoying his time off. After the events of Brighton and Galveston, he had understood the need for a break. The rest of the team had been offered downtime, but all had declined. Keeping the Alliance territories and its ambassadors safe was a full-time proposition. Still, the mental, emotional and physical demands of the fledgling republic had been a drain on Bishop and Terri... and they all knew their leaders needed to get away to refresh their spirits.

Nick was more than a suitable replacement. The ex-contractor pondered the differences between the two team leaders. Bishop was far more laid back, slow to invoke force or violence. But when he did... Lord have mercy.

Nick, on the other hand, seemed more comfortable applying a constant pressure. The big man's style was to keep the foe off balance... guessing... unsure. In contrast, Bishop would play nice, give the other guy every chance in the world, and then unleash absolute fury when nothing else seemed to work.

Taking his knife to the now browned hare, Grim decided both men were equally worthy of his loyalty and respect. He'd been lucky, serving with high-speed, low-drag individuals over the past few years. For a moment, his thoughts turned back to Deke, the face of his former superior and friend still clear in his memory. In all the years, all the campaigns, all the missions, Deke's death had touched Grim in a way unlike any of the hundreds of good men he'd watched fall. Deke had been the ultimate warrior, an elite among professional operators. But in the end, it hadn't mattered.

Grim could see the light fade from his friend's eyes as if it were yesterday. Shuddering, he quickly pushed the images aside – that night in Memphis still haunted him.

"Haunted," he whispered with a grunt, taking another slice of meat. "I'm using the word haunted while thinking about a fight to the death in a graveyard. That damn Bishop and his cornball way of looking at things are rubbing off on me."

"What did you say?" Cory asked, wandering up to the flame.

"Oh, nothing," he said, picking up a stick and poking at the campfire. "I was just thinking about Bishop and that sick sense of comedy. Sometimes I just want to slap him."

Cory grinned, nodding his head. "Yeah, but when I first joined the team, his stupid jokes and innuendo made me relax. I would be scared shitless, and he'd pop off one of those little jewels. It helped me chill."

Grim's focus drifted off, his vision fixing on an empty point in space just inside the flickering campfire. Images of that night... the night Deke was killed by the grave robbers... of the bloodlust he'd seen in Bishop's eyes. "Cornball or not," he said in a low, serious voice, "I'm awful glad he's on our side."

It was soon Cory's turn to stand watch, allowing Kevin to come in and eat. While the remote location of their encampment made discovery unlikely, it was standard procedure for one of them to always remain separate and alert. Grim was pleased to see his teammates perform the switch without thought or discussion. It showed cohesion and professionalism.

"I'm off," Cory announced after wolfing down his meal. "If they kill me, please bury my bones in West Texas. I don't like all of these trees and their gnarly roots."

Grim smirked at the comment, "I think Bishop's rubbing off on both of us."

Cory threw on his ragtag pack, spinning once like a runway model so Grim could sanction his disguise. Nodding, the senior man said, "You look like a vagrant to me. We'll see you tomorrow - if everything goes to plan. Good luck."

And with that, Cory was gone, wandering into the darkness with his newly acquired, rambling gait.

Grim lowered the night vision monocle and peered at Kevin. "They've reduced the number of sentries even more. My bet is your dad must be kicking some serious ass."

The kid merely nodded, as if to say, "What else would you expect?"

Using a combination of hushed whispers, curt hand gestures, and a small map drawn in the dirt via Grim's finger, the two raiders quickly outlined their plan.

Patting the younger man on the shoulder to reassure him, Grim pushed off. Kevin watched the skilled warrior zigzag toward the high, chain-link fence surrounding what was essentially a massive parking lot filled with semi-trailers.

Grim managed the outside of the barrier without incident, quickly scanning up and down the fence line to make sure a patrol wasn't in sight. Kevin was scanning as well, ready to warn his teammate if anything went astray.

The fence was cake. Designed more as a psychological barrier than a serious security tool, Grim easily climbed over and dropped down on the other side of its eight-foot height. There was no barbwire.

Kevin's turn to mount the metal enclosure was next, the young shooter unloading the round from his rifle and racing toward the fence. He tossed his long gun over to Grim and then began climbing. In less than 30 seconds, the two men were inside the compound and moving off.

It was easy to tell which trailers were empty – they weren't locked. The two men progressed inward, covering each other as they passed through the open spaces separating the seemingly endless rows of cargo haulers.

They had just passed into the fourth row when Grim motioned Kevin to stop. Eyeing the padlocked rear door of a nearby container, Grim removed a short crowbar from his assault pack and moved closer with an obvious look of ill intent on his face. "Time to become a felon," he whispered to the nodding boy.

The door's hinges actually gave way before the lock, but the ex-contractor didn't care. A few seconds later, he was shining a flashlight into the interior.

Furniture. Bedsprings, mattresses, and cardboard containers all labeled from some manufacturer in Georgia.

It then dawned on Grim that he should be paying attention to the lettering on the outside of each unit. One row later, Kevin recognized the logo of a nationally known drugstore chain boldly painted on a nearby example. Its padlock was no match for a little elbow grease and the iron lever. Again, Grim's torch illuminated the interior with bright light. This time they hit pay dirt.

The cargo hold was stocked full of medical supplies and household goods. There were boxes and crates labeled with everything from "feminine hygiene products" to "pain relief."

Two large footlocker-type containers were secured with secondary locks, each stenciled with the letters, "Narcotics – Pharmacist Only."

"Painkillers," Grim supposed. "Antibiotics, heart medications, insulin... who knows what all else."

"Why wouldn't they have passed this stuff out to the people?" Kevin asked.

Grim shot the lad a look, his expression clearly indicating that the boy still had a lot to learn. "Power," he whispered back. "The guys running that town have a clenched fist on the jugular of the community... loosening its grip only as much as necessary to maintain control."

"Didn't dad say that Cartersville had lost a lot of people to sickness after the collapse?"

"Yes, he did," replied Grim, hopping down from the rear of the trailer.

"So their leaders... just let people die? Wow... those are some cold dudes."

Grim shook his head, marveling at the naivety. There had been so much conflict, death, and horror pass in front of his eyes. He couldn't even remember what it was like to believe the world was a benevolent place. "We're going to show everyone in that town the truth, and then those assholes really will be cold dudes... dead and cold."

They found several more egregious examples, one bay stuffed to the brim with canned soup, another packing at least 20 generators. Grim pocketed a few samples as evidence of the heinous activity.

"It's still an hour before we are supposed to be at the rally point. Let's chill out inside one of these empty trailers until it's time to raise a ruckus," Grim said.

"You said that almost like you're looking forward to it," Kevin smirked.

Grim smiled brightly, a rare reaction from the normally serious contractor. "Putting down the bad guy is one of life's more refined pleasures. The only problem with this line of work is deciphering who is good and who is evil."

Of all the rugged men Kevin had worked with, Grim was by far the most intimidating. He'd found the best way to get along with this moody co-worker was to remain as quiet as possible, listen intently, and keep his thoughts private.

On the other hand, he couldn't ignore this rare philosophical opening. It addressed a question that he knew often troubled Bishop... and sometimes his father. "How do you tell, sir? How do you separate such complex creatures as human beings, especially in a world like we live in now?"

There was a pause before Grim answered, the question seeming to take him by surprise. "I can't," he finally responded. "I gave up years ago. I found the only way to reconcile the whole ball of wax was to believe in my leaders and follow orders. That's why I offer my rifle to the likes of Bishop... and your dad... and the council. Sometimes things are clear, like in black and white. But that's rare. The rest of the time, I put my faith in the leadership and trust their judgment. That's why the collapse occurred, Kevin. The world lost confidence in the management, and everything went to hell."

Just as Nick had said, Cory had been instructed to set up camp in what had been the city park. After being questioned and frisked for weapons, he had finally been allowed to enter Cartersville via the south gate with directions to the park.

His next step had been to barter ammo for Gospel dollars, a relatively straightforward exchange executed by surly looking men manning what had been the First Community Bank.

With his wad of currency in hand, the Alliance man had wandered the few booths that still remained open in the Exchange. Given the darkness and late hour, he was surprised to find anyone still doing business. He procured two apples and a fist-sized hunk of bread.

Trashcan fires illumined the grounds, the strategically placed blazes emitting enough light for the heavily armed patrols to keep an eye on the town's visitors. Restroom facilities were available in a building that had formerly housed the city pool's locker rooms.

Cory had packed an ultralight tent, courtesy of a looted sporting goods store in Alpha. It was easy to set up and would provide him shelter against all but the foulest of weather.

Despite the hike into town, touring the sights, bartering for food, and pitching camp, he knew sleep wasn't going to come.

He was too keyed up about the next phase of their mission. It would be the most dangerous part. He was also uncomfortable being disarmed, having grown accustomed to having a weapon as a constant companion. "It's like walking around naked," he whispered to the tent's roof.

The chirping of his watch alarm startled him, feeling confused over having actually drifted off. The sun wasn't up yet, another hour of earthly rotation necessary before the light would signal the people of Cartersville to begin their day. Cory knew it was going to be a morning unlike any other.

Parting his tent flap, Cory scanned for patrols. The fact that he didn't see any of the local sentries did little to sooth his nerves. Visibility was poor given the trash barrel fires had burned down, and it was difficult to be absolutely sure he wasn't being watched.

Keeping in mind an excuse of having to use the men's facilities, Cory quietly left his tent and kept to the shadows. When he finally reached the repurposed pool locker area, he again scanned for any observing eyes. The campground was completely still.

It was another half mile to the town's northern-most edge. Adhering to the dark areas, Cory stalked soundlessly toward his goal, always watching for the random patrol or stationary sentry.

The town's makeshift fortification finally came into view, two school buses blocking what could have been a residential street in any American neighborhood. There didn't appear to be any guards assigned to security.

Cory smiled at Nick's apparent success. The team leader had made it clear that he intended to divert resources away from the town and keep the patrols busy chasing him through the forest.

"Security is so prevalent in Cartersville," Nick explained. "We could prove the local honcho is Satan himself, and there would be little the locals could do about it. Now, if we thin out their sentries, then the community might decide to revolt... or at least start asking some hard questions."

From the look of the unguarded street, Nick had succeeded.

Cory crept closer, now able to spot the barbwire strung underneath each bus – an obvious move to keep unwelcome visitors from simply crawling into town.

The razor-like wire continued past the two yellow roadblocks, filling the space between a warehouse type building on one side of the road, and what had been the local pizzeria on the other. Cory wondered how Grim and Kevin would get inside.

Glancing at his watch, he realized his teammates were late.

That wasn't overly concerning, given the unknown territory and estimated distances Nick had noted on the map.

Scanning right and left along the block, Cory decided to approach a little closer. It was possible Grim and Kevin were waiting on him, hiding just on the other side of the barrier, and looking for a sign from him.

He scrambled over the last cross street, making for Mac's Pizza Palace. There was a roadside sign sitting in the small parking lot, the now dark promotion touting that a large, two-topping special was only $8.99.

He ducked down behind the hefty advertisement, again trying to peer beyond the school buses and into the wilderness. The crunch of a boot on gravel caused him to turn.

The three men behind him didn't wear uniforms or have badges. Two of them carried AK47 battle rifles, the third pointing an automatic shotgun. It was clear from their demeanor that they belonged there, and Cory did not.

"What are you doing out after curfew?" the leader barked. "And what are you doing here at the fence?"

"I couldn't sleep and decided to stretch my legs," Cory lied. "I thought I heard something down here, so I decided to come take a look."

"Bullshit," growled another of the men. "You know it's against Gospel's rules to be out after midnight. So let's have the truth. What are you doing out here?"

Corry stuttered, not having to pretend he was scared. "I… I… I am telling the truth. I heard something."

"Search him," commanded the leader. "I bet he stole something and is trying to sneak out with it."

"Let's just pop his ass and be done with it," another countered. "My shift is about over, and I'm tired as hell."

"I ain't no thief," Cory responded, trying to sound indignant. "And no one told me about any curfew. I only came through the gate a few hours ago."

The man who wanted to end his shift with a murder raised his weapon, pointing the rifle directly at Cory's head.

Grim's voice rang out, stopping the execution. "He's here to meet me."

All heads turned to see the new arrival, casually strolling out of a dark pool of shadows by the warehouse.

"And who the fuck are you?" challenged one of the guards.

Grim didn't answer right away, using an acceptable amount of time to close the gap. "It's Jones, asshole… from the south gate."

The closest sentry tilted his head, squinting to see through the darkness. "Who? I don't know anyone named…."

A brief, sharp hissing interrupted the question, the insect-like sound followed by a loud thud. Cory watched as the man challenging Grim jerked and then stared down at his chest.

The fellow's face filled with wonder, his hand moving to cover the small, dark dot that appeared on his shirt. He never finished the gesture, falling to the street, dead with one of Kevin's .308 bullets having wreaked havoc with his internal organs.

Before the stricken man had even hit the ground, Grim charged. The two remaining guards, still trying to process what had just happened to their friend, didn't recover in time.

By the time they did, Grim was among them.

Cory, though not the target of the assault, couldn't discern any details of the carnage. He detected a blink of movement... followed by a grunt... and then a sickening crunch. There was the flash of a steel knife edge, a fleeting, animal-like howl of pain, and then silence.

Grim stood in front of his teammate, bending to wipe the blood from his blade on the closest sentry's shirt. "Come on," he calmly directed. "Help me get these bodies out of sight before another patrol happens along."

Cory did as he was instructed, dragging one of the dead men by the leg.

After they disposed of the patrol, Grim waved his thanks to the darkness beyond the buses. Cory knew he was letting Kevin know he'd done an excellent job, perhaps saving their asses.

Pulling a small pack from his back, Grim handed Cory the strap and said, "Here are the samples we found at the trailers. We can hide out in the yard for a day, maybe two. If you decide to bring anyone out to see the stash, make sure you exit via the north gate. We'll be watching for you there."

Nodding, Cory started to ask a question as he looked inside the pouch. When he looked up, Grim was gone. That seemed like a pretty good idea, so he spun around, scampering off into the pre-dawn darkness.

Chapter 7

Nick had a pretty good idea where the town's hunters would gather to organize before starting their sweep through the woods. There was the main highway, leading out of the south gate, another two gravel roads slightly to the west and north. It was the prefect jump-off point.

In the center of the three approaches were a series of fields, fence lines, and open ground before the pine forest grew dense. He had spotted a large barn in the area, the roofline visible during one of his elevated scouting ascents to the low branches of a sturdy pine. He was almost certain that the structure served as his opponent's headquarters, that hunch bolstered by the number of footprints leading in that general direction from the previous day's search.

He was tired, irritated, and growing weary of the constant diligence required to stay one step ahead of the men hunting his carcass. Most times, he was confident he could continue the game indefinitely. So far, the guys with the infrared had been the only close call.

But pragmatism wasn't part of Nick's extensive training. He was well aware that anything could happen, especially when there were hundreds of men streaming through the woods with weapons in their hands, and killing in their minds. It only took one lucky patrol, one guy with a keener eye than all the rest.

Besides, he thought. Grim and the guys should be executing their part today. Regardless if they fail or succeed, my job in these woods is about over.

For the first time in days, he left the cover of the pines, venturing out into an open field. While he knew the sun would be rising soon, he was also well aware that it was the best opportunity to make a dangerous approach.

Humans, he knew, were the least alert in the wee hours of the morning. While opinions varied over the exact range of hours, Nick had always believed the time between 3 and 5 a.m. were when most men's sensory input and logic skills were the dullest.

He proceeded along a fence line, the waist-high weeds providing excellent concealment. Every 50 meters, he stopped and scanned with his night vision, always planning his next hiding spot before exiting his current position.

The first sentry was 120 meters from the barn, the man's presence indicating Nick had made a good guess regarding the location that the local leadership would sensibly coordinate its efforts.

While it was well within Nick's capability to take the sentry out, that wasn't his purpose. Smoothly, quietly, he maneuvered around the man, moving ever closer to the building.

There were only a handful of pickup trucks and one church bus parked near the structure. As Nick had discovered, the men of Cartersville seemed uncomfortable with hunting him in the darkness. That thought caused the big man to grin.

Another scan with the night vision confirmed the sleepy state of affairs at the barn-HQ. There was one fellow asleep in the cab of his truck, another seated in a lawn chair near the main entrance.

With each footfall carefully plotted, Nick continued his trek around the back of the massive structure, spying a few small, glassless windows cut into the fading red planks. Most of them had recently been boarded shut, but one opening remained clear, no doubt providing circulation as the day's temperature began to rise.

Shaking his head at the sloppy sentry placement and lack of security in general, Nick approached the unencumbered window in the rear of the building. A quick glance inside showed rows of card tables erected in the barn's center – maps, pencils, and empty cups adorning their surfaces.

Folding chairs of all varieties were strewn about the room. Someone had even brought in a blackboard and chalk, the schoolroom device well used, displaying a hand-drawn diagram covered by an assortment of lines and arrows.

With the NVD pressed against his eye, Nick looked up, pleased to locate the anticipated loft, complete with bales of hay neatly stacked here and there. The stall on the other side of his peeping window was open, allowing an unhindered view. He didn't even detect any dung on the floor.

With a grace so rare in such a large man, Nick hoisted himself through the opening, only moments later landing in a combat crouch before re-scouting the interior. No one had detected his invasion.

As he made for the ladder leading to the hayloft, Nick noticed a large table of food nearby. Glancing to make sure he was still alone, he took a moment to see what sort of fare the locals were enjoying during their hunts. He was surprised at the menu.

The feast included cans of everything from salted almonds to pretzels and dried fruits. Several rows of canned soups, vegetables, and even mandarin oranges were available. A few of the items had obviously been grown on the local farms, but those foodstuffs were only a small percentage of the total booty. Mr. Gospel clearly had access to a secret stash – just as Nick had suspected.

Deciding he'd eaten enough pack food, Nick helped himself, stuffing two cans of fruit into his pocket. A few moments later, he was scaling the ladder.

He chose a spot secluded in the hay, quietly maneuvering a few bales to provide cover if he were discovered. There wasn't any retreat. If they found him, he would be "Alamo-ed" with no possible avenue of escape. But he would take a lot of them with him.

After minimally rearranging his space, Nick opened the pop-top fruit, using his knife as a utensil and savoring every morsel. "If for no other reason than hoarding this, you should be shot, Mr. Gospel. Damn, this is good," he whispered to the empty loft.

His bedding was quickly laid out, along with three magazines lined up on a nearby bale. If shooting started, he'd have reloads at hand.

Next, he found the partial roll of duct tape, an always-present item in his pack. Careful to peel off a 1.5-inch section without making a sound, he pressed the sticky strip across his nose, pulling it tight via the skin of his cheeks.

"It wouldn't be good if I gave myself away by snoring," he chuckled under his breath, remembering the old Special Forces trick.

A few moments later, pleased with hiding right under the enemy's nose, Nick drifted off.

Cory made it back to his tent undetected. After allowing his nerves to settle, he began to inventory the small package of goods Grim had delivered.

The first and largest item he pulled from the pack was a bottle of bleach. Frowning with a question over the choice of a cleaner, he moved on.

A bottle of antibiotics was next. "Now we're getting somewhere," he whispered.

A can of pears, small tin of coffee, bottle of bourbon, and the instruction manual for a gasoline generator rounded out Grim's grocery acquisitions.

He almost missed the scrawled note on the bottom of the list, recognizing Grim's handwriting instantly. The list read: "Bleach for water purification, pills – tons of them, still within their expiration, bourbon – lots of booze here, coffee – 'nuff said. We found one truck full of brand new generators."

Cory nodded, now understanding Grim's shopping trip. Nick

had said much of the town had been wiped out by disease from contaminated water. A small amount of the chlorine could have gone a long way to purify the city's water system.

Some of the items were targeted for personal comfort, such as the coffee and booze, while others would and could ease the population's suffering. The antibiotics were worth more than anything else on the planet.

Returning the incredibly valuable items back to the bag, Cory hid the goodies as best he could under his sleeping bag. He just never knew when the authorities might decide to check inside his tent.

A deep yawn made him realize he hadn't slept much, a glance at his watch indicating it was still a few hours before the Exchange would open.

"Nap time," he whispered, resetting his watch alarm. "Now we can get this show on the road."

The sound of several engines interrupted Nick's slumber. If that disturbance wasn't enough, someone had started brewing coffee, the aroma easily overwhelming the smell of the straw that surrounded him.

Before the collapse, the arrival of internal combustion engines would have been expected. Much the same could have been said of the coffee, an everyday occurrence when large groups of men were gathering to work in the early hours of the day.

Now, Nick found himself analyzing such things, always trying to figure out the source or supplier of such amenities. Did Gospel have some sort of refining capability, or did they just figure out how to preserve the content of dozens of tanker trailers?

How did they keep the vehicles running? Even when the Alliance secured a fuel supply, spares required scavenging auto parts stores and dealerships. "Just in time" inventory practices had made the effort frustrating at times, especially for the military with its high portfolio of machines and tools.

The coffee was another valuable commodity, the source bean not indigenous to Texas, or even North America. Hell, Nick thought, inhaling the aroma. The java is probably more valuable than the gasoline.

As he lay in his fortress of hay, Nick could hear the distant hum of voices. As he had anticipated, there were hundreds of men gathering outside.

It wasn't long before the activity increased inside the barn as well. Twenty minutes after the trucks, buses, and other transports started arriving from Cartersville, the people in charge began gathering inside the organization's leadership hub.

Nick, raising up on one elbow, prepared to enjoy the show.

"Today we're going to perform a pincher movement," a voice bellowed over the others, demanding the attention of the crowd. "I want every man in group A to disembark from this line. Group B will proceed from the lake, and group C will act as a blocking force. Any questions?"

The ex-Green Beret had attended hundreds of such briefings in his day. While he couldn't risk exposing himself to spy on the management meeting below, it was easy to envision the gathered leaders checking their maps, making notes and asking for clarification on one point or another.

Less than ten minutes later, he could tell the session had ended.

Shouted commands and orders began to fill the air outside the barn, men being commanded to head here or there while the drivers revved engines and piloted the ragtag assortment of transports.

What a waste, Nick thought, lying back onto his bed of soft straw. My biggest problem is going to be where to use the bathroom here in a few hours. Have fun, guys.... Elvis has left the building.

Cory found the Exchange open for business, just as Nick had indicated it would be. He also noted there were far more vendors than customers at the early hour.

He assumed the lack of shoppers was partly because of the time of day, but also due to Nick's antics, hundreds of men having been reallocated to the woods. Whatever the reason, low consumer foot traffic was perfect for Cory's mission.

With his satchel draped over one shoulder, he made one complete tour of the marketplace. Just like his team leader had reported, it was very much like Meraton's Market, an open-air bazaar offering everything from foodstuffs to candles and cloth.

But Cory wasn't shopping for goods or services. No, he was carefully observing the vendors themselves, looking for the telltale signs of respected, established, professional merchants.

The first indicator of a potential contact was the size of the booth. The more prominent vendors were likely to have been in business the longest and have the most resources.

Secondly, he was scouting for respected individuals, taking note of how each interacted with browsing customers and neighboring booths. He needed to find people who could raise a stink, rally their fellow citizens, and not be afraid to confront the man everyone called Gospel.

It actually took two passes before Cory identified his first candidate. The vendor's setup was one of the larger along the street, offering a variety of tools and other household items ranging from spatulas to weaving looms. The proprietor was obviously a woodworker of some skill, the collapse providing a market for household goods that had been made of plastic or metal before everything had gone to hell.

The proprietor was a balding, slightly overweight man in his late 50s. He appeared to know everyone, smiling and waving to practically every passerby. But it was the framed photographs hanging from a support post that drew Cory's attention. There was a picture of a woman, probably his wife. Below that was a family portrait of a younger couple, complete with two small children and a dog. Someone had carved a beautiful inscription in the frame that read, "R.I.P. You will not be forgotten."

Cory entered the display of goods, nodding and smiling at the owner, who graciously returned the greeting.

After browsing a reasonable amount of time, Cory pointed to the photographs and asked, "Is that your family, sir?"

Nodding, the proprietor responded sadly, "Yes, I lost my beloved Sadie to dehydration… my daughter, too. My son-in-law and grandson succumbed to the fevers."

"Those must have been terrible times," Cory responded. "I lost most of my family as well."

The two men stood in silence for a moment, each consumed by horrible memories.

Extending his hand, the older man introduced himself, "My name is Victor Morten."

Cory returned the handshake introducing himself to the local businessman with a warm smile. "I'm traveling to Louisiana, hoping to find my brother. He's got a small farm out that way, and I pray I'll find his family doing better than I was up in Oklahoma City."

"I hear things were rough all over, friend. Has the road been safe?" Victor asked.

"There have been a few times I thought I might be in a fix, but in reality, I've encountered very few people. Most towns don't cater to strangers; some even enforce their point of view with a warning shot if you get too close. I mainly keep to the secondary roads and avoid other folks."

Victor looked his customer up and down. "Looks like you're doing pretty well, Cory. I've seen my share of travelers come through here who looked a lot worse."

Leaning in close, Cory acted as if he were sharing a big secret. "I got lucky and stumbled onto an unbelievable treasure trove just north of here. I couldn't believe my luck."

Vic was skeptical, having heard it all before.

Cory glanced both directions, ensuring no one was close by. Reaching inside his pack, he produced the bottle of bleach and flashed it to the booth's owner.

Victor knew the value of the liquid immediately, a few drops able to purify water without boiling. "There are truckloads of this stuff," Cory continued. "And I found a huge stash of medicine as well," he added, showing his new friend the bottle of antibiotics.

Taking the offered bottle of pills and turning his back to the street, Victor read the label and then opened the lid. Despite finding the seal still in place, he was skeptical. "How do I know these are real and not just sugar pills? A lot of people have pawned off placebos as medication, you know."

"Open them," Cory suggested. "Surely a man with your experience and savvy can tell a counterfeit from the real thing."

Taking his customer up on the offer, Vic pried off the foil seal and then raised the bottle to his nose. After inhaling the medicine-like aroma, he poured a couple of samples out in his hand, examining the manufacturer's stamp and the firmness of the tablets. "Well I'll be…" he mumbled, returning the pills to the bottle. "How much are you asking for these?"

Cory waved him off, pretending like he wasn't concerned. "That little bottle? Why you can have that, Vic. There are entire cases of those less than a mile from here."

It was Victor's turn to glance both directions, a signal to Cory that he'd landed his first Cartersville fish. "Less than a mile from here? Really? Cases?"

"Yes, sir. I found semi-trailers full of goodies. Check this out," Cory said, showing Vic the can of pears. "I don't know why no one has raided that bonanza yet, but there wasn't anybody around when I came through. I've gorged myself like a king for two days."

It all fell into place for the merchant, the mention of tractor-trailers, the distance from town, the supposed huge cache of valuables. Still, being a trader in a post-collapse world left a man with a healthy dose of skepticism. "What are you after?" he asked, frowning at the anticipated answer.

"I need to get east… to my brother's place. A truck with gasoline would be great. I've only got an old shotgun for protection, so a better weapon and ammo would be of value to me. There are entire trailers of canned goods out there but not any bread. Basically, I want to equip myself to make the trip as fast and safe as possible."

Vic thought about the stranger's request, eventually clearing his throat and saying, "Would you be willing to show me and perhaps another person I know this treasure trove? I promise my friend is trustworthy."

It was Cory's turn to be contemplative. "I don't know… it's hard to trust anyone these days. No offense, but surely a man in your position understands how things are."

The vendor made to reassure his now-skittish acquaintance. Patting Cory on the shoulder, Vic responded, "The other man I'd like to see your discovery is a doctor… one of the few that survived after the collapse. He's an honest, older fellow, who could tell us the true value of the medical supplies and the other items you've mentioned."

Cory started backing away, doing his best to act like the frightened bird who was about to fly away. "I don't know… those guys running this town seemed awful harsh. Downright mean, if you ask me. I don't trust men like that."

Victor tried to reassure the young trader, "Oh, no, no, no. I wouldn't bring those animals in on any deal." His voice then dropped to a whisper as he added, "Doc and I don't care much for Gospel and his henchmen. We tolerate them because we have to. Believe you me, stranger, Stan and his gang of bullies are the last people we want to know about your discovery."

Their conversation was interrupted by the passing of an armed patrol. As Cory moved away, pretending to examine a wooden cup from a table, Victor called out, "Good morning, gentlemen. Looks to be another great day."

The passing security men merely nodded, both appearing exhausted despite the early hour. Victor couldn't let it go. "Any news on that thieving madman you guys have been hunting?"

The question caused the two enforcers to pause, frowns flashing on both their faces. "No," reported the older man. "We've been pulling double-shifts while they track him down. The chief says we're getting close though. Shouldn't be much longer."

"Well, best of luck, guys," Victor replied. "And as always, let me know if there's anything this old peddler can do to help the cause."

After nodding their appreciation, the patrolmen continued on, scanning the Exchange's growing crowd. Victor turned to Cory and then spat on the ground. "Assholes," he mumbled. "Most of them were truck drivers Gospel lured here with the promise of protection and security. Now they think they own the damned town. It's so ironic… no one hated the law more than truck drivers. Now, they strut around here with their tin badges and guns, acting like they are a force for the public good."

Cory watched the two armed men fade into the distance and then glanced up. "Do a lot of people hereabouts feel like you do?"

"Some do; some don't," came the candid response. "As time goes on, more and more people are becoming impatient with their oppressive rules and Gospel's constant skimming. Still, they did protect the town and establish order. Cartersville has fared a lot better than most places from what I hear."

After digesting Vic's words, Cory smiled brightly. "I'll be happy to show you and your friend my stash," he confided. "When would you like to go?"

"My assistant can take over for me after lunch. I'll send word for the doctor to join us here. Are you sure it's safe to go in the daylight?"

"I think we'll be okay," Cory responded, visions of Grim's assault from the night before still fresh in his mind.

"Okay, we'll meet you here around 12:30."

Cory shook hands with his fellow-conspirator, secretly pleased with his progress on the mission. "And so the games begin," he mumbled as he stepped away.

There was another reason why Cory was content with his new friend, Victor. The merchant's booth was easily visible from several good hiding places.

Grim had always stressed to stay away from potential traps and double-dealings, and Cory knew enough to take the advice to heart.

He found an area mostly obscured by landscaping hedges with just enough "pinholes," that he could sit privately and observe the activity around Vic's enterprise. If several enforcers arrived shortly before their meeting time, he would have to slink quietly out of town and scratch the mission.

But it didn't happen.

Only one man showed up a few minutes before the scheduled rendezvous, a salt and pepper-haired gent who matched the stereotype of a small town sawbones.

Despite his continuous observation, Cory approached cautiously, finding the doctor examining the bottle of tablets he'd left with the proprietor.

"This is Dr. Hanes," Victor introduced as Cory walked up. "He is the man I told you about."

After shaking hands with the physician, Cory looked around anxiously. "Are we ready?"

The three men casually strolled through the Exchange, making every attempt to appear normal to any observer. Eventually, they left the crowded confines of the market, making their way to the north gate.

There were three security men working that portal to Cartersville, all of whom knew both Victor and the good doctor. "Where are you going?" one of them asked bluntly.

"This man has an ill companion," answered the doctor. "I told him he can't bring the patient into Cartersville, so I'm going to make a house call."

The explanation was accepted without further challenge, and soon the trio was traveling through sparsely populated countryside, with only the occasional abandoned building or farm adjoining the road.

"I wish I'd brought a firearm along with me," Victor commented, scanning a dilapidated structure that had once housed a small convenience store. "I've been inside those walls so long it feels weird not to have any people around."

"I agree," stated the doctor. "There might be any number of nomads, vagabonds, or ne'er-do-wells roaming the countryside."

Cory wanted to tell his friends about Grim and Kevin, but decided against it. They would be meeting the rest of his team soon enough.

They continued north, signs of civilization thinning as they trekked further away from the town. It was Victor who saw the two men appear out of the waist-high weeds bordering the highway.

Both men were armed, one with a shotgun, the other with a sizeable revolver in his hand. Their clothing was filthy, with holes in the knees and several tears. Long, unkempt hair, soiled faces, and dark teeth left little doubt that the duo had seen better days.

"Highwaymen," Dr. Hanes announced unnecessarily.

"Now looky here," one of them drawled. "We have gone and stumbled upon three unarmed travelers."

"No shit," replied his co-robber, spitting for emphasis. "And while they don't appear to be carrying much, their clothes sure do look to be in better shape than ours."

Cory took a few steps forward, moving in front of his guests from Cartersville. "Move on," he said in a strong, clear voice. "You're signing up for more trouble than you can even imagine... so move on and live another day."

The man with the shotgun laughed, his head scanning the

immediate vicinity. "I don't see any trouble. I think you're just blowing hot air."

"Just shoot him," added his partner in crime. "There's a town up ahead, and this might be a busy road."

"Why waste the shells," came the response. "I'm sure these fellas won't mind shucking off those fancy duds and taking out whatever they got in the pockets."

"I'm not going to warn you again," Cory stated. "You have no clue what you're dealing with. Move on."

The two bushwhackers threw a glance at each other, the man with the shotgun shrugging his shoulders. "Maybe you're right," he said, lifting the 12-gauge to take aim. "I should just kill 'em and be done with it. Shame to put double-aught holes in them nice duds."

Cory saw Grim rise up from behind the two nomads, his outline magically appearing less than 50 feet away from the highwaymen. "He's not going to like that," Cory asked, pointing over the shoulder of the 12-gauge's owner.

The robber grunted, a smirk cracking the lines of his dirty face. "You expect me to fall for that old trick?"

"I got no problem shooting you in the back, friend," Grim snarled.

The sound of a voice so close and so unexpected panicked the scattergun's owner. Reacting on pure instinct, he tried to swing the weapon around to cover Grim, but instead smacked his partner in the head with the barrel. Cory charged.

It was only three steps to the thieves. They were bone-thin, under-nourished, and in shock over Grim's sudden appearance. All of this flashed through Cory's mind as his shoulder slammed into his target's sternum. But what overrode all other thoughts was the man's body odor.

Spearing his opponent to the pavement, Cory heard the sickening snap of bones, followed instantly by a howling of pain. He saw the shotgun rattle across the blacktop.

His next thought was of the pistol in the other bandit's belt.

Rolling free of his initial target, Cory tried to orientate himself on the new foe, but he wasn't there. The sound of footfalls explained the absence, the crook evidently deciding he didn't need a new wardrobe after all, and choosing to run like hell instead.

The three men from Cartersville watched the escaping outlaw as he made his way across a section of thigh-high grass and weeds that had once been a roadside pasture. It occurred to Cory that the guy was showing an exceptional amount of spunk for such a low looking and horrible smelling creature.

Bounding, hopping, and scurrying across the field, it looked like a clean getaway, until another coyote brown figure rose up from the undergrowth directly in the escaping man's path.

Kevin's rifle stock struck the man's head with a vicious butt-stroke, the impact so brutal the renegade practically did a back flip.

After verifying his opponent was out of the fight, Kevin looked back at Cory and shrugged his shoulders. "Ooops."

"Pick him up and bring him back over here," Grim ordered, strolling up to join the trio from Cartersville.

Nodding, Kevin bent over the unresponsive man at his feet, and then recoiled. "I ain't picking him up, sir. No way."

Grim, thinking the pistolero was putting up some sort of resistance, began jogging toward his youngest team member, M4 carbine snapping shoulder high.

Kevin clarified his disobedience quickly. Backing away in horror while aiming his rifle at the threat, he wrinkled his nose and said, "Ewwww... this guy's got head lice crawling all over his scalp. I ain't picking him up... no way... sir."

Pulling up short from his rescue-assault, Grim started laughing at Kevin's reaction. The humor was contagious, every man on the road joining in with a hearty chuckle.

"What?" Kevin questioned. "What's so funny?"

Shaking his head, Grim replied, "Nothing, son. Nothing at all. Just tie a piece of paracord around the vermin's foot and drag him over here."

"But he smells really bad," came the response.

Much to Kevin's puzzlement, another round of chuckles rose from the onlookers, Cory regaining his composure first. "Is he still breathing?"

"I don't think so. I... I crushed his skull," Kevin replied, scowling down in disgust at the body.

"Well, just take his weapon and come on back here," Grim ordered, shaking his head at the kid's bug-revulsion.

With two fingers extended gingerly, Kevin bent over. He reemerged holding the old revolver at arm's length, examining it for lice eggs or creepy crawlers.

"Good move on the take down," Grim said to Cory. "I'd been watching those two scumbags for the last 15 minutes and could have shot them any time, but the gunfire might have drawn unwanted attention."

Nodding his understanding, Cory turned to his two guests from Cartersville. "Gentlemen, I'd like to introduce you to Grim and Kevin. They're part of my SAINT team. We're all from the Alliance of West Texas."

It took less than ten minutes of conversation before Victor and the doctor got the picture. After deciding both of them were trustworthy, Grim even went so far as to fill them in on Nick's diversion plan.

While Cory and Kevin tied up the surviving bandit, Grim explained their association with the big man who was causing such a ruckus with Mr. Gospel's security forces.

The doc got it first. "So all of this has been staged intentionally to undermine Stan's control of the town. You're trying to sow the seeds of an uprising."

"Yes, yes we are, and we need your help," responded Grim. "We don't give a rat's ass if the town overthrows the local dictator or not. What we do care about is the citizens being able to travel and trade freely. Our experience has been that if people see things are better elsewhere, they'll take the steps to improve things at home."

Victor chimed in, "If this Alliance is all you say it is, why you didn't just show up at the south gate with hundreds of armed men?"

"We've done that before," Grim explained, "and it didn't work out so well. The ruling council is trying to walk a fine line between ensuring everyone's basic freedoms and being a conquering force. We are authorized to induce and promote internal changes, but invasion isn't an option."

Both of the men from Cartersville seemed to accept that logic. "So Mr. Gospel has hundreds of semis full of goods... medicine and supplies that might have saved my family's lives."

"If there are more of the antibiotics Cory showed me, he could've saved thousands of lives," the doctor added.

"But that would have caused a problem with the hordes of truckers showing up," Cory said. "I bet if you go back and looked at the mortality rates of Cartersville's citizens versus the new arrivals, the survival rate was much higher for those men who were loyal to Gospel."

Grim waved the group toward the discovered treasure, clearly worried about the time. "Come on, I'll let you see with your own eyes."

As the group began walking north, Grim turned to Kevin and instructed, "Move on ahead. Give me 30 meters off-center to the right; I'll take a 40-meter flanking position to the left."

Kevin nodded, jogging off to get ahead of everyone else and make sure there weren't any surprises along the road.

Grim spun and informed the men from Cartersville what was going on. "I'll meet you all a half-mile up the road."

No one seemed to mind having the two armed men for protection.

Dr. Hanes climbed down from the semi-trailer, a look of pure disgust all over his face. "This is a crime... nothing less than a crime against humanity. I've known Stan since he moved to Cartersville, and I would have never thought the man capable of such an atrocious act."

"With these supplies, we could have saved thousands and thousands of people," Victor added. "I've always heard power was corruptive, but this is just insane."

"We've seen it over and over again," Grim responded. "I hope you both understand why our team has been so deceptive and has had to resort to violence."

Victor looked at his friend. "So, Doctor, how do we go about sparking a revolution in Cartersville?"

The physician rubbed his chin, deep in thought. "We can't be overt with this information. Stan and the chief still command the loyalty of hundreds of armed men known for their trigger fingers. There has been enough death and destruction already. We need subterfuge and sedation."

"We are willing to help," Cory added. "But as Grim said, we're limited in our scope."

Kevin's voice sounded from atop a nearby trailer, "I've got another security patrol coming down the east fence. You guys should take cover."

After helping the two older men climb into the empty hold of an adjoining semi, Grim said, "Whatever you decide to do, it has to happen quickly. Our man Nick can't stay out in the woods forever, and as soon as Gospel gives up hunting for his head, he'll put all those guards back here to protect this stash. I don't think there's much doubt that will make your job all the more difficult."

"You're right," whispered Victor. "Our community has suffered enough already. We need to take advantage of this window of opportunity to improve our situation."

"If I know Stan's heart, the word of your Alliance is going to make him tighten down on the town even more. Now's definitely the time to act," the doctor added.

A few minutes passed before a soft thud sounded on the semi's wall, the result of Kevin tossing a small stone to indicate the "all clear."

All four of the occupants squinted when Grim pushed open the rear doors, bright sunlight flooding their hide. "We need to get you men back to town," the ex-contractor stated. "That way you can plot your treason in the comfort of familiar, secure surroundings."

The return trip back to Cartersville passed without incident, Cory and the two locals strolling the distance in silence. Everyone was deep in thought.

They cleared the north gate without much harassment from the guards, then entering the Exchange and returning to Victor's place of business.

Dr. Hanes turned to Cory with an inquisitive expression. "I've got an idea, but it is going to require some research. Can you and your team give me another day or two?"

"We'll try. I don't know Nick's status. Like Grim said, he can't be the rabbit indefinitely, and if Gospel does manage to corner him, a lot of people are going to die before my boss goes down."

Victor's grunt signaled his agreement. "I saw him take on four of the chief's deputies. Clearly, he's not a man to be trifled with."

"Then I'm off to my reference books," announced the sawbones, turning to exit. "I'll be in touch through Victor as soon as possible."

Nick was bored.

While the loft provided the most comfortable sleeping accommodations he'd experienced in days, by late afternoon he was experiencing cabin fever.

It was a common problem in his line of work. Over the years, he'd been deployed on countless hide and observe, scouting, stakeout, and intelligence gathering missions. Hours upon days, days upon weeks, and finally months of doing nothing more than hiding, watching and waiting.

He often mused that he would have never applied for Special Forces if he'd known of the boredom, been aware of the monotony. The tedium, and its mind-numbing effect, was increased exponentially as a result of the intensive training and discipline imposed on the teams.

Nick thought "the teams," were men of action, trained specialists in the science of violence, death, and destruction. And they were.

But those duties seemed minimal compared to the countless hours spent doing nothing, much of that time requiring the utmost restraint and non-action.

Rising up on one elbow, he peered down into the barn's central area, cautious that his movement didn't draw the human eye. There were only two men still inside the structure, the rest having moved out hours ago to scour the forest in search of his skin.

How many times had he carefully peeked through a jungle canopy, hoping to catch a glimpse without being spotted? He'd lost count of the desert washes that had hidden his body, forgotten more of the spider holes, dugouts, trap doors, and ghillie suits than he could remember. They were all used to conceal his presence, so much of his lifetime's work spent where he wasn't wanted – or expected.

Silently, he smiled, thinking back to a miserably muddy, excessively cold hole in the Afghan mountains. A buzzing barn fly reminded him of a camel spider, the six-inch beastie deciding to visit his hide in the Syrian Desert. Those monsters have pinchers that can take off a man's finger, he remembered. Maybe the hay loft isn't so bad.

The dichotomy was a strain for men like Nick. They were immersed in the finest training available, instructed, drilled, and tutored in the art of ultimate violence. Each man was skilled to a high degree in the application of firearms, explosives, sabotage, and maneuver. Physical prowess was required to make the cut, the ability to endure extreme hardship, mental duress, and grueling standards of personal discipline all being minimum requirements.

Yet, the finest, most highly trained killing machines available spent copious amounts of time hiding, stalking, sneaking, and remaining as absolutely still as they possibly could. It was torture of a nature, a necessary evil that most accepted, but never embraced.

As time wore on, Nick's restlessness continued to build, forcing the big man to resort to mental games of distraction. Images of Diana and Kevin were always near the surface of his conscious mind, his occupational downtime leading to the usual wonderings of what his loved ones were doing, how their days were progressing, and if they were thinking about him.

His thoughts of Kevin were especially poignant, his only son now carrying a rifle in harm's way, probably no less than a few miles from his present position. He tried to redirect that negative energy, but didn't succeed. If something happened to Kevin, he knew it would be a struggle to remain on the reservation.

With an extreme effort, he pushed it aside, entertaining himself by guessing the time of day from the scarce shadows within view. He made a serious attempt to eavesdrop on the limited conversations nearby. Tried to catch up on his sleep.

Nibbled on the salted beef from his pack.

A ray of sunlight brought him back to the job at hand, the narrow slice of light finding a small gap in the planks that comprised the barn's wall. About two hours of daylight left, he judged. The men hunting him in the woods would soon be returning, moaning and tired, bitching about yet another day of fruitless activity. The thought made Nick smile.

He then had an interesting idea, a concept that could make his new friends from Cartersville adore him even more.

There was only one man in the barn turned command center, an older gentlemen who seemed to be enjoying his afternoon nap. Nick listened carefully for several minutes, trying to determine if there was anyone else nearby. He heard only the occasional bird and buzzing insect.

He repacked and shouldered his ruck carefully, eyes darting between the main door and the snoring gent below.

A last minute idea popped into the operator's head. Taking his Shemagh from around his neck, he quickly folded the square cloth into a triangle and then began wrapping it around his face and head, Palestinian style. When he'd finished, only a small slit reveled any part of his face, an inch-wide opening for exposing an assassin's eyes.

Down the ladder he stepped, gradually letting his weight settle on each rung, hoping to avoid squeaks and creaks. The solid, packed earth ground felt good under his boots. It was only four steps to the sleeping man, Nick's knife drawn and carried low to thrust. He gave the dozing occupant a rude awakening.

With one large hand, his cupped the poor fellow around the mouth, jerking up and back with unbelievable force, tipping chair and man over, and pinning both to the floor.

Nick was just above his victim's shocked face, staring though his cotton mask with steely, green eyes that promised death. For a moment, the big man thought about screaming "Allahu Akbar," the traditional Islamic battle cry, but decided his new friend's heart probably couldn't handle it. Bishop would do it, he decided.

The barn-keeper must have thought terrorists had invaded the Texas countryside, his face growing instantly pale as he peered up into the nightmare hovering just above his nose. Nick's voice did little to settle the man's heart rate, growling low and harsh. "Make a sound and I separate your head from your body," he stated.

With his eyes darting between Nick's knife and the unblinking, fanatical stare, the older gent nodded a rapid agreement.

Before removing his hand-gag, the big man let his victim

feel the point in his throat.

"When are the patrols coming back?"

"I... please... I," muttered the terrified prisoner.

"When!" hissed Nick, pretending to be on the edge of homicidal rage.

"Dusk," came the whimpered response.

"How many men are guarding the transports outside?"

Nick saw a flash of bewilderment pass behind his new friend's eyes, the man more frightened of not knowing the answer than anything else.

"Transports?" came the honest question.

If he hadn't been playing crazed-madman, Nick would have laughed at the situation. "Transports. The buses and trucks used to haul the men from Cartersville. How many men are guarding them?"

The guy started to nod his understanding, but the tip of Nick's blade made him reconsider the expression. "Three I think, maybe four."

"Okay, friend. Here's what we're going to do. I'm going to let you up, and we are going to stroll to the door. You are going to call to the guards, instruct them to come inside the barn. Tell them you just received some good news. Tell them anything you have to, but get them in here. Do you understand what I am telling you to do?"

"Yes."

Nick raised up, pulling the much smaller fellow up by his shirt. Making sure his new acquaintance could clearly see the safety coming off his carbine, the big man waved his captive towards the door. "Fuck this up, and I will cut you in half. Do as I ask, and you'll see your family tonight."

After a few hesitant steps to the door, Nick listened as his instructions were followed to the letter. "Hey! Hey, you men! Come on inside. I just found out they've got him! We can all go home soon."

Nick could hear the message being passed around outside as he motioned his captive to move away from the door. The prisoner did as he was told.

The sound of footfalls came from the entry, the first arrival finding Nick standing inside, rifle three inches from his head, finger on his lips. He grabbed the new arrival's lever-action 30-30 and shoved him out of the opening.

The next two came in at the same time, one of them trying to be clever and raise his shotgun. Nick's left fist knocked the poor fellow staggering into his mates.

"Any more?" the big man grumbled.

No one seemed to want to answer. "Hey guys, where did

they catch him at?" a new voice just outside the threshold queried. The question never received a response.

Nick found himself with five severely frightened locals, all of them staring at him as if he were the devil just arrived from the gates of some Middle Eastern hell. He also had collected quite the respectable stash of weaponry.

Covering the detainees with his carbine, Nick ordered one of them to toss the weapons outside the door. That task completed, he issued a final set of orders.

"I'm going to leave you guys inside of this barn. Come out, and I will shoot you. Make a ruckus, and I'll set the place on fire and watch you all burn alive. Remain quiet, and you can all enjoy meatloaf at home with your wives and kids tonight."

All five heads signaled their agreement with the plan, but then again, they didn't really have any viable options.

Nick stepped outside, pulling the heavy wooden door shut, and then securing the latch with a small length of paracord. That ought to hold them until I'm done, he thought.

Most of the cars, buses, and pickups were parked in a relatively straight line. There were at least 50 vehicles. Deciding to "work" on every third unit, Nick began moving down the row, his knife visiting each fuel tank.

It seemed to take forever, moving along, rolling under the bumper, and issuing the fateful thrust.

After 20 minutes, he finally made it to the end of the line, the smell of petrol growing thicker in the air.

Again using a small length of paracord, he tied a handful of hay into a bundle, and then wrapped the torch onto a scrap piece of lumber he found lying along the route. After blowing to make the flames good and hot, Nick reversed his direction, pacing back along the line of leaking tanks, sticking his torch underneath each one until a whoosh sounded, and the fire began licking out from underneath.

With his arson now complete, Nick trotted off, needing to put some distance between his crime and the men who would be rushing back from the woods as soon as the smoke became visible.

After crossing a nearby field, he paused and looked back. It was an unusual sight, every third car in the long line appearing as a glowing red ball of fire. The first tank exploded just then, sending a column of red ash and yellow flame high into the sky. The two neighboring cars were burning just a few moments later.

"Now that is really going to piss them off," Nick grunted. Without looking back, the big man swerved, jogging toward the setting sun.

Chapter 8

Dr. Hanes pushed open the screen door leading to his back porch. Under one arm was an old medical reference, its yellowed, dog-eared pages indicating a life of toil from a time before the internet came to exist.

Like so much of his library, The Forensic Guide to Poisons was once again proving useful, the hardcopy tomes lining his office shelves in vogue since the collapse.

He casually meandered over to a bushel basket of potatoes, bending to lift one of the small tubers he had intended to plant for the last two weeks.

Holding the specimen up to the light, the physician squeezed the skin, taking careful note of its softness and color. The now-sprouting eyes were another positive indicator. He then used his fingernail to slice a small cut in the soft exterior peeling.

A slight tinge of green just under the skin made him smile. Returning the sample to the basket, he whispered, "That's the ticket."

After making his way back to a cluttered desk, he reopened the book and reread the page that had sent him on the potato quest.

He remembered his grandma's warning when he had been just a lad and confirmed his suspicion with the manuscript. There was a toxin in potatoes. Called solanine, it only developed in the tubers' eyes and green portions just under the skin of near-spoiled specimens. The poison would make anyone consuming it very, very ill.

Most spuds grown in North America had been genetically modified to remove the potential threat, but the doctor had joined the all-natural, non-GMO crowd a few years before everything had gone to hell.

He began reading the necessary dosages required, noting the milliliters that would cause symptoms ranging from a mild stomachache to vomiting and severe diarrhea. If too much solanine was ingested, death could occur.

Once satisfied with his calculations, the physician made his way to the kitchen. It took him several minutes of searching, eventually finding the lemon squeezer in a seldom accessed drawer.

A few minutes later, he was squeezing one of his potatoes, using pressure to milk the liquid from the mash. After three such samples had been drawn, he began spinning the beaker of cloudy liquid in tight, centrifuge-like circles.

His arm began to tire after a short time, but that was just

fine. He turned up the oil lantern to its brightest setting, holding up the clear container and pushing his wire-rimmed glasses back to their most effective perch.

"So there is a separation," he said, observing a small layer of green-colored liquid residing at the bottom of the beaker.

He verified his theory with a slide and microscope, the magnified image of the solanine matching the pictures in his guide. "Poison from spuds," he whispered, rising from the scope's eyepiece. "Who would have known?"

He closed his book and destroyed his notes. The potatoes' remains were thrown out, the small amount of liquid in his beaker the only remaining evidence of his treachery.

"Time to recruit a co-conspirator," he mused, slipping on his jacket and heading for the door.

He approached Victor's booth with a neutral expression. "How do we get access to the security guard's meals?" he asked bluntly.

Initially taken aback by the inquiry, Victor soon caught on. "Poison?" he whispered.

"Just to make them sick. They'll think they have the flu or some other nasty crud. When they come and ask for my help, I'll tell them they are all about to die. 'Too bad we don't have any antibiotics,' I will say. The guards will spill the beans to save their own hides, and the secret will be out."

Victor's smile made it clear he understood. "They use the school's cafeteria as a dining hall. That place is like a fortress though… no way we could get in there."

"Maybe our new friends can help with that. They seem quite capable."

"Can't hurt to ask," the shopkeeper responded.

"In the meantime, would you happen to have any lemon squeezers handy?"

Victor rubbed his chin, thinking about his friend's odd request. "No, but I've got a Tofu press at home. Would that work?"

The physician threw the merchant a questioning glance, "A what?"

"Don't ask," responded Victor, waving off his friend's next question. "I'll send one of my helpers home to get it."

"No," came the firm reply. "You go by yourself. I want to keep this just between us in case something goes badly wrong."

Grunting his agreement, Victor responded, "You're right, of course. We wouldn't want to trouble Stan with having to execute more than just the two of us."

Gospel watched the twisting, serpentine queue of grumbling, dog-tired men trudge through the south gate. Turning to the chief, he said, "This Nick fellow is a demon. He didn't kill anyone, yet the patrols seem to believe we got our asses kicked."

"The bigger problem is that once retold, the gossip morphs into a tale completely different from the truth. One of my men overheard some rumblings today. He said that the stories are beginning to elevate our fugitive to an urban legend status. They are talking about him in the same terms as Bonnie and Clyde or John Dillinger, giving him the prestige of an outlaw folk hero," replied the lawman.

Gospel understood and didn't like it. "I'll fix that later. For the time being, we have to raise morale. Look at these guys; they're plodding along with their heads down, shuffling their feet, and hardly saying a word. I'm no military commander, but I sure as shit can see when an army is beaten and in retreat."

"It's more than just the physical exhaustion and lack of any success. I've heard some of them complaining that their families aren't going to have enough to eat because they're spending so much time on our manhunt. The reward you're offering doesn't seem real to them anymore. No one thinks they're going to find the fugitive."

The chief's words resonated with Stan. He hadn't encountered a problem like this in a long time. It reminded him of those early days, shortly after society had dropped off the proverbial cliff.

Those had been desperate times. The people of Cartersville had appeared much the same as the men marching past him now, shiftless, struggling, and without hope. He remembered thinking there was a vacuum of leadership, that the townspeople were nothing more than lost souls, wandering through life aimlessly. There wasn't any direction, path, or plan. He had stepped in and filled the void.

Now, two years later, Stan firmly believed it was his vision and charisma that had filled the gap. Yes, the supplies available via the influx of truckers had helped, but he was convinced that his own personal magnetism had saved the day. After all, they didn't call him Mr. Gospel for nothing.

An idea consumed his thoughts, a stone that would kill two, troublesome birds.

Turning to his lieutenant, he said, "We need to organize a party... a feast. We can use some of the trailer food, buy more from the market, and throw a real shindig in the square. Let's have music, free meals, and of course, I'll give a speech. It will be a church social on steroids."

The concept surprised the chief, his eyebrow movement indicating he hadn't expected anything like what his boss was suggesting. "Interesting," he ventured. "You might just be on to something there."

"Someone once said that an army marches on its stomach. Well, I believe a town does as well. We'll have a celebration, make sure everyone in Cartersville knows society here is stable, and we're making progress, despite this little setback from our friend Nick."

"When do you want me to pass out the party invites?"

"As fast as we can organize it. Tomorrow evening would be best. I want to nip this wave of unrest right in the bud. I want to get things back to where they were before that asshole showed up and started spouting off about his Alliance. I'll announce that we have word he's headed on back from the cesspool he crawled out of... blah, blah, blah."

The chief wanted to remind Stan that he'd suggested the exact same thing two days ago, but held his tongue. The man standing next to him had a delicate ego and was unpredictable when challenged. He kept his mouth shut, secretly happy that they were abandoning the ill-advised hunt for the single fugitive.

"Get your best men working on it," the boss ordered. "I want this gala happening as soon as possible. You can access the treasury to buy whatever is available from the market. You have my leave to use whatever you need from the trucks. Make it a banquet to remember."

"Yes, sir. I'm on it."

Bishop had an idea.

Standing in the doorway of the small hut Rocco had assigned for quarters, he surveyed the comings and goings of the local villagers.

In reality, his mind was elsewhere, trying to solve the problem. He needed to reunite with Terri and Hunter, and that was going to be extremely difficult with a range war in progress.

While he had little doubt he could infiltrate the Culpepper ranch, Rocco had described the property as a maze of outbuildings, trailer homes, and other structures. "It's like a small town," the local leader had said. "There's no telling where your wife and son are being held."

"They have scouts and outposts surrounding the ranch," Rocco claimed. "They move them all the time. Believe me, Señor, we have tried to raid the enemy camp several times, and carried back numerous bodies after each attempt."

Bishop snorted, recalling the conversation, his confidence unaffected. There was an enormous difference between detecting a raiding party and identifying a lone, stealthy individual. He was sure he could get in, but then how would he find Terri?

And even if he could locate his wife and son, how would he get them out? While he loved Hunter more than anything on earth, the lad hadn't exactly mastered noise discipline. One single cry, giggle, fart, or belch at the wrong time could spell trouble. If the boy were upset, his healthy lungs would let everyone know about it… everyone for miles.

Bishop had determined that a late night rescue was out of the question. That left only two alternatives – end the war, or negotiate with the Culpepper outfit.

Bartering for his wife's release was fraught with peril. He didn't possess much of value, and if the Salineros had any hint of the rank of his wife's position within the Alliance, they might demand a hefty ransom. He wondered for a moment if Mr. Culpepper realized he had the leader of the free world staying at his hacienda.

Even if Bishop could strike a deal, he was sure Rocco and the Tejanos wouldn't appreciate the Alliance strengthening their sworn enemy. Culpepper would likely want food, arms, or ammunition in exchange for his family. While Bishop had little doubt Diana and the council would pay practically any price, the ransom would increase the lethality and longevity of the Salineros' effort. Not a good deal for his current hosts.

Bishop finished the mental round trip, ending up right back where he'd started. The only way to pull this off gracefully was to end the war. In his mind, that meant providing both sides with what they wanted. Silver, and a steady supply of food.

If all the fighting and killing were really over silver, why not provide the Tejanos with another source of the precious metal to keep their people healthy? That solution would allow the locals to thumb their noses at the dreaded Culpepper overlords and get on with peaceful coexistence.

The Texan knew there were plenty of silver coins throughout the Alliance. He was also well aware that precious metals had held little value in post-collapse civilization. You couldn't eat, shoot, or stab with gold, so what was the use?

As the recovery had begun, the value had risen somewhat,

people wanting to barter and trade with the rare metals. Ammunition and pre-issued US greenbacks were still the currency of choice.

As he worked through the concept, Bishop found very few negatives. If the Tejanos had really found a cure for TB, their experience with refining and knowledge of dosage might become priceless if the disease spread through the Alliance. Besides, Rocco had said that colloidal silver was thought to cure many other ailments.

"That's how I will solve this and get on with my vacation," he whispered. "I'll broker a peace deal with the Salineros and a trade deal with the Alliance. Meraton isn't that far from here, so my new friends could use the market there."

But what would the Salineros get out of the deal? Bishop knew they had manpower, land, and expertise in raising cattle. He could broker an arrangement with Mr. Beltran to restock their herd, and in the meantime work out something with the council so the cowboys could eat until things got going again. Culpepper had salt; maybe the Alliance needed another source.

Bishop's thoughts returned to Terri, sure his wife would be proud of his solution. She was typically the diplomat, always his better half that dreamed up the complex, non-violent deals.

"You're not the only one who can play ambassador," he mused in a soft voice. "I've got game, too."

"You've got what?" sounded Rocco's voice from the street.

"Game. I've got game," Bishop responded with a smile. "I was just thinking of my wife."

A huge grin crossed Rocco's face, "Ohhh, Señor. I see. You miss your wife, fantasizing about the reunion," he said in a husky voice while grabbing his crotch. "I knew right away you were a macho hombre, my friend. Going to give her a good one, eh?"

Bishop snorted at the man's misinterpretation, but decided to play along. "Damn right. She's got some catching up to do."

Rocco leaned in close, his eyes roving up and down the street, his voice low and confidential. "I've heard that some of the local women are very interested in you. I'm sure I could arrange some temporary companionship until your reunion. After the beating you gave Carlos, rumors of your physical capabilities are spreading."

Bishop pretended to be considering his host's most gracious offer. In reality, he was thinking, "You think I gave Carlos a beating... that wasn't shit compared to what Terri would do to me if I strayed."

Finally, the Texan responded, "Thank you for the offer, my friend, but I'm not planning on being a burden to you much longer. I've got a scheme that I think you'll find is a win-win for all parties."

Thoughts of pimping for his guest quickly evaporated from Rocco's mind. "Go on, Señor, I'm intrigued."

"What would you say if I could provide a steady supply of refined silver? You would still have to barter and trade, but it would be on an open market where competition would keep the prices reasonable."

"Yes... yes, that would solve one of our problems, but what about the Salineros? I don't see how helping us is going to free your wife and child."

"I will negotiate a separate deal with Culpepper – one that would allow him to feed his people without squeezing your village dry. After tempers have died down, if you both want to open up again for trade, then that will be up to you."

Rocco put his finger to his lips, contemplating Bishop's words. "Go on," he said, evidently waiting for the rest of the outline.

"I can broker an arrangement that would allow both of you to trade with multiple parties for what you need. The Tejanos could basically ignore Culpepper and his lot, or you could mend fences and become good neighbors again."

"But what about the discrimination, Señor Bishop? You seem to think our struggle is purely about salt, and while that mineral has been the catalyst, our fight is over having to live like second-class citizens. For 150 years, the ranchers like Culpepper have treated my people like dogs."

Bishop was shocked by his host's words. "What? What are you talking about? Culpepper's men and you both told me this war was over salt. Nobody said anything about discrimination."

"I think you've misunderstood," Rocco replied. "Salt is a simple thing, and we are well aware that there may be other sources. But that isn't the primary fuel that burns the fire of our cause. We want equality... we want to be treated the same as everyone else."

Bishop's anger started to build, a burning frustration welling up inside him. "I don't get it. I'm sorry, Rocco, but I just can't understand. If Culpepper and his lot treat you like shit, then don't go around them. If every Texan on the other side of the Rio Grande is a horrible racist or bigot, then don't do business with them. Do you genuinely hope to change their minds by exchanging bullets?"

The local jefe's temper rose a notch as well. "The people of this region have suffered from those holding power on both sides of the border for 100 years. If it wasn't the Mexican government, then it was the cartels. If it wasn't either of those, it was the army or local police. Corruption, mismanagement, and graft have held these people down for generations. And then... poof! It was all gone; the veil of repression was lifted. After the collapse, there wasn't any government, or army, or police force. For the first time in over a century, the people here controlled their own destiny."

Bishop struggled to regulate his voice, well aware of the men nearby who ran the town. "So you're telling me that you are fighting to keep the Salineros from reestablishing that same oppressive dominance?"

"I know it may sound silly to you, Señor. But to us, the Salineros and their demands for salt are a prediction... a glimpse of the future. They know why we need the salt, yet they demand ever more in trade. Why? It's not because they are in need; it's because they want to push us down. They want our people to die; they desire nothing more than to keep my village hungry."

Bishop didn't respond, his mind trying desperately to sort it all out.

Rocco continued, "If you can provide any other explanation... give me any other logic regarding why they have acted in such a way, I will listen with an open heart and mind. But I will tell you, Señor, you won't be able to do so. There's no justification for their actions. They simply don't want us to walk as equal men and are willing to do just about anything to keep us in our place."

"Have you said this to them? What was their response?" the Texan asked.

A frown crossed his host's face. "Yes, in the early days of the war, I tried to reason with them. This was the response."

Rocco pulled up his shirt and turned around, displaying several rows of raised lash marks across his back. Bishop found it sickening, but his host wasn't done. Turning back to face the Texan, Rocco lifted the cloth even further to show the star-shaped scar of a bullet wound. How it had missed the man's heart was nothing short of a miracle.

"They whipped me for over an hour," he said. "I had approached the Culpepper ranch alone, unarmed, and carrying a white flag. They didn't even try to negotiate or talk. They tied me to the corral gate and used a bullwhip until their arms got tired. Mr. Culpepper himself then shot me in the chest."

Bishop looked down, hating what he was being told. The injustice of it was bad enough, the fact that his wife was now under the control of such men adding to his emotions.

"They sent my horse back into the desert with my body draped on its back. I was lucky, our healers telling me that the bullet could have only missed my heart by a hair's breadth."

"I'm sorry this has happened to you, Rocco. I can't explain or justify Culpepper's actions. But I have to ask you this, can there be peace between you, or has this all gone too far?"

Bishop determined the village leader hadn't expected that question. Either that or he didn't have an answer. Rocco partially turned away, almost as if he didn't want any stranger to see his face. He sighed loudly and said, "I don't know the answer to that, Señor. Honestly, I just don't have any idea. I am focused only on killing and winning; I can't think about peace anymore. The concept is beyond me... out of my reach."

And then, without another word, Rocco ambled off, leaving Bishop with an even deeper dilemma.

Terri sat on the main house's back porch, snapping beans. Hunter, utterly fascinated with an old set of tin measuring cups, was playing on a blanket at her feet.

Pausing to study her son's activities, she grunted as his face furrowed in concentration, each tiny hand sporting a utensil. "You're just like your father," she whispered sweetly. "Fascinated with cup sizes."

The joke was lost on the boy, but it didn't matter. The always-welcome sound of his mother's voice elicited a toothless smile across his baby-fat cheeks.

Terri had rolled up her sleeves and demanded to do her share around the house. Part of that drive was due to an internal value system, always feeling the need to contribute when there were chores to be done. Nervous energy, fueled by constant images of her husband being beaten, tortured, or worse, was also a credit to her work ethic.

Returning to the unsnapped bushel basket of beans, Terri reinitiated her task, thankful the mindless activity allowed her time to think.

Hampered with Hunter, without transportation or communication, she couldn't come up with a solution. With a baby in tow, there was no way she could attempt any sort of cross-desert excursion without a vehicle. Calling for help was also out of the question.

Instinct told her that brokering a peace treaty of some sort was the answer, but the Culpepper crew had been adamant – the Tejanos were near savages, untrustworthy and bent on slaughtering anyone associated with the ranch.

The fact that she didn't buy into that argument 100% wasn't an overly important factor at the moment. Mr. Culpepper and his management team did, and they were the ones who would have to agree to any sort of arrangement.

Reflecting on the current state of affairs, Terri's mind settled on a curious introspective, a realization the council's directives had indeed been sage. A single line of communication could have solved this regional problem... one radio or phone line or messenger could have prevented a lot of needless butchery, agony, and grief.

The Salineros, as they liked to call themselves, wouldn't have depended so much on the villagers if they knew about the markets and recovery available in Alpha and Meraton.

Mr. Culpepper would have been able to work with other ranchers in the area, perhaps salvaging his herd without all this drama. Less than 100 miles away were solutions to all the problems, assets and services available that might have kept things from spiraling into a shooting war. Yet, neither combatant had been aware. Communications, she thought, another vote for the fourth directive.

Her analysis was interrupted by the kitchen's squeaky screen door. Terri glanced up to see Mr. Culpepper coming to join her.

The elderly rancher rarely made eye contact, something that at first, had bothered Terri. After a few days, she'd come to understand that her host was always checking his land, scanning the horizon for trouble or opportunity. The habit wasn't due to any shifty avoidance or dishonestly, but based on the need to know what was happening around him. It was probably how he'd survived all these years.

"How did it all get started?" Terri asked after the two had exchanged greetings.

"What? The war?"

"Yes. Tell me more of the early history, if you don't mind."

Mr. Culpepper hesitated, unsure of where to start. "I guess it all got started years and years ago. If you want to really understand the root of the problem, you have to go back to when white settlers moved to this part of Texas."

"Oh?"

"Yes, I'd say that is a good place to start dissecting this whole mess. There's always been a rub between the two different cultures. European whites came from a background of individual property ownership, fence lines, and borders. Our Mexican and Indian friends, on the other hand, held more to a sharing of community assets, tribal usage of the land, a more nomadic utilization of natural resources. This fundamental difference has probably fueled the vast majority of the clashes between the two sides."

Terri nodded her understanding, "I've read where the

concept of land ownership was completely foreign to the native peoples, that they didn't even have words to describe it in their languages."

Culpepper continued, "But it wasn't just land. My daddy fought rustlers for years. On the few occasions when he did catch someone stealing cattle, more often than not they were from the other side of the Rio Grande. Not always, but mostly. They weren't professional thieves, just deprived people who saw a cow wandering the desert and decided it would feed their family for weeks."

Pausing for a moment to scoot his chair over and grab a handful of beans, the old rancher then continued. "On most occasions, I ignored it after taking over for my dad. While there were years when a few less losses would have made a big difference to our operation and profitability, I also knew those folks over there were dirt poor. If they culled out some meat once or twice a year, it wasn't the end of the world for us. I didn't like it, sometimes calling the sheriff, other times walking over myself and warning them to leave my livestock alone. It didn't do much good, and jurisdictional boundaries prevented law enforcement from eradicating the problem."

Hunter chose that moment to fuss, one of his toys slightly out of reach. He was soon content, thanks to his mother's longer limb.

After kissing her son's forehead, Terri said, "So this war y'all are fighting has deep roots. Most do, I suppose."

Culpepper frowned, "Yes, yes I suppose it does. But things didn't seem to get out of control until about four months after the civilized world vanished. That's when the rustling got really, really serious. Sometimes four or five head per week."

"I assume you went to the village and confronted them?" Terri replied.

"We tried. You have to understand that there's not just one village. There is an entire conglomeration of hamlets, outlying ranches and farms. Everybody denied knowing anything about rustlers."

Terri mulled over the statement, choosing her next words carefully. "But you were sure."

"We caught three of them red-handed," Culpepper remembered. "They had two of our branded steers roped and in tow. We backed them into a small box canyon and they came out shooting. I lost my first two men that day. But we killed all of them."

"And you knew they were from the villages?"

"No, not at first. We took the bodies across the river and rode up into the square, asking if anyone could identify the men we had killed. The wailing wives and mothers confirmed our beliefs. I lost another two riders getting out of there after they opened fire on us."

Culpepper grimaced, the memories flooding back. "That night, my riders wanted blood. One of the dead men had three brothers working our spread, another of the casualties was survived by a father and uncle. There was still hard liquor in several of the hands' lockers, and before I knew it, there was a large mob of angry, drunken cowboys demanding revenge. When I forbade it, they up and quit on me, taking off in a full gallop, brandishing whiskey bottles and Winchester rifles."

"Did they ever come back?"

"No, never laid eyes on 'em again. But I heard later that they did horrible things to some Tejano women... some things I would never have sanctioned."

Terri shook her head, the story familiar and not uncommon. It was easy to see how the situation had spiraled out of control. "So I have to ask, is this mendable? Can there be peace between the two sides? Are you like Israel and Egypt, where a treaty and lasting peace can be negotiated, or like Israel and Palestine where so much bad water has passed under the bridge there's no hope? Are both sides so entrenched in their hatred that neither will be able to see a better way? Are the Tejanos leader and you wise enough to walk the path to armistice if it presents itself?"

The old rancher's head snapped up at the analogy, a flash of anger flickering in his eyes. A harsh reprimand formed in his throat, but then he stopped himself.

The young woman sitting across the basket of beans wasn't afraid of him. She stared back, firm in resolve, confident in her place. True, she didn't work for the ranch, wasn't in his employ. But there was more to it than that.

It took Culpepper a moment to put his finger on his guest's attitude. She's playing poker with me, he finally realized. And she knows she has the winning hand. Be careful with this one, you old fool. She'll turn you inside out and laugh while your guts spill out on the ground.

Some men would have been angry. Some would have dismissed Terri's posture as nothing more than a bluff. Despite the fact that she was sitting on his back porch, snapping his beans, and being an uninvited guest in his house, Mr. Culpepper realized he respected the woman sitting across from him. There was an authority there... a level of self-assurance he rarely encountered from man, woman, or beast.

Why? He asked himself. What gives some folks that rod of steel in their cores?

124

The rancher's thoughts then returned to the instant the woman had first learned her husband was a prisoner of the Tejanos. Her angry, blurted words came back into his mind. "I need to get to Alpha," she had said. "I need to get there right fucking now. I will have 10,000 men with battle tanks and Apache helicopters hit that village in less than two hours." An interesting reaction from a woman stranded alone in the desert.

"I don't know the answer to your question, young lady. I do know this; there's more to you than meets the eye. I think you're holding back on me."

Terri didn't want to go there, still regretting her previous outburst. She instantly flipped on the innocent charm, fluttering a smile and dismissing her host's observations. "Why, Mr. Culpepper, would you hold it against a proper lady if she kept a few aces up her sleeve? Think about my current predicament – I'm alone with a small child in tow… without the benefit of my husband or other resources. I am completely at the mercy of strangers, depending wholly on the benevolence of men I've never known. Wouldn't you hold a few things close to the vest if you were in my shoes?"

"Yes, ma'am… I suppose I would. But like most things on this earth, it's what I don't know that concerns me the most."

"I'm no threat to you, Mr. Culpepper. Hunter and I are peaceable folks," she said, bending to pick up her son and rest him on her knee. "I only want to find my husband and get back home."

"I wish I could make that come true, ma'am. But for the time being, that's a problem I can't solve."

"My experience has been there's always an answer, sir. It will come…. I have to keep the faith…. It will come."

The announcement of a town-wide feast surprised Victor. Turning his booth over to a subordinate, he immediately headed for the doctor's home upon hearing the news.

When the loud knock had sounded at his door, Dr. Hanes had nearly suffered a coronary. He'd been working tirelessly on his potion of venomous potato juice, the evidence of his crime spread all over the kitchen.

Victor's face peering through the front door glass, rather than the mugs of the chief or his goons, had brought immediate relief.

"Why are you out of breath?" asked the merchant as he

was shown in.

"You scared the shit out of me," replied the physician. "I could feel the noose tightening around my neck."

Cory appeared around the corner, a large butcher knife still in his hand. After seeing Victor's glance at the weapon, the co-conspirator flushed with embarrassment and lowered the blade. "Sorry," he explained, "I'm not going to be taken alive."

For some reason, Cory's statement brought home the seriousness of their activities. All three stood silently with their thoughts. It was the doctor who spoke first, "So did you come over here to help us press potatoes, or just to make it easier for Stan and his thugs to gather all of us up in one place?"

"Neither," responded Victor, shaking himself out of morbid thoughts of capture. "Mr. Gospel, savior of our town and benevolent leader of all that surrounds him, has declared a feast will occur tomorrow afternoon right on the courthouse square. It occurred to me that your concoction might spice up the festivities."

Grunting at his friend's choice of words, Dr. Hanes nodded. "That's excellent luck. I would think debuting my little witch's brew there would be a whole lot easier than breaking into the school and poisoning Stan's henchmen. Still…"

"Why not do both?" Cory interrupted.

"Because I can't be sure of how much each person will consume," replied the doctor. "If we spray our potion on the chicken, and some fool eats three times the normal serving, then our potion could kill. On the other hand, we need to make sure enough people get good and sick, or Stan won't be concerned enough to tip his hand."

"We need to make sure Stan is one of the victims," added Victor, the bitterness bleeding through in his voice. "That's the only way to be sure that asshole will break out the goodies and expose his greed and deception."

"I still say we do both," Cory said. "My friends are scouting the school. If anyone can get inside and apply the poison, it will be them."

The doctor considered Cory's logic, looking at the beaker of greenish liquid they had extracted. "I think our friend is right, Victor. We have to do both. If Stan's men don't get sick, he'll just blame the illness on food poisoning. If people who never visited the banquet show the same symptoms, then he'll have to know it is something more serious."

"When will you be ready?"

"We have another half bushel to process, and then we have to separate the concentrated toxin. We'll be finished in a few more hours."

126

Chapter 9

Grim handed Kevin back his sniper rifle, blinking his eyes after peering for so long through the high-powered scope resting atop the weapon.

They were 800 meters from the school that now acted as Mr. Gospel's headquarters, hiding in the dense brush, and trying to determine a way inside.

"That's one nasty setup," Grim commented to his younger companion. "Even at night, it's very risky."

"There has to be a way," Kevin responded, returning the rifle to his shoulder to scan the distant structure. "It's just a school, not a military base or prison."

"Oh, if we could take out a couple of the guards, it would be cake to get inside. But this op calls for accessing the interior without leaving any trace of the visit. That building has unobstructed fields of observation for hundreds of yards, well-placed sentries on the rooftop, and random patrols. It's a tough nut to crack."

Kevin didn't comment, his comrade's tone indicating he needed time to think. He continued studying the complex, looking for any weakness or access point.

While he watched, three women appeared at the makeshift gate someone had erected, one of the female visitors carrying a mop bucket, another toting a broom. There was a brief conversation with the guards manning the checkpoint, and then the cleaning crew was allowed to pass.

"I have an idea," Kevin teased. "Can you dress up like a wash woman?"

"What?" Grim asked, recoiling from the young man and his suggestion.

Handing the rifle back, Kevin said, "I just saw three women get past the guards. They had cleaning supplies. You can see them just strolling into the complex."

Grim was silent for a long period, watching the women enter the building and disappear from sight. "Brilliant," he finally responded. "Absolutely brilliant."

"So you're going to dress up like a woman? I've got to see that. Can I use the solar charger to power up my phone? I want to take pictures to show Bishop and my dad."

A light chuckle came from Grim's throat. "No, I'm not becoming a cross dresser. I don't have the legs for it. But it does give me another idea. Come on, we've got some work to do."

An hour later, the two Alliance men were on the opposite

side of the school, perched on the second floor of an abandoned home.

"Do you see it?" Grim asked, waiting for Kevin to focus the rifle's big optic. "Twenty meters away from the double doors, just to the right of those bushes."

"Yeah! Yes, I see it."

"Can you hit it? From here?" The older man asked anxiously.

"Sure can," Kevin responded, checking the range. "But I'm not sure how much damage I can do. This is a .308, not a 50 caliber with armor piercing shells."

"It's a pump, for Heaven's sake. It can't be armored."

The sniper studied the target, trying to analyze the machine's operation. "Are you sure that's the water pump?"

"Positive," replied Grim. "My uncle was an industrial plumber by trade, and I used to help him before I went into the Army. If you look a little to the left, there's a gas generator hooked up to the pump. They will run the unit for about an hour a day to fill that big tank on the roof. Gravity provides the water pressure for the school. A lot of rural, commercial buildings are configured the same way."

Kevin scanned the setup, slowly moving to the roofline of the three-story school. Just as Grim said, he could spot a hefty storage tank, complete with silver piping running in and out.

"Why don't I just shoot the tank at the bottom," he asked. "The water will leak out, and they'll have to call a repairman."

"It would be too obvious that the tank had been hit with a pretty, round bullet. It would put them on high alert. The pumps, on the other hand, do occasionally rupture on their own. I thought we'd have a better chance of pulling off that deception."

"I know!" Kevin brightened. "How about I shoot the pipe? Wouldn't a pipe give way if it was old and corroded?"

Grim rubbed his chin, "Yes, it might. Especially one that was exposed to the elements outside. Can you hit that small of a target from here?"

Kevin pulled a laser range finder from his vest, steadying his hands on the window frame. "It's 910 meters, but the wind is calm. Might take me two, maybe three shots."

"Are you able to do it with the CAN on your rifle?"

"Yeah… the cancelation device doesn't affect the ballistics. What I can't do is use the sub-sonic rounds. They won't reach that far."

"So what will the guards around the building be able to hear? Will they know it's a bullet?"

Holding up a finger to signal he needed a bit of time, Kevin began digging around in his pack. The first thing he extracted was a notebook and pencil, second came a calculator.

Grim watched as the team's best shot ran through a series of calculations, punching the buttons of the solar-powered calculator and scratching the results on a blank sheet of paper.

Next, the number cruncher made another pass through the pack, finally producing a plastic box of cartridges labeled "200 gr." Opening the lid, Kevin sighed in disappointment. "I've only got three left."

"You only have three rounds left? Period? Total?" Grim questioned, his tone indicating he was about to go ballistic himself.

"No, no. I have plenty of regular ammo left for my weapon. But these are extra heavy bullets. I rarely use them, but they would work for this target because they slow down quickly while in flight."

The expression on the older man's face indicated he didn't understand.

"The speed of sound is 1,127 feet per second. My bullet has to be going slower than that before it reaches the school, or the guys on the ground will hear a sonic boom, the crack of the round passing through the air faster than sound."

"So you need heavier bullets because they slow down?"

"Yes."

"And you only have three?"

"Yes, sir."

Grim paced back and forth, trying to contemplate the risks versus reward. They had to create a need for the men inside the school-compound to contact an outside service, and it had to be something unusual. He was sure the cleaning crew and other regular visitors were well known by the guards. But a plumber surely wasn't an everyday guest. Besides, after working with his uncle, he was sure he could talk the talk and walk the walk.

The risks were many. Kevin could miss. Three shots might not be enough to bust the pipe. The guards could realize someone was shooting at them. A patrol could hear the sniper rifle and pin them down in the house or chase them away.

Any of those options would cause the men running the facility to lock it up tight – water or no.

But they had to do something… and quickly. Nick couldn't last forever out there, and the men in Cartersville had their side of the plan ready to go. "Bishop once told me that a half-assed plan today is better than a perfect plan tomorrow. Do it, Kevin."

The kid nodded, setting the three heavy shells to the side, then working on a proper brace and shooting position for his shots. Grim rotated between scanning their surroundings and watching his teammate prepare. While few men could stand against the ex-contractor inside of 200 meters, he had never been able to develop long distance shooting skills. He just didn't possess the patience and special mindset required, but was fascinated by those who did.

The house they occupied was full of random junk, cobwebs and all kinds of post-occupational debris. After scanning the scraps of cloth, furniture, and crumbling plaster that littered the floor, Kevin lifted a dilapidated, old dresser to a position just inside the window.

Using his pack as a seat, the kid steadied his rifle's bipod on the dresser and then set about making himself as comfortable as possible. "This is at the edge of my effective range," Kevin noted as he worked on the setup. "When I talked dad into letting me join Bishop's team, I never thought I'd have to shoot much further than 1,000 yards."

Grim glanced through the glassless window at the distant school. He shook his head at the seemingly impossible distance. "You're doing great, Kevin. You've bailed our asses out I don't know how many times. Do your best – that's all anyone can ever do."

Watching as the kid returned to rummage in his pack, Grim was surprised when the shooter pulled out a pair of rolled-up socks. "Do your feet itch?"

Kevin laughed, acting like he appreciated the joke. After he'd settled down, he looked at Grim soberly and said, "Thanks for that. That's something Bishop would do to help my nerves. I really appreciate it."

Grim wanted to tell the kid he wasn't joking, but decided against it. "Just trying to do my best to help."

After taking his perch, Kevin picked up the socks and inserted them between the rifle butt and his shoulder. "At extreme range," he whispered, almost as if repeating past instructions, "you want the least amount of human body on the weapon as possible. The shooter's heartbeat, pulsing through the rifle's stock, could throw the shot off. Try to brace the weapon to the point where there's nothing more than your finger on the trigger."

It seemed to Grim that it took hours for Kevin to prep for the shot. He watched impatiently as the kid adjusted, braced, shimmed with cardboard, and at one point put the weapon down while he placed a thin piece of cloth under one edge of the dresser.

Finally, Kevin looked up and announced, "Ready as I'll ever be."

Grim hustled to the back of the house, scanning all around for any sign of humanity that might be sneaking up on their hide. He observed no one. He quickly double-checked all around, still identifying no threat in the vicinity. "Send it," he said calmly.

It was another minute before the rifle barked. With the noise cancelation device screwed onto the end of the barrel, the report was much calmer than Grim expected – more like someone hitting the bottom of a soup pan with a wooden spoon.

With only his finger on the trigger, the heavy rifle jumped considerably. Kevin was ready, quickly realigning the weapon's position so he could view the impact of his bullet.

It took almost three seconds before Kevin looked up from the optic and admitted, "Shit. I missed."

Again assuming the role of leadership, Grim tried to respond smoothly. "That's okay. That was just the sighting round. You've got two more opportunities."

The process of setting up the rifle went by quickly this time, Kevin having all of the components he needed at hand. "Ready," he stated calmly.

"Send it," Grim responded, not feeling a need to check the perimeter.

The spoon hit the saucepan, and then Kevin was rearranging to see the results.

Grim would have sworn it took the bullet an hour to reach the target, but the wait was worth it. "I hit it!" Keven reported with a smile, his face never leaving the scope.

But then he frowned, looking up at Grim with a questioning expression. "I know I hit the pipe," he stated coldly, "but it didn't bust. There's no water leaking out."

It was Grim's turn to cause a delay, pacing back and forth while he considered their options. "Are the guards reacting in any way?"

It took another few minutes before Kevin reported absolute calm around the school.

"Try the third shot," Grim stated.

The rifle fired the third and final heavy bullet, both men waiting anxiously for the result. Kevin pulled back from the optic, grinning widely. "It's like a thunderstorm has hit the school," he said with joy. "Here, take a look."

Grim didn't need to be asked twice, trading places with the kid and putting his eye up to the scope. What he saw made him whistle.

A steady stream of water was spraying in a considerable arch across the school's flat, tarpaper roof. Hundreds of gallons were pouring out of the massive tank, indicating a significant rupture of the pipe. "They ain't going to patch that leak with duct tape," Grim said, obviously pleased.

The celebration was short lived. "Come on, we've got to get in touch with Cory and let him know what we're doing."

A few moments later, the duo was exiting the home, hustling for the edge of town.

It was the smell that led the security team to the bodies. With the continued shuffling of assignments, no one had noticed three of their own were missing… until now.

The chief, his nose and mouth covered with a handkerchief, examined the three corpses, their personal effects identifying them all as part of Stan's security force.

"They've been here for at least two days," observed one of the deputies. "Other than that, we would need a full autopsy to determine the cause of death."

"Well, it's pretty damn clear to me two of them were killed with a knife, the other guy shot in the chest," replied the senior lawman. "That's cause enough for me."

Hurrying outside to gulp the fresh air, the chief ran into Stan. "What's all the ruckus about?" the head man asked.

"We just found three of your security people in there. All three died violently. I'm not sure what to make of it just yet. No witnesses… no obvious clues."

Mr. Gospel pondered the announcement for a moment, reaching a conclusion quickly. "He's got help, damn it. That fucking Alliance goon has people inside of our town helping him."

"Could be," responded the chief. "But why kill those men? Why here, completely on the opposite side of Cartersville from where he's operating."

"It doesn't matter," came the angry response. "They are among us, and no doubt up to no good. Let's run every stranger at the park out of town. Right now."

The lawman became worried about his friend, Stan's reactions getting more and more paranoid. "If you say so, Stan. But I've got to tell you, I think we're overreacting. We don't know that these men weren't slain by a completely independent party. Maybe someone managed to steal something valuable and was trying to get out of town? Hell, for all we know, some of our own people might have begun an uprising."

Stan's eyes darted left and right, and for a moment, the chief thought they might roll into the back of his head. "Don't fuck with me on this!" the man screamed, veins popping out on his forehead. "I'm sick and tired of everyone second guessing my decisions. Get every damn stranger out of this town and do it right this minute! The only people I want to see at our feast

132

tonight are the loyal, happy citizens of Cartersville."

"Yes, sir," came the brisk reply, the lawman retreating as quickly as possible, rushing off like a sergeant eager to execute an officer's orders.

After his adrenaline had a chance to burn off, the chief used the walk to gather his thoughts. Stan was losing control, the signs of a breakdown plain to see.

Moving with a purposeful stride toward the school, the experienced lawman pondered his options. Was it time for a change in management? Was it time for his old friend to have an accident that would force new leadership to be appointed?

His analysis was interrupted by one of his men rushing up. "We've got a problem at HQ," reported the out of breath man.

"What now?"

"A pipe on the roof has burst; the building no longer has water. The second shift will be coming in soon, and they're going to want showers and food."

The chief's first reaction being that someone had executed an act of sabotage against his forces. For just a moment, it flashed through his mind that perhaps Stan wasn't so insane after all.

After a few questions and answers with his deputy, he determined it was just a maintenance issue and not an attack. Exhaling, the top lawman said, "Don't worry about it for now. We've got new orders to execute. We need every available man in town. Stan has ordered the park cleared out, as well as every non-resident. That's going to take a while."

"The men aren't going to like that," reported the lieutenant. "A lot of them have been out searching the woods for the last few days. You're going to hear lots of bitching about Stan's promise of a hot meal and a little down time."

An idea then occurred to the chief. "Tell them they can still get a special supper. We'll just cut in line at the festival tonight and make sure our guys get their share first."

The deputy was skeptical. "Are you sure Stan is going to be okay with that?"

The senior lawman's initial reaction was to bark a reprimand at his subordinate, but he held his tongue. "What choice do we have? Not five minutes ago, he ordered me to clear out every stranger in town. I don't see how we can safely accomplish that and provide security for the festival at the same time. He'll be okay with it."

Cory and the doctor finished their task late. By the time the physician was handing over his share of the poison, the Alliance man realized he was going to miss the scheduled meeting with Grim at the fence.

While he was still trying to figure out the next move, Cory heard whistles blowing outside. He ran to the window in time to see several of the security men walking through the streets. "Oh shit," he said. "They're on to us."

But the local thugs passed by the doctor's house, continuing on toward the Exchange and the park. A nervous looking Victor arrived a short time later, sneaking in the back door like he had just robbed a bank. "Stan has ordered all non-residents to leave town immediately," he reported. "I think they're suspicious about something, maybe even our plan."

"Shit," Cory snapped. "I better get back to the park and pack up my stuff. I'll do my best to deliver our little liquid package here, but now with all this going on, it is probably a long shot."

"It's okay," replied Dr. Hanes. "Our scheme will still work even if we only manage to spray the festival food. Do your best, but if it's too risky, don't worry about it."

Cory shook the hands of both men, pledging to see them soon. Tucking the small bottle of poison into the top of his boot, he exited the doctor's home and made for the park.

As expected, he found the local enforcers bullying the temporary residents of their camps. Moving quickly, so as not to draw their ire, he began folding up his tent and packing the few belongings he'd brought into town with him.

Twice, one of the local goons had passed by, ordering him to hurry up and get out of town. Cory had just smiled, thinking about the man puking up his socks after he consumed the doc's special sauce.

And then he was hustling for the north gate with the rest of the visitors, everyone grumbling and cussing the town of Cartersville. Cory wished he could have let them know they were better off not being able to partake in the feast, but again, he kept his mouth shut.

And then he was hiking along the same road where the bushwhackers had tried to rob him just a few days ago, wondering how he was going to make contact with Grim and Kevin.

Not knowing what else to do, Cory headed for their camp, not expecting to find anyone there, but not relishing the thought of wandering around the countryside at night – alone and unarmed. If Grim and Cory didn't show up pretty soon, it was going to be too late to seed the poison in the guard's headquarters.

It was almost dusk when he approached the abandoned home they'd been using to conceal the pickup. It seemed like a year had passed since they'd left Fort Hood, the four-man team excited over having a new leader and a new mission. In reality, it had only been 10 days, but to Cory's bone-weary body and exhausted mind, much more time seemed to have passed.

"SAINT, coming in," he announced to the empty-looking abode that had been home for most of the mission.

He found their truck undisturbed, Grim deserving credit for finding the excellent hiding spot. Cory found the secreted key, right where it should have been, and was soon pulling his weapon and radio out of the cab.

The radio! Grim and Kevin still had their radios!

He flipped on the still-charged device. Keying the mic, he said, "SAINT C to anyone. SAINT C to anyone. Do you read me?"

His heart fell when no one responded immediately. He tried again.

Finally, distant and riddled with static, he received a response. "SAINT C, this is SAINT N. Do you copy?"

Nick! It was Nick's voice he heard over the airwaves. The boss must be close.

"Roger that, N. I read you."

"I'm two miles south of camp," came the response. "I should be there in an hour, if the creek don't rise."

"Copy, N. It will be good to see you. If you hear from K or G on the way in, let them know I need to talk to them ASAP. It's critical."

"Copy that, C. Heat up some coffee for me, would ya?"

"You got it, boss. C out."

Grim checked his watch for the tenth time, worry painted all over his face. Kevin and he had been late arriving at the rendezvous point; Cory had never showed. It weighed heavily on the temporary team leader.

He had moved in as close to the blocked street as possible, switching his radio off so as not to give away his position, and save battery time. It never occurred to him to keep the transceiver operational. Cory hadn't taken his communications device into town, afraid of getting caught with equipment would make him seem like anything but a poor, barely-managing traveler.

Kevin was acting in his usual role as overwatch, guarding Grim's flank with his high-powered rifle. The combination of their positions would make it nearly impossible for their teammate to slip through unnoticed.

When Grim first spied a group of men walking away from Cartersville, the contractor relaxed. While he had no idea why Cory wouldn't come alone, the fact that his man was safe eased the stress somewhat.

But Cory wasn't among the group.

Before he could react, another small band of pedestrians appeared. What? Grim thought, we haven't seen this much foot traffic since we've been here. Something is wrong.

Knowing Kevin had his back made things easier. Rising from the shallow ditch that had been providing cover, Grim slung his rifle around to his back and approached the small group of walkers.

"Howdy," he greeted, the strange Texas custom sounding weird coming from his mouth. "Have you folks been to Cartersville?"

There were four men, two women, and a small child huddled together as he approached. They did not seem happy or eager to make new friends.

"I mean no harm," Grim stated explicitly, stopping several feet away and trying to look non-threatening. "I'm just seeking information."

"Yes, we were just thrown out of Cartersville, stranger. It's not a very friendly place at the moment," stated the oldest of the bunch.

"Sorry to hear that," Grim answered. His concern over his teammate immediately escalating. Still, he did his best to conceal the elevated anxiety. "I was there some time ago, and while they were pretty strict, it was a fair place to hole up for a while."

"Yes, yes it was," replied one of the others. "But today, something went wrong. They started rounding up everybody who wasn't a full-time resident and forced us to leave. We didn't have time to gather any supplies - barely got out of there with our belongings."

"Any idea what happened?" Grim questioned, trying to pry as much Intel out of the frightened exiles as possible.

"There's been a lot of unusual activity lately. They had some man come visiting from something called the Alliance a few days past, and that's when the trouble started. Ever since then, the local goons have been high-strung and mean as hell. But today... today was really off the charts. They kicked everybody out and were damn rough about it."

"Well, thank you for the warning. I think I'll avoid visiting for a while, maybe give things a chance to settle down."

Grim started to turn, but then remembered something the man had said. "Hey mister, before we part company, did I hear you say something about the Alliance?"

"Sure did. There was some guy meeting with Mr. Gospel, the man who runs Cartersville. Rumor had it the visitor was from a new group taking over a lot of central Texas. They call themselves the Alliance."

Grim smiled, nodding his understanding. "Not long ago I passed through an Alliance town. It seemed to me they really had their act together. It was the nicest place I've been in a while. If you folks head south and west of here, I'm sure you'll run into them."

"Thanks. We might not have much choice. Appreciate the advice."

Both parties continued on their way, Grim circling back to Kevin's position. After filling in his comrade with the news out of Cartersville, he said, "I think something bad has happened to Cory. Either he's been detained or hung or is in hiding."

"It's not like him to give up on meeting us so easily. I wish he'd been able to take his radio in there."

Grim announced their next step. "Kevin, this is going to be dangerous as hell, but I don't see any option. We don't leave a teammate behind. I wouldn't abandon you and would expect you guys to burn down the gates of hell for me. We are going to have to go in and look for him."

Kevin nodded, "You don't have to tell me that, Grim. I'd die for any of you. We are a team."

"Glad to hear you say it," Grim replied. "This is going to be extremely tricky given their security people seem to be on high alert. But if we're careful and work together, I think we've got a good shot at pulling it off."

"I'm in, 100%. Just tell me what you want to do."

Bishop awoke from his catnap, his dreams interrupted by the sound of excited voices. While he couldn't understand the language, it was clear something was happening in the village.

He stayed inside the tiny, single room adobe, watching through the narrow door as women, children and men moved along the street at a quickened pace. Everyone appeared to be heading for the square. He decided to follow.

A significant crowd had gathered by the time the Texan

arrived. Fortunately, he was taller than the average citizen, so standing at the back of the throng didn't limit his visibility.

A procession came down the main street, several of the village's younger men brandishing their rifles while being kissed on the cheek as they passed through the clusters of local maidens. Everyone was expressing congratulations, patting the armed party on the back and sharing hugs of celebration.

Toward the end of the parade, Bishop finally saw the reason for the merriment. A single horse was being led into the square. In the saddle sat a cowboy, his hands tied behind his back. The man looked nearly dead, blood streaming from his nose, mouth and ear. Red welts covered his face and bare chest. Somebody had beaten the captive badly.

Then another horse came into view, a body tied over the saddle. The villagers hurled insults and pointed angry gestures at the passing dead man.

Rocco appeared on the church's steps, the default, elevated speaking platform for the tiny square. After the horses were led to a stop in front of him, Rocco clasped his hands together in victory and waved them above his head. The throng went nuts, cheers of support filling the adobe lined streets.

"Viva Tejanos!" Rocco yelled over the crowd. "Viva Tejanos!"

Several voices took up the chant, it soon sounding like the entire village was shouting at the top of its united lungs.

While the mob continued to celebrate, several men pulled the prisoner from his saddle, roughly manhandling him up onto the stage. Bishop noted they had to support the poor fellow, his legs unable to bear his own weight.

While he couldn't catch every Spanish word, it soon became clear to Bishop that Rocco was telling his supporters that the captured Salineros rider would be interrogated throughout the night and hung in the morning. He warned everyone that their sleep might be disturbed by the prisoner's screaming and begging for mercy. The crowd didn't seem to mind, many of the people around Bishop calling for the man to be skinned alive – right now, right there on the church steps.

And then the party was over, Rocco's troops lead the doomed man away, as well as the two horses.

Bishop hung back, trying to appear as disinterested as possible. In reality, his mind was moving a thousand miles per hour. A solution had just appeared before his eyes, the answer to all of his problems appearing out of thin air.

After the mob had dispersed, Bishop made for the place he knew Rocco would be. Sure enough, the local jefe was congratulating his fighters, listening to their excited bragging about how they'd come to execute one rider and capture the other.

Like any good leader, Rocco rode the wave of victory, soon ordering tequila and cigars for the brave Tejanos soldiers.

Bishop stayed back, having no desire to dampen the festivities, but wanting to talk to Rocco before they accidentally killed the Salineros rider.

Someone showed up with a guitar, soon followed by several young ladies in brightly colored skirts. The tequila flowed, and the dancing began. The Texan grimaced when the partiers starting firing celebratory gunshots into the air. What a waste of ammo, he thought.

After an hour, it became clear that Rocco had more serious tasks on his mind. Slowly, politely, his two top lieutenants and he began shooing the revelers away, gently guiding them to take their celebration elsewhere.

Bishop stayed put, listening as the merrymakers moved a few streets over, their voices, gunshots, and shouting now held down to a dull roar. The Texan checked his carbine, thumbed off the safety, and began walking toward Rocco.

'Evening," he announced, startling the three Tejanos leaders as he appeared out of the shadows. "I understand I'm no longer the only gringo in town."

Rocco didn't seem displeased to see Bishop's approach, smiling broadly at the new arrival. The two subordinates weren't so happy, eyeing Bishop's rifle with wary eyes.

"What can I do for you, my friend?" Rocco asked.

"I would like to have a word with you in private," Bishop replied, his tone making it clear something important was on his mind.

Glancing at his two remaining soldiers, Rocco shook his head. "There is nothing my men can't hear. I trust them explicitly."

"Fine with me," the Texan responded. "I'll get right down to business. I want the prisoner and the two horses. They're my ticket to get my wife and son back, and our ride home."

A hurt look replaced Rocco's smile, almost as if Bishop had insulted the man.

"Señor, while you are my honored guest, your request is impossible. We don't turn captured Salineros killers loose. I cannot do as you request."

"Don't fuck with me, Rocco. I want my wife and child back, and I don't have any other option. I'll give you my word that I'll come back and make a serious attempt to broker a peace between the Culpepper outfit and your people."

Rocco spread his hands wide in the air, "How about a

compromise? I'll grant you the horses and as many of the supplies from your truck as you can pack. You can ride the animals to the ranch? I think this is a fair bargain, no?"

"No. If I show up at Culpepper's front door with two of his men's horses, he might think I murdered them. I need the survivor to guide me in and tell those people that I rescued him."

Rocco shook his head, his voice becoming less friendly. "I'm sorry, Bishop, but I cannot grant your request. My men need to see the conclusion to their efforts. My people have to know we are winning."

The two men with Rocco noted the change in their boss's tone, both of them becoming stiff and ready for action. Bishop remained calm.

"Give him to me, along with the horses, or there's going to be trouble. I've got to get back to my family and make sure they're okay. Don't press this, Rocco. It's not a fight you want right here in the middle of your hometown."

Bishop saw an odd light pass behind Rocco's eyes, a glimmer of something cold and cruel. "As you wish," the leader replied. "I'll have our captive brought out for you," he added, turning to step to the back of his home. As he passed close to his men, Bishop heard a whisper in Spanish. "Kill him."

It was a poorly executed move, the Texan primed and ready for just such a play. Both of Rocco's troops brandished AK47 battle rifles, but they weren't experienced enough to bring them into play while moving at the same time. Bishop, on the other hand, already had his carbine at his shoulder, centering his red dot before either man on the porch could even raise his weapon.

The M4 barked once, twice, three times, its report blending in with the occasional gunfire still erupting from the nearby celebration. Both lieutenants crumpled to the porch's wooden planks.

Rocco paused, his hands in the air, his back still turned to Bishop. "Will you shoot me in the back?" he asked the Texan.

"No. Like I said, this is a fight you don't want," Bishop replied, walking closer to his former friend. "Bring me the prisoner and the horses. Now!"

Rocco nodded his agreement, taking a half step and then spinning quickly. Bishop saw the flash of shiny steel in the man's hand just as a knife came hurling through the air.

The blade struck Bishop dead center in the chest, but bounced harmlessly off of the Texan's body armor, clambering down to the packed dirt surface at his feet.

Rage swelled inside the Texan, the underhanded attempt to kill him sparking an eruption of fury. With his head down and heart pumping, he stepped into Rocco. It would have been too easy to slay the man with his rifle; he wanted the pleasure of thrashing his foe with his bare hands.

Rocco was furious as well, the death of his men combined with the Texan's unreasonable demands making him regret ever letting Bishop live. The two men collided.

The larger and stronger of the two, Rocco still was handicapped, his one arm hampered by the injury suffered during the ambush. Still, he was a brave and potent fighter.

While Bishop was the more skilled, his efforts were restricted by the rifle and heavy kit strapped to his chest.

The Texan was far more motivated than his opponent. In addition to the pent up stress from not knowing Terri and Hunter's status, he knew the engagement had to end quickly, or local reinforcements would arrive.

Stepping in close, he ducked a powerful roundhouse, popping back up to deliver a punishing series of quick jabs to Rocco's face.

Backing away from Bishop's swarming fists, Rocco took a few breaths to recover. "You are no better than the Salineros trash we fight every day. I should have killed you back in the Valley of Rocks."

Bishop ignored the taunt, stepping in with a feigned right while launching his best left. Rocco somehow managed to duck under the punch, delivering a solid kick to Bishop's stomach as he passed. It was the Texan's turn to stagger back and regroup.

"You're too stupid to realize what I'm offering you, Rocco," the Texan managed between heaving breaths. "I'm giving you the best chance you'll have at peace. To end the killing. To end the suffering. You're so wrapped up in hate and loathing, you can't see anything other than revenge."

The words seemed to sting Rocco. Growling, he dove into his opponent, good arm throwing two quick punches that insulted nothing but open air. Bishop wasn't there.

A sharp pain bolted through Rocco's ribs, courtesy of Bishop's elbow. Another blow landed on the larger man's ear, ringing-white lines of pain vibrating through his head. Rocco went down to his knees, unable to stand any longer.

"Being blind to reality is always the way it ends up, Rocco. Really, it's not your fault. The passion required to lead people through a war doesn't mix with the wisdom it takes to find peace. I'm sorry it had to end like this. I really had hoped you would see the light and put a stop to your people's suffering."

Bishop stepped close, but then stopped, something in his adversary's eyes making him halt the final onslaught.

"Wait... please wait, Señor. I can't give you what you want, my people would never trust me again...."

Bishop was out of time and in no mood for pleading. "Night, night, my friend. I'll see you later," he whispered.

The blow to Rocco's jaw sent the now unconscious man tumbling over, Bishop grabbing his shirt as he fell, laying him gently on the earth. He disagreed with Rocco's position, but understood and respected the man's passion.

Seconds later, the Texan entered the barn and was helping the astonished Culpepper rider up and into his saddle. He found Rocco's assault pack, securing the small amount of food, ammo, and water to the cowboy's saddle.

Few in the village heard the two horses race off into the night, most of the residents hoping the loud party would soon end so they could all get some sleep.

Chapter 10

The Cartersville festival was in full swing by the time Victor and Dr. Hanes arrived. Country and Western music drifted softly across the courthouse square, the lack of electrical power dampening the volume considerably. No one seemed to mind.

The basement of a local church had provided a long row of tables, each in the process of being stacked with food, desserts, and, according to Mr. Gospel, a recently uncovered stash of paper plates and Styrofoam cups.

Along with the miracle of disposable eatery were other staples of a time long past. Cases of soft drinks had been discovered as well as an enormous amount of canned foods. The sugary beverages were being eyed by the eager throng, generating serious crowd appeal and the most finger pointing. Few of the residents had tasted anything sweet in years.

Stan stood over the fruit table, greeting the occasional passerby as if he were Santa Claus at a corporate Christmas party. Cases of canned peaches, oranges, pineapple and other delicacies drew the attention of the townsfolk. Their eyes glimmered, and their mouths salivated at the prospect of the buffet feast being assembled.

"We'll be open in a bit," Mr. Gospel would smile and announce. "We're going to have a party unlike any since the collapse."

Earlier in the day, Gospel's men had made the rounds, informing every vendor in the Exchange that they were expected to contribute to the evening's feast. Victor had eagerly agreed, hoping to gain easy access to the foodstuffs, and use the spray bottle that the good doctor had in his pocket.

The merchant had closed up shop early, rushing home to put an old family bread recipe into his wood-fired oven.

The two conspirators made their way past the guards and into the food preparation area, Victor carrying one basket of loaves, the doctor another. Stan's voice, so boisterous and close, served to motivate both men to complete their treachery with haste.

The doctor's serum filled a small spray bottle, the green liquid forming a mist in the hurried backyard testing conducted just a few minutes ago. It was the best they could do.

People were hustling about everywhere, unpacking the crates Stan had so mysteriously uncovered, arranging prepared dishes, and working manual can openers at a furious pace. It was barely controlled bedlam.

A small army of backyard BBQ grills had been wheeled in,

another crew responsible for providing the appropriate supply of timber to fire the battalion of grills. No one involved thought it was a textbook example of how to prepare for a festival, but few complained.

Victor and his accomplice were directed to a specific table reserved for breads. The two connivers began unloading each loaf, nervous eyes casting around to get a feel for the ever-present security men.

After the first few rounded hunks of bread were on display, the doctor reached into his jacket pocket and palmed the bottle. He wasn't a magician, his sleight of hand technique lacking in dexterity and stealth.

Victor tried to block his friend's clumsy attempt, peering around with nervous glances to make sure they weren't discovered. "Are you going to be able to pull this off?" he asked.

"I somehow imagined this would be easier. I'm trying to stuff the bottle up my sleeve, but it won't fit. Give me a minute, will you?"

Stan was fifteen feet away, standing next to the chief. "What's up with those two?" he asked the lawman, nodding towards Victor and the doc.

"They sure look nervous. What is that in Dr. Hane's hand?" the chief responded.

The two bio-terrorists were motivated, but unskilled. Neither had the experience nor training to conduct such an operation, and it was becoming more apparent with each passing moment.

Frustration and nerves began to work on the good doctor. At one point he dropped the spray bottle, bending far too quickly to scoop it back up. Victor wasn't helping, his hand-wringing and too quick head movements drawing attention to the pair's nefarious activities.

"Screw this," the physician finally stated. "I'm just going to stroll down the line and keep the bottle in front of me. Try to block me with your body as much as you can."

Victor nodded, his head pivoting back and forth, eagerly looking for any security men.

As if he was reaching for a wallet, the doctor moved the spray bottle to the inside of his jacket. Victor and he made every attempt to stroll casually to the first food table where the trays of carved meat steamed into the evening air.

Glancing right and left, the doctor uncovered and aimed his poison, pulling the small trigger pump once, twice and then a third time. Nothing came out.

"What's wrong?" Victor hissed, now having second thoughts about their scheme.

"Nothing... it just takes a bit to prime the pump," came the response.

Both of them jumped when Stan's voice sounded behind them, "Good evening, gentlemen. Are you trying to spice up our meal?"

The doctor tried to return the bottle to his jacket, but the chief's burly hand darted out of nowhere, clutching the physician's wrist and securing the evidence. "What do we have here?" asked the lawman.

Holding up the bottle so Stan could see, the chief then unscrewed the cap, sniffing the foul smelling substance, and then pulling away with a scowl. "Damn, Doc, what the hell is this shit?"

Neither the sawbones, nor his partner wanted to talk. Stan took his turn, smelling the pungent liquid. "Whatever it is, it's toxic as hell. Even my untrained nose can say that for certain. What kind of poison are you trying to slaughter us all with, Doctor?"

"I'm not trying to kill anyone," replied the doctor. "It's not deadly. I'm not an inhumane animal like you are, Stan."

Mr. Gospel laughed loudly, the outburst intended more for the benefit of the gathering group of security men than due to any real humor. Stan knew he had to be careful here. Victor and the doc were well liked and respected. "Do tell, gentlemen, do tell."

"We know about the semi-trailers," Victor managed to confess and accuse at the same time. "We know you've been hoarding medications, water purification supplies, and tons of cargo that could have saved hundreds of lives here in Cartersville. We are fully aware you've been keeping these critical items back so you could stay in power."

Ignoring the accusations, Stan held up the spray bottle. "And this?"

"It will make people slightly ill," the doctor chimed in. "Nothing more. My plan was to make you reveal the existence of the supplies after you and hundreds of others got sick."

Again, the town's honcho laughed. "Very, very clever, gentlemen. There are just two problems with your betrayal. The first is that you got caught. The second is that I'm obviously not hoarding anything – look around you at all the cases of food. Does that look like I'm hiding vital supplies? By the time we took inventory of all those trailers, the sickness and disease had passed. I was merely managing that stockpile for a rainy day."

"And to feed your security men… to keep them happy and on the payroll," added Victor.

Stan was obviously done with the conversation, waving a hand through the air to dismiss his accusers. "The penalty for treason is death, my friends."

Gospel then turned to the chief and said, "Our discovery of

this skullduggery will provide additional entertainment this evening. Handcuff both of them and take them to the central podium."

The chief nodded, turning to issue instructions to his deputies. A few moments later, a small parade of law officers, Mr. Gospel and the two prisoners approached the main stage.

A hush fell over the crowd, most thinking Mr. Gospel was going to announce the much anticipated opening of the food tables. Things got really quiet when the bound physician and merchant were hauled up onto the elevated platform.

Stan bent, lifting a pre-positioned bullhorn. "Ladies and gentlemen, I bid you welcome and best wishes," Gospel began. "We, the good citizens of Cartersville, have cause to celebrate this evening. As most of you know, a single fugitive has been troubling our good town, pulling off seemingly impossible acts that have impacted each and every member of our community."

Pausing for effect, the smiling ruler swept his gaze over the gathering of his subjects. "For days, the chief and I have been amazed at how one man could have pulled off such miraculous feats. This evening, an explanation has been uncovered, as well as a plot of terrorism that would have killed hundreds of our friends and neighbors."

A murmur shot through the crowd, whispered voices and grunts of surprise rising into the air.

"But thanks to the professionalism and ever diligent eye of our security forces, this barbaric plan has been foiled, the conspirators captured red-handed in the act."

Stan motioned for the two captives to be pushed forward while at the same time holding up the spray bottle for all to see. "We just apprehended these two men with this bottle. They have confessed that it contains a deadly poison, which they were about to spray on our food line. All of you would have been seriously ill, if not dead, a few hours from now."

Voices of outrage and shock followed the announcement, irate faces gaping at the stage.

"But fear not, fellow citizens. Our security forces have performed admirably and apprehended these criminals. So this evening...."

The doctor's voice rang out, overriding Stan's bullhorn. "He's lying! He's been lying for two years, and we have found out the truth!"

One of Stan's men pulled up hard on the physician's handcuffed hands, bending Dr. Hanes over in pain and cutting off his speech. It was a mistake.

The crowd didn't like the bullying, a few strong voices rising over the din, "Let him speak!" someone shouted. "Let's hear what he has to say!" came another.

Stan nodded at his man, the muscular ex-trucker backing off. It took a moment before the doctor could gather himself. "You all know me. I delivered half of your children, saved a good many of your lives. Let's have a trial... a jury of my peers... and the truth will come out. Mr. Gospel might as well be named Mr. Stalin... he's been deceiving all of us since the beginning."

In the flickering light of the burning trash barrels, Stan saw several heads nodding up and down. The mood of the crowd was turning against him, any sort of trial completely out of the question.

Standing close, the chief inhaled deeply. He could tell by his boss's body language that the man was barely controlling his temper, hardly able to keep his emotions in check. It reminded him of the moments before Greyson's execution.

"What? What am I accused of doing?" Mr. Gospel screamed at the captives, spittle flying from his mouth. "What heinous falsehoods do you want to spew?"

The crowd grew silent, watching their leader's vivid hand gestures, taken aback by his wild, darting eyes. Victor answered the question, "Have a public trial. Examine the evidence. Let the people decide what you've done. That's all we ask."

Mr. Gospel's head trembled with rage; his jowls vibrated with wrath. In a lightning strike, he struck Victor in the head with a crushing blow, the handcuffed man knocked backward, bowling into the deputies behind him.

It was a mistake. Cries of outrage rose from the mob, several men surging forward in anger. Stan's henchmen, manning a security picket in front of the platform, pushed back. Someone threw a rock, a woman screamed, another cried out from the crush of the throng.

The chief knew his boss was out of control, the experienced lawman keeping his regard focused on Stan, ready to intercede. When Mr. Gospel reached for the holstered pistol at the small of his back, the old cop's instincts sent his own hand toward his weapon.

"I got your fucking trial; you son of a bitch!" Stan screamed as the nickel revolver came free of its holster.

The chief was three feet away, his service weapon clearing the holster just as Stan put the barrel of his pistol against the doctor's temple. The cop fired three rapid shots, two hitting Mr. Gospel in the torso, the final bullet entered the brain.

Bedlam erupted across the Cartersville square.

Like a school of fish trying to escape an attacking shark, people scrambled, ran, and clamored in all directions at once. Shrieks of panic filled the air, elderly men and women knocked to the ground in the ensuing mayhem, children trampled under the pressing mob.

Stan's body thumped hard onto the platform, Victor and the doctor flung aside as deputies and security men all reached for their weapons. One of the ex-truckers and a stalwart supporter of Mr. Gospel was drawing his gun when the image of the chief's smoking pistol came into view.

Furious that someone had attacked the man who had saved his life, he opened up on the chief, several shots slamming into the senior lawman's chest and head.

Grim and Kevin were above it all, observing the town square from the third story window of what had once been a furniture store in the center of town. "Holy Mother of God," Grim cursed when the shots rang out, the entire scene unfolding less than a 100 yards away.

The two Alliance men stayed low and back, shocked at how quickly things spiraled out of control.

In a matter of seconds, the security-teamsters were squaring off against the town's deputies. Pistol shots filled the air as the two sides rushed for cover. Grim could see the occasional head pop up, followed by one or two hastily fired rounds.

Throughout it all, Victor and the doctor laid prone on the stage, both men still handcuffed and unable to bolt for freedom.

"Both of the town's honchos are dead, and it looks like a civil war is taking shape right before our eyes," Grim observed, watching the half-assed firefight between the divided security forces. "That's not what we were supposed to accomplish on this mission. Nick is going to be pissed to high heaven."

"No kidding. The two guys who are on our side are going to get hit eventually. I see more and more men joining both sides of the fight."

It occurred to Grim that they might still be able to salvage the situation, but it would take well-known local figures to calm things down. "Let's go pull those guys off the stage and save their bacon. Maybe they can help us reestablish order."

Kevin looked at his superior as if Grim was insane. "Seriously? You want to go into that square and get our butts shot off?"

Grim smirked at the kid's reaction, "What's the big deal? It just a bunch of scared shitless cowboys plinking at each other. Hell, I've not seen a single man get hit yet."

Shaking his head, Kevin said, "You're in charge, sir. Lead the way."

They climbed down the rickety old fire escape, more confident in the descent since the rusty metal had supported their earlier climb. Grim hit the ground first, moving to the corner to cover his partner.

Sensing Kevin at his back, the former contractor hustled across the street, zigzagging to throw off anyone thinking of sending lead his way. Once Grim was safe on the opposite side, Kevin zipped around the corner, and then the two men headed for the square, their weapons high and ready, sweeping both sides of the street.

When they approached the next corner, Grim shouted, "Cover me from that park bench," and then sprinted onto the courthouse grass. Kevin was on a knee, using the thick wooden backrest as both support for his rifle and as a barrier against incoming fire.

When Grim was 20 yards away from the stage, he flipped his carbine around to his back. Rather than mount the steps to the platform, he leaped aboard head first, using Stan's body as cover.

After waiting a moment to see if his movement drew any fire, Grim rolled over to the chief's prone body, finding the handcuff key where all cops kept it. He belly crawled toward Victor and the doc.

One of the Stan's security men noticed the movement, yelling, "Who's that on the stage?" to his friends.

Someone answered, "They're trying to flank us," and just like that, several pistols began firing rounds in Grim's direction.

Kevin saw it, sensing the change in sound and the brightness of the muzzle flashes. The outline of a shooter was in his crosshairs a moment later, the roar of his rifle echoing off of the surrounding buildings. He didn't miss.

Both the cops and truckers realized the game had changed. An eerie quiet filled the square – the only sound coming from the platform when Grim grunted to lift Victor into a fireman's carry. The doctor was able to walk on his own.

Kevin noticed another fellow rising from the cover of a parked car, his pistol arching in Grim's direction. Again, the .308's thunder cracked through the air, a cloud of red mist replacing the shooter's head.

Burdened by the slow moving physician and the unresponsive Victor on his shoulder, Grim felt like he was watching a movie in slow motion. He heard, rather than saw, Kevin's high-powered rounds doing their work. But in the mayhem, there were still rounds zipping past his head.

Spinning to give the doctor a head start, Grim fired several wild shots one-handed from the hip. He didn't expect to hit anything with the poor technique, hoping only to force his enemy's head down.

A few seconds later, Grim dashed past Kevin, shouting out the instructions, "Cover me!" as Victor's body bounced on his shoulder.

It took Stan's thugs a few moments to realize that their game was up if Victor and the doc survived. Mere seconds after that, one of the faster thinking of their ranks began issuing commands and organizing their force.

More men were arriving all the time, drawn by the sound of gunfire and screaming. Kevin, trying to give Grim and Dr. Hines a reasonable head start, noted more and more long guns were amongst the forces now assembling on both sides.

The deputies and ex-lawmen were vastly outgunned, and they knew it. Stan's truckers had numbered in the thousands, the able-bodied men in the hundreds. The majority had been drafted into the security force.

With their chief dead, an inferior sized force, and no clear leadership emerging, the lawmen seemed content to barricade themselves in one corner of the square and wait it out.

Stan's security heavies, on the other hand, started moving toward Kevin's bench.

When the kid fired the next shot, he hoped seeing one of their own fall would give the approaching shooters reason to reconsider. Firing into the teamsters had the opposite effect.

Rifles began pounding lead in Kevin's direction, splinters and dirt filling the air. He dove, rolled, and crawled across the street.

Grim appeared at that moment, unburdened by Victor's body, and dashing like a demon. In a flash, he was between the scuttling kid and the oncoming attackers. Like a drummer pounding out a cadence, Grim's finger began squeezing the trigger.

At a rate of two to three shots per second, the battle-hardened man's fire tore into the approaching skirmish line, shot after shot finding flesh, sinew, and bone.

Spewing 28 rounds in less than two breaths, Grim's empty magazine was rattling across the pavement, a new one inserted faster than the eye could follow. Another volley of high velocity death then followed.

So accurate was Grim's barrage, the gaggle of security men scattered, many of them running in retreat. More than a handful of moaning, withering bodies littered the sidewalks, another number unable to move at all.

And then like a ghost, the figure that had sprayed death into their ranks was gone, the swish of his shadow disappearing around the corner.

It took a moment for the terror and fear to morph into anger. As more and more reinforcements arrived, the security force began to regroup.

Grim, Kevin and the two locals didn't have much of a head start, but they would take what they could get. Pushing aside his frustration at how slowly they were moving, Grim said, "The only thing I know to do is get the fuck out of here."

They continued running, using a dark side street and trying to make their way north. At the next crossing, Grim announced, "We're way outnumbered, and it's going to take the friendly locals a while to get organized. We have to get our two friends to safety, and that means out of this town."

For such a small berg, it seemed to the Alliance men like it was taking forever to reach the edge of Cartersville. Both Grim and Kevin knew they'd feel better once they reached a more rural environment.

Finally, three blocks ahead, Grim spied the same roadblock where he'd met Cory just the night before. "Now we're cooking with gas," he yelled between breaths. "Let's get out of Dodge."

Rather than respond, Kevin pulled up short and then dove for cover.

Several rifles opened up from the barricade, incoming rounds throwing sparks and chips of pavement into the air. Grim leapt as well, Victor's limp body hitting the ground hard. "Sorry about that, bud," he whispered as his rifle came up.

Just as Grim had centered the first man in his sights, more rounds began impacting around his position – these coming from behind.

Grim spun, catching a glimpse of several outlines moving up the street behind them. "Fuck, Kevin! We're cut off! I got the rear; keep those assholes at the barricade off of us!"

Their position wasn't ideal, tactically or strategically. With only two abandoned cars and a single utility pole for cover, Grim could think of a hundred other places he'd prefer as a Fort Apache.

Nor was maneuver an option, the nearest cross street now held by the enemy, oblong one-story buildings flanking both sides of the lane. There literally wasn't any place to go.

Grim scanned both high and low between shots. There weren't any manhole covers to open for escape, no trees to climb. He seriously doubted any angels or helicopters were going to swoop down and save them.

More and more rounds shredded the cars and earth around

them, an increasing symphony of pings, thwacks, and zings signaling their opponents were growing stronger by the second.

The air became harsh, difficult to breathe, polluted with a fog of cordite gun smoke, fragments of bullet-cut concrete, and snowflakes of lead-shaved metal. It burned the throats of the Alliance fighters, stung their eyes and denied their lungs.

Neither impending death nor fear burdened Grim's mind. He was in his element, a state where all of his senses worked in harmony to derive an advantage, any advantage, to win the fight. The ricocheting scream of a near miss invoked a mechanical string of computations and commands, his carbine's barrel adjusting to address the threat. The sharp stab of ear-pain from a heavy bullet just missing his head automatically adjusted his targeting priority.

Marathon runners often claimed to reach a state of mental euphoria called a "runner's high." Grim was now in a place his comrades called a "gunner's high."

But his internal, business-like calm of combat was about to be shattered.

"I'm down to 40," announced Kevin's frightened voice, informing Grim he was going to run out of ammo soon.

"Make 'em count, kid. Hurt 'em bad," was the only thing he could think of to say.

Nick is going to skin my dead carcass for getting his boy killed, Grim thought. I'm sorry, my friend. I did my best. He went out fighting as well as any man I've ever served with.

Despite the deadly accurate return fire, the men at both ends of the trap were growing impatient. Grim saw them bunching up, ready to execute a multi-pronged assault.

"Here they come, right and left," he yelled to Kevin. "I've got the left side."

A blizzard of debris, glass, concrete, metal shavings, and hot lead filled the air around the two Alliance defenders. Despite every natural instinct to duck and stay low, Grim and Kevin rose and began returning as much hell as they could dish out.

It worked, the enemy's charge faltering after three men in front dropped down, tripping others behind them. "Amateurs. You fucked up," Grim whispered. "You were bunched too tightly."

He also knew they wouldn't make that mistake again.

"I'm out," sounded Kevin's excited voice.

Grim drew his sidearm, throwing the pistol across to his partner and then following the toss with his only spare magazine. "You've got 15 rounds. Make 'em count."

Checking his own ammo supply, Grim frowned. He was down to three magazines, each holding 28 rounds. His hand felt for the knife on his belt, but the hilt didn't generate much comfort.

The operator knew instinctively the opponents were regrouping for another charge. Without Kevin's rifle covering the other side of the street, he figured the kid and he would be overrun in the next 30 seconds, maybe less.

And here they came.

With better spacing than the previous attempt and moving at a faster pace, they surged with twenty men on each side of the road. It was a mad rush at Grim and Kevin's position. Again, a wall of bullets tore into the Alliance defenders' cover.

Grim took his time, making sure every one of his precious bullets dropped a man. But the aggressors were too close and too numerous. Again and again, he dropped one of the charging outlines, but they kept coming.

When the combatants managed a position within 50 yards, Kevin started firing with his pistol. Grim wasn't sure how accurate the kid could be at that range, but at least he would distract some of the blistering, incoming fire.

Grim noticed one, and then another man on Kevin's side of the street fall. Then a third went down, immediately followed by a fourth. Damn, he thought, I knew the kid was hell on wheels with a long gun, but that is some serious combat shooting with a pistol.

Returning to the cluster of attackers on his side of the road, Grim was amazed to see two of them fall as well. "What the hell?" he muttered, emptying another magazine.

Again, the assault stalled, confused men peering all around them as it trying to determine where the death was coming from.

A huge shadow appeared out of nowhere, bright muzzle flashes illuminating a new presence on the battlefield. Accurate, debilitating, fire began pounding into the flank of the clustered attackers. Down they went, one after another. Grim laughed, raising his newly-reloaded carbine to add to the carnage. "We just found your dad," he shouted over to a wide-eyed Kevin. "Looks like Cory is with him as well."

Despite the champions being comprised of only two men, Nick and Cory's attack on their flank was too much for the ineffectively led and lightly trained security forces. In less than a minute, they broke, scampering wildly in retreat.

"Come on!" Nick waved at his besieged teammates. "Are you waiting for an engraved invitation?"

They still had the smaller group of defenders at the barricade to worry about, but their enthusiasm to fight seemed to have faltered after seeing their comrades take a serious ass whooping.

As Grim started to lift Victor onto his shoulder, Nick appeared at his side. "I've got him. You need a break," the larger team leader announced.

Effortlessly, Nick hefted the tiny looking merchant. After glancing over at Kevin and nodding, the four SAINT members, along with the two locals, faded away into the night.

"I'm damn glad to see you, but where the hell did you come from?" Grim asked as the team moved away from Cartersville.

"When Cory explained to me what was going on, I decided we'd better see if we could lend assistance. We heard the gunfire, so we drove the truck and hid it closer to town. I figured if there was shooting going on, you were probably in the middle of it," Nick grinned.

"Well, thank the heavens for small miracles. That one was getting close," Grim responded.

"We'll talk about my son's welfare while under your charge later," Nick stated. Grim couldn't tell if the big guy was kidding or not.

They found the pickup, left behind a barn in waist-high weeds. Victor's moaning signaled he'd regained consciousness, the merchant's nose broken by Stan's mighty blow. Nick tossed the doctor a first aid kit and then observed as the physician went about tending to his friend.

Satisfied the injured man was receiving excellent care, Nick then moved to Kevin's side. He watched as his son tried to reload a magazine, the young man's hands trembling so badly he couldn't hold onto a cartridge.

Gently placing his hand over Kevin's, Nick said, "It's okay, son. Everything is going to be fine. You're safe now."

Kevin peered up at his father, trying desperately to hold back the tears. Nick knew exactly what his son was feeling, had experienced similar emotions a dozen times in his early career. A soldier taking a life for the first time was one thing, facing one's own certain death was another. The young teen's brain was dealing with still being alive after he'd prepared himself to die. Survival, under such circumstances, is often extremely difficult to reconcile, and the older soldier knew how it felt. When father pulled son close, the kid couldn't hold back anymore, bursting into a deep sob.

Nick didn't say anything, keeping a tight hold on his son. Waves of weeping racked Kevin's body, his father feeling each and every shudder. Despite every man at the camp being well aware of what was happening, no one said a word.

After a bit, Kevin worked it out of his system. Wiping his face on a sleeve, he glanced at his father and nodded his thanks. "I've pulled it together," he said bravely. "I'll be all right."

"No, you won't," Grim's voice sounded as he stepped to Kevin's side. "We've all been right where you're standing, kid. You'll never be like you were - never be the same again. Eventually, you'll manage to keep it under control, and that's about the best any soldier can ask for. It's a skill just as important as being able to shoot or run or reload. And let me add this; you can fight beside me any day of any week. You did well, and I don't say those words to many men."

Kevin nodded his thanks to Grim and then returned to reloading his magazines. Still, he couldn't control the shaking. "You go heat up some coffee, and check the perimeter with my carbine," Grim ordered. "I'll take care of your mags."

When the kid hesitated, Grim squared up. "That's an order, trooper. Do it."

Nick and Grim watched the younger man leave. After he was out of sight, Nick looked down at Grim and mouthed the words, "Thank you," and then spun away quickly, moving off to talk to the men from Cartersville.

Bishop and Reed rode hard for about 10 miles, finally slowing so their animals could recoup. Near the boulder field where the ambush had taken place, both men dismounted for a break. Reed was thirsty, his body trying to heal from the beating suffered at the hands of his captors.

Checking him out as best he could, Bishop didn't think the cowboy had suffered life-threatening injuries. "You're going to be sore as hell for a month," he advised. "But you'll live."

"Thanks to you," the ranch hand replied. "How did you pull that off?"

"We can talk about that later. Right now, I have one pressing question. 'How are my wife and son?'"

Reed detected the edge in his rescuer's voice and was glad he could deliver good news. "They're just fine," he responded. "Mr. Culpepper has been treating them as honored guests. That boy of yours is as cute as a bug's ear from what I hear."

The relief that flooded Bishop's body was beyond description. That one statement lifted a tremendous weight from the Texan's shoulders, instantly improving his energy and mood.

The two riders continued for another few hours until they

reached the valley's summit. "There's not enough moon to guide the horses down," Reed advised. "Besides, Mr. Culpepper's patrols are probably a little trigger happy right now. I suggest we hide out here until daylight and then ride on in."

Bishop agreed.

Reed tethered their steeds, giving each animal a handful of grain from the saddle bags. He pulled a small bowl from the same area, pouring each horse a trifling amount of liquid from his canteen. "I saw the Tejanos water these animals," he informed Bishop. "They'll be okay."

"So I assume you know how to get into the ranch without getting us shot?" Bishop asked.

"We should be fine," the cowpoke responded. "They'll change the patrols and lookouts if they think I was captured. The Tejanos have a way of making a man talk if they take one of us alive."

Satisfied with the answers he received, Bishop continued on to the next task. "You've had the shit beat out of ya, so I'll take the first watch. I'll wake you up a few hours before dawn."

"You're a good man," Reed nodded. "I hope to pay you back one day."

A few moments later, with his hat tipped low over his eyes, loud breathing drifted through the otherwise still night air as the cowhand drifted off to sleep.

Bishop was so elated to hear his family was well, that he probably wouldn't have been able to rest anyway. Taking a perch on a nearby high rock, the Texan's thoughts drifted to what Terri and he would do once they were reunited at the Culpepper spread. There was still the problem of an ongoing war.

Unless Terri had formed some grand idea, Bishop didn't believe a solution was possible.

The subject was complex enough that it commanded most of the Texan's time. Before he knew it, the eastern sky was glowing with its announcement of the coming day. Reed would indeed be grateful for the extra shuteye.

Wishing they could build a fire and sip some coffee, Bishop finally nudged his co-rider awake. "I let you sleep all night by accident," he stated. "Besides, you looked like you needed the rest."

"Again, I'm in your debt," came the yawning response. Like most men who made their living on the range, Reed was ready to climb into the saddle in less than 10 minutes.

Down from the ridge they rode, eventually reaching the desert plain. Yellow-brown sand stretched off into the distance as far as Bishop could see, the featureless terrain looking sun-bleached and barren.

The pace was faster on the flat earth, the two riders continuing north at a steady pace. There was little conversation, only the occasional comment such as, "Going to be a hot one today," and "Your water supply holding up?"

The flatlands eventually turned into gradual slopes of sand and rock. At the crest of one such formation, Reed signaled for Bishop to stop. "We're getting close," he said. "The ranch is less than two miles away."

They continued, ultimately spying the outline of low, hazy rooflines in the distance.

Through the heat mirages rising from the hot sand floor, Bishop spotted the riders approaching. Five men met them face on, Reed's reunion with his friends tainted by Bishop's presence. "He saved my ass," Reed informed. "The Tejanos were sharpening their skinning knives and giving me the evil eye, but my friend here busted me loose."

"What about Frank?" one of the riders asked.

Staring down at his saddle horn, Reed delivered the bad news. "He didn't make it, but he didn't suffer none. They took him out with the first shot right through here," he reported, pointing at his heart.

They rode on in, Bishop dismounting just inside the main gate and handing his reins to one of the cowboys. His only thoughts were of Terri and his son.

Chapter 11

Terri was making her bed when she heard the floor creak behind her. Subconsciously reaching for the pistol resting on the bedside table, she jumped when a familiar voice said, "I know I've been away for a while... are you really mad enough to shoot me?"

"Bishop!" she shouted, rushing to his arms.

He lifted her off the ground, spinning in circles of joy. "I've never been so happy to see anyone in my life," he said honestly. "You don't know how much I've worried about...."

Terri smacked his chest with her hand, interrupting his words. "Don't you ever take off and leave me alone again or I'll..." she began, but then stopped, staring into his eyes.

She kissed him passionately for several moments, then abruptly pulled away and struck him again. "If you ever...." The protest was stopped short, her lips returning to his.

Hunter soon joined in the family embrace, the three of them forming a triangle of hugging and kissing. Bishop couldn't remember ever feeling so good.

The sound of someone in the hall clearing his throat interrupted the reunion. Bishop and Terri turned to see Mr. Culpepper standing outside Terri's room.

Tipping his hat, the old rancher said, "I hate to break in like this, but I'm getting ready to head out to the east fence. I was wondering if I might have a word with my new guest before I leave."

Bishop extended his hand and introduced himself. Mr. Culpepper responded in kind, showing the younger man a firm, confident grip.

The two men ambled to the front porch, Terri staying beside her husband, not about to be left out. If Culpepper was bothered by her presence, he didn't show it.

"First of all, I want to thank you for returning my man. Reed's been with me for a long time and losing him would have been agonizing."

Bishop smiled, "I was just saving both our hides. Wasn't any big deal, Mr. Culpepper."

"What can you tell me about the Tejanos? Are they planning any sort of major attack in the next few days? How are they holding up? Things like that."

Sighing, Bishop looked the older man straight on. "I really didn't see much. I saved their leader's life the night of the ambush. In return, he let me live after his men arrived. I wasn't a prisoner, but then again, I wasn't an honored guest. Since he

159

believed I didn't fight or ride with your outfit, I was just someone passing through."

"Do they think they're winning?" came the real question, the same inquiry every weary general wanted to know during difficult campaigns.

"Yes, the people do. But my read on Rocco is that he knows it's a stalemate, just like you."

Culpepper wasn't used to someone putting words in his mouth, especially like those just aired by a stranger in his house. He started to reprimand his new guest, but then changed his mind. Bishop was right, and they both knew it.

"So Mr. Culpepper, here's the deal. I'm going to take my wife and son, along with those two horses I returned, and we're going to ride to Meraton. I'll send the horses back to you."

"Now just a damn minute, son. You just got here... just rode in on my animals and are standing under my roof. And you're already telling me how it's going to be?"

Bishop glanced at Terri, his question needing no words. He doesn't know about my role in the Alliance, came the unspoken message. And I don't want him to.

Sighing, Bishop looked back at their host. "Mr. Culpepper, I mean no offense, but if we don't get back to a friendly town pretty soon, our friends are going to come looking for us. There will be a lot of men combing the countryside... and they won't be overly friendly to anyone who objects to their search. If they end up between you and the Tejanos, who knows how many innocent people, on all sides, could get hurt?"

Again, Bishop managed to raise Culpepper's ire. There was a thinly understated attempt at intimidation in that last statement, and the rancher didn't like being threatened.

"I don't give a shit who comes looking for whom, anyone comes trespassing on my land is going to meet the business end of our rifles," the older man spouted.

Terri stepped between the two men, attempting to restore calm. "Mr. Culpepper, you've been a kind and generous host, but I'm sure you don't want to be responsible for feeding Hunter and me forever. My husband is only trying to say that there will be a lot of people worrying needlessly about us if we don't get back soon. Some of them are hotheads and might get a little passionate if they think we are in danger or have been mistreated. Wouldn't your friends and employees feel the same way? We just don't see any need to add stress to anyone's lives."

Bishop would have grunted if the conversation hadn't been of a critical nature. His spouse, as usual, had used her charm and diplomatic prowess to rescue his blunt honesty. He could tell from the rancher's expression that Terri's logic had defused the old man's wrath.

"I suppose you're right," Culpepper finally responded. "But I want to think about things for a bit before I let you two go gallivanting across the desert with a couple of my horses. I'll be back tomorrow afternoon. Please accept my hospitality until then."

The couple returned to Terri's room in silence, Bishop closing the door to keep their conversation private. "Sorry about that, I should have let you deal with him from the get go."

"So... we both have a lot of catching up to do. You go first."

Bishop spent the next 20 minutes describing his adventures since their separation. She sat and listened intently, only occasionally asking for clarification on a specific point.

After he had finished, Bishop scooped up Hunter and began bouncing the blissful boy on his knee. "Your turn," he stated flatly.

Terri's tale took less time, much of the duration spent at the ranch.

Both expressed their frustration at not being able to arrive at a solution to the ongoing range war they had bumbled into.

"I don't trust our host," Bishop stated, changing the subject. "After our little interaction a moment ago, I get the feeling he's just as desperate at the Tejanos. I wouldn't put it past him to try and hold us for some sort of ransom or payoff."

Much to Bishop's surprise, Terri agreed with his analysis of the ranch's owner. "I think you're right. But here's the real news from this side of the trenches. This war has been going on for so long, our friend Culpepper no longer believes peace is possible. The only end to this mess that he can see is the complete genocide of the Tejanos."

Bishop grunted, "Same goes for Rocco over on the other side. They're fighting based on hatred and events that occurred before any of the current generation was born. When I asked him if he could envision an armistice in his people's future, he admitted he couldn't."

Again, Terri surprised her husband. "Well, one thing's for certain. Hunter and I don't want to be hostages. Let's get our things packed up, rustle a couple of horses, and get the hell out of dodge."

"Whoa, there little cowgirl. Just hold your powder for a minute. We can't just meander out to the barn and abscond with a man's livestock. We're going to need water, food, and diapers. We'll be riding through some very dry terrain for quite some time before we reach Meraton."

"I've made friends with the lady who runs the kitchen," Terri said in a low, confidential voice. "She'll help me gather whatever supplies we need."

Bishop exhaled, his mind wandering to the next problem –
viable transportation. "I just saved one of the foremen from being
skinned alive," he announced. "Maybe he can arrange for us to
borrow a couple of steeds."

"Even though Mr. Culpepper ordered us to wait here?"

"Well, he didn't specifically order us, if I recall correctly. I
believe he suggested we be his guests," Bishop replied with a
touch of deception inflected in his voice.

Terri rolled her eyes, "Whatever. Do what you have to,
Bishop…. Just get us out of here. I really, seriously think it's wise
that we leave."

"Let's try for tonight. It will be cooler then, and I hear the
stars provide a wonderful view out this way."

Terri demanded Bishop wash up before he slept in "her"
bed. Mumbling uncertainties about the wisdom of marriage and
commitment, the Texan took a dip in the adjoining bathroom's
tub, buckets of hot water hauled in from the kitchen.

After drying off and ignoring the ring of dirt at the waterline,
he was further frustrated to find his clothes had disappeared.
"They smelled like an old army mule," Terri stated firmly. "They'll
be back by the time you eat and get some rest."

Sitting on the bed, wrapped in a towel, Bishop wolfed down
some excellent stew, the hot meal accented with oven fresh
bread and slices of prickly pears. The experience made his
eyelids heavy, and in a short time, he was in a deep sleep.

Terri's rustling around the room woke her husband several
hours later. She was busy packing two bags, one for her, the
other for Hunter. "You'd better get to work on our horses," she
reminded. "It will be dark in a few hours. I've got all of our stuff
ready. Your clothes are over there."

Bishop found his garments clean, soft, and smelling like
sunshine. He had to admit, it felt good to put on duds that
wouldn't stand in the corner by themselves.

He found Reed in the bunkhouse, sporting two bandages
on his face and a wrapping around his ribs. "They want me to
stay in bed for a few days," the cowboy complained. "I'm afraid
the boredom will be the end of me."

"Sorry to interrupt your beauty rest, but Terri and I have
decided we need to head out tonight. Mr. Culpepper isn't around,
so I thought you might be well enough to help in getting a couple
of horses ready."

"Sure," replied the hand, his legs coming off the bunk. "Let me get on a shirt and boots, and we'll head over to the tack room."

A few moments later the two men approached the main stables, Bishop with a saddle on each shoulder, Reed complaining that he wasn't hurt so bad as to be unable to fetch leather. Still, he hadn't protested too much when the other man had hefted the load.

The armed guard standing duty didn't even bother to challenge Reed, instead greeting his co-worker with a friendly, "Glad to see you back," and a nod of his head.

They entered the stables, Reed trailing down the long row of stalls until he found what he was looking for. "This is Bluebird," he said, pointing to a healthy looking mare. "She is gentle and not easily spooked. I think she's a good match for your wife and child."

They continued for a few more cubicles and then stopped, both men standing in front of the same horse Bishop had ridden the night before. "This is Zeus," Reed introduced. "He's strong and knows you now. He'll get you to where you're going."

Twenty minutes later, Bishop was leading the two horses to the ranch's main house. Terri was waiting there, Bishop's pack, rifle, and assorted luggage sitting nearby.

They rode out at dusk, passing through the rings of security surrounding the ranch without incident.

When they were a few miles to the north, Terri spurred Bluebird in order to ride beside her husband. "Doesn't it strike you a little odd that no one even challenged us?"

Bishop shook his head, "No, not at all. The sentries are there to keep people from getting in, not getting out. I didn't really expect any trouble."

"So what are we going to do when we get back?"

Bishop chanced a glance at his wife, flirting eyebrows moving up and down. "I was going to raise the subject of that second honeymoon," he teased.

Hunter, riding in a papoose on his mother's chest, giggled loudly, thinking his father's funny face was directed at him.

The couple got another good laugh out of that, the fresh, desert air and even footing providing an enjoyable ride.

"Seriously, Bishop. I want to know your opinion about trying to make peace back there."

The Texan glanced at his wife in an effort to get a read on her mood. "I spent a lot of time trying to work out how that could be accomplished. I think both sides are in the wrong, but both have some reasonable grievances. But, in reality, none of that matters. When I boiled it all down, I came to a conclusion that you're not going to like."

"What's that?"

"That the only option is to let them fight it out."

Terri's outburst was expected; her reasoning was not. "What? I disagree completely," she began. What followed raised Bishop's respect for his wife to new heights. "If the Alliance doesn't act, that conflict could boil over into our territory. The two warring parties aren't that far from our breadbasket along the Rio Grande, and if those farmers become embroiled in their quarrel, our food inventories could become collateral damage."

Bishop grunted, not having considered that aspect. "Go on," he said, trying to catch up with her.

"I spent my time trying to figure out which side we should support, and then pressuring the other into peaceful coexistence," she answered.

"I pondered that as well, but historically, that hasn't always worked out so well. Look at Vietnam, where we funded and died for the south while the Soviets supported the north. Neither of the superpowers got the return on investment they expected. We lost over 50,000 guys in the process."

Terri nodded her understanding, but quickly countered. "True, but that strategy has also been extremely successful. Take Israel, for example. We poured money into that country for years and years. In the end, they were our only true ally in the region and grew into an incredibly strong nation."

"But Israel didn't conquer her enemies, and they ended up hating us for our support. I don't think you can chalk that one up to a completely successful implementation of such a doctrine."

They rode along for a bit, Bishop always keeping close watch on their surroundings, Terri trying to solve the Alliance's problems.

After four hours in the saddle, Terri announced she, and her bottom, had endured enough of the genuine West Texas experience for one night.

"We'll set up camp down in this gully," Bishop said. "We can build a small fire, and it won't be visible in such a low spot. I'll even fix us something to eat."

After tethering the horses, Bishop found dry kindling at the bottom of the wash, the flatland transitioning into a streambed during the rare desert rains. Most of the fuel was finger-thin, but the Texan knew that even skinny mesquite would burn for extended periods of time. It smelled pretty good, too.

As Terri unpacked and tended to Hunter, her husband went about setting up their campsite.

Bishop considered putting out tripwires but quickly decided against it. The desert here was too flat and open, making hiding and securing the devices difficult and ineffective. Besides, the horses would probably warn them of any approaching man or beast.

The meal was simple, reheated stew from the Culpepper kitchen and fresh green beans. Hunter enjoyed a small helping of each, as well as a bottle of goat's milk warmed over the fire.

Bishop strung his survival net between an outcropping and a makeshift tent pole scavenged from the streambed. It provided a comfortable hammock when padded with their sleeping bags, allowing plenty of room for mother and son. "I'll lean against that rock over there," Bishop said. "If I doze off, fine, if not, I had a long nap this afternoon."

Terri was too exhausted to debate the subject, she and Hunter soon snuggling in the thick covers, rocking gently back and forth while suspended in mid-air.

Bishop spent the night watching for shooting stars, searching the desert with his ears, and thinking about his family. He was happiest when they were together, whether it was the desolate regions of West Texas, the luxury RV his wife used as a mobile office, or the cramped confines of the camper at his ranch. The "where" didn't matter, it was the company a man kept that improved the quality of life.

He fantasized about moving back to the ranch, of building a house, a herd, and having a nice, green garden. Chickens would be another staple, plus his skill with a rifle would supplement their diet with venison or game birds now and then.

But he knew it wouldn't be. Terri was so critical to the Alliance, the people having seen her in action and trusting her judgment. He couldn't blame them; his wife's abilities to read people and originate creative solutions to big problems were a constant source of amazement to him.

How long could she last? Betty's death in Galveston had been the first event to negatively impact his wife's energy and determination – at least that he'd noticed. His battle wounds from the Brighton mission had given her pause, but when Terri had lost her best friend in the hurricane, it had wounded her soul deep and wide.

Then there was the complexity of her role. As the Alliance expanded its territories, more and more people wanted to play a part in the new government. This led to a nearly continuous state of disagreement with local officials, wanna-be lawmakers, and a host of other power-hungry folks. So many of them looked at his wife with disdain, their snarky attitude betraying unvoiced questions like, "What qualifications do you have to lead a government," often bleeding through. She constantly had to prove herself, and that would wear on anybody, in any role.

Yet, despite all that, Terri seemed to relish her job. Improving people's quality of life provided a tremendous reward, the progress being made with the five directives a constant source of gratification. Bishop didn't blame her, held no ill will over his wife's recognition and power. His only regret was that they didn't get much quality time together.

"I guess that's a worthy sacrifice," he mumbled under his breath, glancing at the moonlit outline of her serene, slumbering countenance. "She's a good mom and loyal wife who is helping millions of people. What man could ask any more of his spouse?"

The sound of morning birds caused Bishop to startle, his neck and back sore from sleeping against the rock. "The false dawn is breaking in the east," he noted. "I must have nodded off."

A quick check of their surroundings told him everything was okay. Terri was still out, Hunter resting comfortably beside her. Neither man nor beast threatened the camp.

He watered the horses and then began packing up their kit. Hunter would get a breakfast of milk; Terri and he would enjoy nibbling jerky in the saddle.

An hour later they were back on the trail, heading mostly north and west towards Meraton. It wasn't the perfect departure. Terri was complaining of a sore backside, Hunter deciding he didn't like the papoose anymore. Bishop shrugged it all off, resolving to take more breaks and act more like a husband and less like a trail boss ramrodding a cattle drive.

There was no hurry, no urgency to rush or push. Other than personal comforts and better food, it wouldn't make that much difference if they arrived in Meraton tomorrow or the following day.

Chapter 12

Victor was doing better, his flat nose and blackened raccoon eyes looking worse than the man claimed they felt. They had moved the truck back to the original hiding place, every member of the team more comfortable after increasing the distance between themselves and the turmoil in Cartersville.

But that sentiment quickly changed, driven by the doctor's concern over who would fill the vacuum left by the death of the top two men.

"The town made a rushed, desperate decision after the collapse," the physician stated. "Stan stepped up, and like his nickname suggests, did an excellent job of spreading the good word and making the tough calls. I'm afraid of what will happen now that he's gone."

Nick spoke up, waiting for his coffee water to heat over a small fire. "My guess is that some folks will side with the truckers; others will go with the remaining deputies. It wouldn't surprise me if the whole thing didn't turn into a miniature civil war."

"That's exactly what we have to go back and prevent," countered Dr. Hines. "There needs to be a clear voice of reason. Someone leading the town towards elections and a government like we once had."

"What's to stop the teamsters or the deputies from shooting you the minute you step foot in town?" Grim asked.

"That's just a chance we're going to have to take," replied the physician, a quiet Victor nodding a painful agreement. "But we've got to move fast before someone with dictatorial leanings moves in and gets one side or the other to rally around him."

"I can take you back," Nick stated coldly, "but we can't get involved in any civil dispute. We'll see you through the gate and hang around for an hour. After that, you're on your own."

"How about a different approach," Victor mumbled, his words difficult to understand. "Are there running trucks that can haul the trailers?"

Grim thought about the question for a moment, brightening when he realized where the merchant was going. "Yes, we saw a couple of refrigerator units still hooked to their trucks. We could hear the diesel motors running."

"So why don't we go hijack a couple of the more valuable trucks, crash them through the gate and pull up right on the courthouse square? We can open the trailer doors and prove to everyone what has been going on?"

"That would make a statement," Nick conceded. "It would get everyone's attention, no doubt about it."

The team's leader stood, towering over the small fire. After sipping his coffee for a few moments, he scanned the faces of his comrades and conceded, "Why the hell not? In for a penny, in for a pound."

Grim smiled, clearly in sync with the idea. He pulled on his chest rig and then started checking his rifle. Kevin and Cory weren't far behind.

An hour later, Nick was approaching the gate that led to the trailer lot Grim and Kevin had scouted. A single sentry appeared from the guard shack, the man raising his arm to signal the approaching truck to stop.

Grim's rifle barrel greeted the surprised fellow as he marched up to the truck. It didn't require any additional persuasion for him to open the gate. Evidently, the sentry had aspirations involving future sexual relationships – promptly answering each and every question after Nick threatened to demonstrate his "castrating knife."

The team learned that several experienced, over the road drivers were in the area, three such experts resting comfortably in the lot's office building, the cots supposedly in the back room.

Describing the SAINT team's entry into the facility as a "rude awakening" would have been an understatement. One of the rousted drivers, staring into the muzzle of Grim's rifle, went so far as to announce he thought it was "damn rude." Less than 15 minutes after crashing the gate, Nick watched as three trucks were being hitched to the trailers identified by Grim and Kevin.

Each truck carried not only valuable cargo in the back, but housed one of the Alliance men in front - just to make sure the driver didn't deviate from the proper route.

Nick, along with his two VIPs from Cartersville, followed in the pickup.

The large Peterbilt tractor didn't slow down for the north gate, crashing through and sending the guards scrambling for their lives. Grim enjoyed flipping the sentries a middle finger as they roared past.

The rest of the convoy rolled by unmolested, Nick noting that the once bullying guards seemed to have lost a lot of their bluster. He decided that was a positive development.

The streets were nearly deserted, most people afraid to come out of their homes after the previous evening's violence. The long row of tables, as well as much of the food, sat undisturbed from the night before. Someone had moved Stan and the chief's bodies. Blood still stained the platform's wooden surface.

"Where is everybody?" Victor mumbled through his still throbbing face.

"They'll show up. Let's get out and walk around. We need to be visible, to let everyone know it's us," the doctor suggested.

After ten minutes, no one appeared.

Cory spied the bullhorn, still resting on the stage where it had fallen from Stan's dead hand. He wandered over and picked it up, pushing the button to test the device. It still worked.

He stepped over and handed the amplifier to the healer. "Let them know you're here," came the suggestion.

The SAINT team watched as the physician walked around the square, broadcasting various announcements and letting the townsfolk know it was safe to come out. For a bit, Nick was worried the noise would attract hostiles as well. He sent his men to cover, instructing them to stay out of sight unless troublemakers made an appearance.

Gradually, one by one, a few of the town's men peeked around or cautiously showed themselves. After 20 minutes, a small crowd had gathered, peering inside the semis at Victor's invitation.

The first armed men to arrive were a pair of ex-deputies still wearing the uniforms from the night before. Both men, after a brief conversation with the sawbones, pledged their support to the promised democratic initiative, agreeing that it was high time the town held elections.

Slowly the crowd grew in size, Victor and Dr. Hines circulating to greet each arrival and explain about the content of the trucks.

Everyone tensed when the first truckers arrived, Nick's men raising their rifles and ready to fight. It was an unnecessary precaution as it quickly became clear the haulers weren't in the mood to cause any problems. They had no place to go and wanted to stay and help rebuild the town.

Not everyone wanted to sit around the campfire and sing songs, however. A few disagreements broke out here and there, but gunplay never became an issue. "Use your vote, not your gun," the doctor repeatedly reminded.

It was early afternoon when Nick ordered his team to mount up. He took the doctor aside and handed the temporary town leader a pre-printed sheet containing instructions on how and who to contact in the Alliance.

"We'll be sending a team back in here in a few days," the big man promised. "They can help you get organized, even set up trade and communications. Until then, you can contact us on these frequencies, or send a messenger to these towns. Good luck."

As they approached the south gate, anxious to get home to Alliance territory, Nick had to stop the truck. All four of the team watched out the front windshield as an oversized farm tractor pulled away part of the barricade, opening a road that had been closed for years.

"Now that's progress," Nick observed with a huge grin. "This is an important lesson for all of us. The council's security directive doesn't mean a bunch of armed men standing around and maintaining order. Convicts in a jail have that, but they aren't free. Cartersville needed to establish order, and while that was an absolute necessity for a while, in the long run it didn't offer true security. The proper meaning of the term has a much broader and deeper definition. Security involves personal liberty, freedom of choice, unrestricted movement, and self-determination. It has always amazed me how easily 'maintaining control' morphs into restriction, intimidation, and authority through fear. I hope our friends back there will never forget the experience."

"Do you really think it will stick?" a pessimistic Grim asked from the back seat. "I have my doubts, and history justifies that lack of optimism. Don't you remember all sorts of trouble with pre-collapse police forces crossing the line? The same with government as a whole, all that bickering and debate over intrusion into private lives versus national security. I don't think you'll ever get two people to agree to a definition of the word, let alone an entire society."

Nick had to admit it; Grim had a valid point. He didn't respond for a while, watching the east Texas countryside pass, formulating his response as they rolled toward home. Eventually, he came out with it, "Security isn't a static thing. It's not fixed, like a set of written rules that once implemented, never need to be modified. You must constantly gauge the needs of the community and adjust. Like my drill instructors used to say, 'How can you improve if you don't measure?' But people don't want to do that. They don't want to take the time or put in the energy until something comes up and bites them in the ass. Then, all of a sudden, the sky is falling. The pitchforks and torches come out, common folks demanding the shroud of tyranny be lifted from their lives. Years later, the whole thing repeats. It's an unfortunate cycle."

"So how do you fix it, Dad?" Kevin asked.

"I wish I knew, son. We, as a species, have been repeating the same mistake since two of us moved into a common cave for safety and convenience. It's always been that way, and I'll be damned if I have a solution. But look at the bright side – guys like Grim and me remain employed because of this madness. If people were perfect, I would be jobless, and Grim would probably be living under a bridge somewhere."

A grunt came from the back. "I can just see your dad holding up a homemade sign at an intersection," Grim spouted. "Hungry. Broke. Will topple third world governments, assassinate foreign leaders, instigate revolutions, or train insurgents for food."

Mr. Culpepper sat on his chestnut bay, stoic and unmoving, the squeak of saddle leather and light desert breeze the only sounds.

Whitey was behind him, as well as two other hands just out of earshot, both diligent and alert. There was a range war on, and taking chances lead to shortened life spans.

It bothered Culpepper that he had to ride with extra men, a state of affairs that he considered wasteful. Whitey and his boys should be out mending fences, checking the herd, or repairing water mills, not playing bodyguard for a man doing nothing more than traveling across his own spread.

Live with the times, he thought. Don't fight them. You'll lose.

The messenger from the neighboring 888 Ranch had arrived yesterday, a layer of trail dust indicating the man had ridden hard and fast to deliver the invitation. Ward Hamlin was the long-time owner of the expansive spread and had sent word requesting a powwow. Culpepper hoped it would be good news.

Waiting next to the fence that separated the two ranches, he tried to remember the last time he'd seen old Ward. Had it been at Christmas three years ago? Four?

The fact that bordering neighbors didn't lay eyes on each other for long stretches of time wasn't unusual. With holdings counted in square miles rather than acres, the neighbor next door might be over two-hour's drive or a full day's ride away by horseback.

Culpepper had been in Alpha before his last visit to the triple-8, purchasing barbed wire, water tanks, and a half-mile of pipe. He'd been waiting at the cash register when a display had caught his eye, a chess set with well-crafted marble pieces depicting western figurines.

Holiday spirit wasn't a normal state of mind for the rancher, but he understood the need and intent for an event that required folks to think of someone besides themselves. On a rare impulse, he picked up the item, thinking of his old friend Ward.

When they were younger, single men of less responsibility, the two ran together. Sometimes they would manage a trip to Alpha, cruising into the "big city" via automobile - If Ward's pa would give up the keys to his baby-blue Cadillac convertible. Those excursions were legendary, the two tall, thin young men rambling into town with visions of carousing, beer, and female companionship at the forefront of their agenda.

But sharing the fast lane wasn't the true basis of their friendship. On many occasions, the chores, obligations, and circumstances of life didn't allow for shenanigans involving Pabst Blue Ribbon beer, Country and Western music, unfiltered Marlboro cigarettes, and swirling dance floor skirts.

Often, they were lucky just to spend time together, a welcome escape from the grueling work and everyday companionship of older, gruffer men. On those occasions, an occasional chess match would break out, both young men learning the game in the bunkhouses of their respective spreads.

Time, marriage, and the responsibility of taking over their outfits had come between the two old compadres. With the chess set tucked under his arm, Culpepper had diverted from his standard route home, surprising his friend with the Christmas gift, and spending the afternoon slacking off and retelling exaggerated stories and outright lies.

He'd left that day, both men promising to stay in touch and carve out some time to rekindle the friendship. But it hadn't happened. Business, the everyday struggles of making ends meet, and then the collapse had gotten in the way.

When the range war had started to go against them, Culpepper had reached out to his old friend for help. He was short on everything from manpower to ammunition. Ward had responded the best he could, sending over a truckload of supplies and five of his toughest hands.

Two weeks ago, the first messenger had ridden up, delivering a handwritten note on 888 stationery. "I'm going into Alpha next week," it read. "I'm not sure what I'll find, but I keep hearing rumors that things have gotten better there. I'll try to secure supplies and spread the word that you're recruiting hardy men who aren't afraid to use a rifle. I'll be in touch upon my return. Ward."

Anticipation wasn't a feeling Sam Culpepper experienced much these days, but when word came that Ward had returned and wanted to meet, he'd felt a flush of optimism. He needed help, or they were going to lose this fight.

The whinny of a horse announced the arrival of the 888 riders. Culpepper was happy to see his old friend leading the small party of men. The appearance of four pack animals, each burdened with rope-secured supplies, made the long ride even more worthwhile.

Ward rode up to the fence line, extending his hand over the

wire. After the warm handshake, he said, "Sam, I'm glad to see those Tejanos haven't managed to nail your hide on the barn door... yet."

The two old ranchers shared a good chuckle over the jest, and then Ward got right down to business.

"Yet again, the world has changed on us, Sam," the triple-8 honcho began. "I couldn't believe what I found in Alpha."

"You don't say? Has the anarchy and bedlam spread, or is everyone dead and gone?"

"No, quite the opposite. There's a recovery in process, and I like the look of it."

Ward went on to recount his visit, informing his old friend of the Alliance, businesses being reopened and electrical power prevalently in use. Culpepper was initially stunned, but as their conversation wore on, he realized he shouldn't have been surprised.

"You know, I've got some visitors staying out at my place. They've made a few comments that struck me as odd, and they seem to be in one big damned hurry to get back to Meraton. Now that I've heard your story, I can understand why."

"I met with the lady who runs the show in Alpha. Her name is Diana Brown. I told her what was going on with the Salt War and the battle you are waging. She informed me you need to get in touch with another gal, the big boss of the whole outfit. She claims that this female honcho is in charge of the military and what law enforcement they've managed to scrape together. Went on to brag about how this Terri woman was a skillful diplomat and negotiator."

The light of realization flashed through Culpepper's brain, Terri's outburst about tanks and soldiers resurfacing again. "Did you say her name was Terri?"

Ward nodded, "Sure did. I tried to hook up with her while I was in town, but she is supposed to be on the road with her husband and child. They expect them to be back in Alpha any day now."

Culpepper didn't respond for a moment, a thousand thoughts racing through his mind. Finally, "Did you happen to catch the husband's name by any chance?"

"Burt... no Bishop. That was it, Bishop. According to rumor, he's not a man to be trifled with, but a fair-minded individual nonetheless."

"Well, I'll be horn-swagged and dipped in chocolate. It all makes sense now."

"What? What's wrong, Sam?"

"Bishop and Terri are at my ranch right now, my old friend. Their truck got shot out from underneath them by the Tejanos, and they found their way to my place."

Ward grunted, "You don't say. Now there's a good turn of events for you Sam. It's not every day dignitaries and powerful people drop in from the sky. What are you doing sitting out here, swapping words with an old fool like me? You should be back there kissing their asses and making nice."

Sam had a good laugh at his friend's perspective. "Yeah, I suppose you're right."

"I brought you back 100 pounds of flour, two bottles of some near-deadly moonshine whiskey, and as much ammo as I could scrape up. I'll send you the bill for all that and the horses, too."

Again the two men shook hands. "Ward, you're a good friend. I won't forget this."

"Before you go, I can't help but give you a word of advice. Things are getting back to the way they were. End this damn war you're fighting, Sam. Life's too short - the trail too rough. Get out of the business of killing and put things back where you can come over and spend a little time playing chess. I've not had the pleasure of kicking your ass in years, and it tasks me."

Culpepper stared down at the ground and then smiled at his neighbor. "Sage advice, I'm sure, Ward. But we both know it's not that simple."

"Yes, I know. Things are rarely clear cut. But you know me, Sam. I've never been shy about telling another man how he should run his affairs. Still, by my way of thinking, I'm right more than I am wrong. Mull my words over, old friend. I think you'll land on the exact same spot that I'm preaching from."

Bishop thought it best that they rest more during the day while it was hot. While shade wasn't an amenity, it seemed to help Terri and Hunter to take a break from riding every hour or so, consuming as much water as possible and stretching their legs. Hunter was happy being free of the papoose.

While it slowed their progress significantly, the Texan decided it was a much easier schedule for his family to tolerate.

During one of their "walk abouts," Terri returned the conversation to her favorite topic as of late, how to deal with the Salt War.

"So if you had to pick one side or the other for the Alliance to support, which would it be?" she queried.

"I would go with the Tejanos," he replied instantly. "The vast majority of people in the villages are simple, honest souls who only want to improve their life. Since the collapse, the border means nothing anymore. Why not add more self-reliant individuals to our fold?"

Terri laughed, enjoying the conversation with her favorite man in the world. "I would choose Culpepper," she countered. "His folks are a textbook example of the American spirit, tough men making the best on a harsh and often unforgiving land. Everything about the Culpepper operation screams free enterprise and determination. Those are the type of people that will make the Alliance stronger in the long run."

"Why not make both of them allies? Why does it have to be one or the other?"

Tilting her head as if contemplating his suggestion for the first time, Terri responded, "I thought about that, but then what would keep them from escalating their conflict? Working with the Alliance would make both wealthier and more powerful, and that could lead to a hotter war and spill over into our interests."

Bishop understood, but he wasn't ready to give up on brokering peace. "If I were in your shoes, I'd make the two leaders sit in a tent and lay it out to them. Either behave and play well with others, or the Alliance will isolate you and let you wither in the fires of war. At least give them a chance to stop this incessant bickering."

Terri didn't comment at first, Bishop's watch indicating it was time for them to mount up and ride for an hour. After she was back in the saddle, she said, "That's not a bad idea, Bishop. Let me mull that around for a while. After all, there isn't much else to do right now."

"I can't believe this!" Mr. Culpepper screamed at his men. "I go away for a few hours, and when I come back, you've let them go. What on God's green earth is wrong with you people?"

Reed and Whitey had seen the boss's temper before, both men knowing that Mr. Culpepper really didn't want anyone to answer the rhetorical question.

After stomping around for a bit, the honcho sternly peered at Reed and demanded, "Well, what do you have to say for yourself?"

"I didn't know, sir. No one told me Bishop and Terri were prohibited from leaving. He came in, said they wanted to leave, and asked for two horses. He'd stated that was his plan while we were riding back from the Tejanos' village. It seemed righteous enough."

Mr. Culpepper didn't like the answer but knew it was honest.

The old rancher paced some more, grumbling and cursing under his breath. His next orders shocked both of the men standing before him. "Get 25 men ready; we're going after them."

"What? Sir?" Whitey spoke up. "Are you sure it's a good idea to split our forces when the Tejanos have been so active lately?"

But Samuel Culpepper wasn't in the mood to debate the issue. "Do what I said, Whitey, and make sure they've got plenty of ammo."

"Yes, sir."

The boss started to turn away, but then stopped. "Oh, and Whitey, I'm going with you. I'll need a fresh horse."

The two stunned cowhands stood and watched their boss amble off. "What the hell is going on?" Reed muttered, puzzled by the strange behavior.

"Beats me," the second in command replied. "That Terri-woman we brought in had messed with the boss's mind somehow. He's not been the same since she landed on our doorstep."

"Her husband seemed like a fair enough man. Do you think they're trying to hurt the outfit in some way?"

"No way of telling. What I do know is that we've got to put together a war party. Are you feeling up to a ride?"

Reed nodded eagerly. "Get me out of that damn bunkhouse, Mr. Foreman. I'll go loco from boredom if I have to stay in there much longer. Besides, I'd like a chance at mending fences with Mr. Culpepper."

"Get your saddlebags packed. I'll put you on the list."

Bishop noticed the dust cloud behind them an hour before dusk. Trying to remain optimistic, he'd pined for the disturbance to be nothing more than a dirt devil or robust current of air lifting sand from the desert floor. But those justifications faded quickly - this problem wasn't going away.

He waited several minutes before pointing the development out to Terri. She wasn't handling the cross-country trip all that well, unaccustomed to life in the field and sore from riding so many hours. He had to admit; his legs and backside weren't exactly in rodeo condition either.

Hunter was probably having the worst of it, the lad's discomfort within the confinement of the papoose making him fussy and grouchy. Of course, when the baby isn't happy, the mother follows suit.

But they had plodded along, eating up the miles slowly, their mood elevated at the prospect of reaching the safety and comfort of Meraton.

Now, the following cloud was the center of his wife's attention.

"What do you think it is?" she asked, already knowing the answer.

"It's a group of riders on our trail," he answered calmly. "My guess is that Mr. Culpepper is unhappy that we absconded with his horses and violated his wishes."

"Really? You think he'd be that pissed?"

"He's like a lot of ranchers in these parts, tough as iron spikes and almost as bull-headed as his livestock. Besides, I think he was beginning to realize you were much more than just some random, stranded traveler. Between both of us opening our big mouths and dropping clues, he had to be putting the pieces together. He's not stupid, you know."

Terri chanced at glance back at the haze again. "So what if he did? I can't do anything to help him if I'm isolated at his ranch. Why chase us down with a big posse of men?"

Bishop shook his head, proud of his wife's faith in the virtuous nature of mankind, never understanding her innocence of the evil that lurked in men's hearts. "You would command a fine ransom from the Alliance," he replied evenly. "That, or he could try to force us to come down on his side of the war. Either way, I don't think we would like his plans."

"That's silly," she replied. "What makes him think I would go along with such a scheme? I think he's underestimating me."

"Really?" Bishop challenged. "Think about that little bundle of joy riding along with you."

Terri glanced over her shoulder at Hunter, the realization of her husband's meaning causing her face to distort in a grimace. "No! You can't be serious. He'd threaten Hunter to leverage me? I don't believe that, Bishop, not for a second. I was around the man for two days while you were off flirting with the señoritas across the border. No way – he's not that kind of man."

The Texan pulled up on the reins, turning to face his wife. "Terri, you are the love of my life and one of the most brilliant people I've ever met... but... you have got to develop some apocalyptic street smarts, young lady. Culpepper is locked into a deadly war that he believes is lost. It might not seem like much to us, given all we've been through and endured. But to him, it's a life and death struggle and the only thing that matters is his survival. If he could hold Hunter's wellbeing over your head to survive, I bet he'd do it without hesitating one second. I know the man leading the Tejanos would do the same without feeling a thimble full of remorse or guilt."

Terri stuck out her lower lip, the exaggerated pout intended to express her displeasure with the scolding, as well as an attempt to lighten the mood. Bishop didn't go along.

"All the electricity, food, manufacturing, and rebuilding doesn't mean squat out here," he continued with a voice firm with resolve. "You need to start thinking like the desperate, downtrodden people that still occupy this land, or you're going to be in for an extremely rude surprise."

"I'm not that naive," she protested. "While I haven't seen some of the things you have, I've been through a lot, and just can't see a man like Sam Culpepper kidnapping babies."

Bishop sighed; Terri's stubbornness and strong will made him love her, and yet those attributes could be a royal pain in the ass at the same time. Nodding toward the following riders, he quipped, "Do you want to wait here and test their goodwill? I'm not a tracker, but I would guess there are 20 to 30 men behind us. If they catch us out in open ground like this, you'd better be right."

Terri's gaze returned to the cloud and then back to Hunter. "I guess you're right. Better to be safe than sorry, no matter what."

He leaned across and kissed her cheek, taking a moment to pat Hunter's head. "Let's keep moving. I think we need to pick up the pace. Maybe we can lose them."

Despite increasing their speed, the men behind them continued to close the gap. Darkness was falling when Bishop made his second unpleasant announcement of the day. "We can't stop to eat. If they come upon us in the night, we won't have a snowball's chance in hell."

"I understand," Terri said. "Can you help me get Hunter around to my front? I can at least put the last of the goat's milk in his tummy and get him out of that prison for a few minutes. I wonder if the pioneer women learned to change a diaper while riding on horseback."

They both laughed at the concept. "We can stop long enough for that. I don't want the boy to grow up with a complex against horses or the trail."

"I think it's too late," she chuckled.

They continued on, Terri passing Hunter to Bishop, letting dad take a turn after she'd performed a change on the move.

Bishop judged the terrain flat enough to let the boy ride behind the saddle horn. Hunter seemed to like the change, his father humming various tunes helping to calm the little man's mood.

Two hours after it was dark, the trio crested a hill and paused. Bishop needed to study the landscape and make a decision on the easiest route.

Handing his son back over, he pulled the night vision optic from his vest and began studying their surroundings.

Something looked familiar to the Texan; the dark shape of the distant mountains combined with the pattern of the foothills ahead caused him to search his memory cache to satisfy that flicker of recognition. He'd been here before.

With excitement in his voice, he turned to Terri and announced, "We're on the ranch's southwestern corner... the ranch I grew up on!"

"Really? Does that mean we're close to Meraton?"

"Yes, but more importantly, we're not that far away from our ranch. We could hole up in our canyon tonight, sleep in the camper. If the people on our trail happen to find us, we will have the bat cave for defense."

The thought of being somewhere familiar brightened Terri's outlook. "Hunter and I could take a bath in the spring and sleep on a mattress. Let's go."

Bishop plotted a course, trying to remember a land that he hadn't visited for years. He then glanced over his shoulder, troubled by not being able to gauge how much distance still existed between them and the pursuit. The dust cloud simply wasn't visible in the night.

Having no choice but to continue, they started down off the hill, heading into the valley that held Bishop's land. As far as the Texan was concerned, they couldn't arrive too soon.

The lights of Alpha served to lift Nick's spirits even higher. The pickup's cab had been mostly quiet during the return trip from Cartersville, each man's mind occupied with what he wanted to do during the team's upcoming downtime.

For his part, Nick had been mulling over his own future. For once, he'd had the opportunity to think about personal things, his mind free of the daunting, monumental problems facing the Alliance on what seemed like a daily basis.

Diana was at the core of his thoughts, his longing to see her while away on the mission cementing emotions he'd ignored for too long. Glancing over at his son, Nick asked what he hoped was a very carefully worded question. "So what do you think of Diana?"

Kevin's reaction was completely unanticipated. "I think she's a perfect match for you, Dad. When are you going to ask her to get married?"

It took all of his training and willpower, all the discipline honed across the battlefields of the world to keep Nick's jaw from dropping at his son's response. "Umm... well... umm... I don't know. I wonder if she would say 'Yes,'" he pondered aloud. "What do you think?" he quickly added, internally cursing himself for the stumbling, undignified reply, and then looking away, not daring to meet Kevin's knowing gaze.

"Well, of course she would, Dad. Can't you see that she loves you?"

When did this kid next to me grow up? Nick wanted to shout. Who is this man riding in the passenger seat?

"I don't know, son. Sometimes things like that aren't obvious to a man."

Kevin chuckled, shaking his head at his father's words. "You can spot a sniper in the woods at 500 meters. I've seen you take out a hostile at 550 using iron sights on an AR15. You can anticipate which arm a man is going to use for the next punch, but you can't see that Diana is deeply in love with you? Come on, Dad, do what you always tell me to do – open your eyes."

Nick almost let the truck veer off the road, completely taken aback by his son's comment. "Don't get uppity with me, young man. You did a great job on this mission, but that's no cause to get too full of yourself. I can still put you on your ass in the blink of an eye."

Grim's laughter from the back seat prompted Nick to remember they weren't alone. "What he's trying to say, Kevin, is that you just put your old man in his place, and he doesn't like it."

An irritated, "who asked you" pair of eyes bore down on Grim from the rearview mirror, but the ex-contractor ignored the threat. "Seriously, Nick, why haven't you made her an honest woman? You two are like peas in a pod... everybody can see it. If I were your commander, I'd order you to get off your lazy, frightened ass, and get it done, soldier."

The big man's first instinct was to pull the truck over, extract both of the smart-ass passengers from the vehicle, and issue both of them a first class, militarily-efficient shellacking – right there alongside the road. He was trying to determine how many bones he could break without permanently disabling Bishop's team when Kevin came to his father's defense.

"He's not scared, Grim. He's just cautious. I know he's not afraid of women because he married my mom."

"He's going to caution himself right out of a good woman," Grim mumbled. "He's not the only single man in Alpha, you know."

That did it! Nick hit the brakes, the veins popping out on his neck.

"Dad! Chill out," Kevin said, reaching across to put a calming hand on his father's arm. "We're just giving you a hard time. Why are you taking this all so seriously?"

With his foot returning to the gas, Nick didn't answer for several miles. Fortunately, for their well-being, the passengers decided silence was a virtue and quietened their friendly banter.

The thought of another man attracting Diana's eye caused his gut to hurt. Was Grim just spouting off in his usually crude way? Had the contractor noticed something? The ex-Green Beret just couldn't accept her being with someone else.

As the miles passed, Nick realized Grim was actually doing him a favor, making him acknowledge how he really felt about Diana. "My apologies, gentlemen. I'm exhausted and contemplating a big step in life. I shouldn't have lost my temper back there."

"Ask her, Dad. Seriously, you should propose."

They stopped in front of the courthouse, Nick assuming Diana would be in her office despite the late hour. Grim agreed to drop the rest of the team off at their homes.

As Nick exited the cab, Grim stopped him in front of the truck. "You almost lost your son on this last mission. You know as well as anybody that shit happens. Marry the woman, Nick. Life is too short."

Nick smiled at his friend, nodding his thanks for the honest advice. "I think I'll do just that."

The big man took the courthouse steps two at a time, nodding to the security guard stationed at the front door as he passed. The light was on in Diana's office. He increased his pace, not wanting to lose the ball of courage he'd summed up.

"I thought I would find you here," he announced, causing her to look up from the report in her hands.

Her smile was bright and sincere, joy filling her face as she stood up and rushed into his arms.

After a lengthy embrace, Nick held her at arm's length and looked directly into her eyes. "I have something very important I need to talk to you about," he stated with a trembling voice.

"You've heard already?" Diana asked, concern crossing her brow.

"Heard what?"

"Bishop and Terri never showed up at Fort Bliss. I received a radio transmission a few hours ago and was trying to organize search parties."

Nick frowned, then walked over to the calendar hanging nearby on the wall. A quick count of the days made him even more concerned. "They should have made it to Bliss two days ago even if Bishop did decide to take an extra day camping. Something must have gone wrong."

"That's what I thought," she started. "But how did you know already?"

Nick ignored the question, not sure how to answer. Instead, he stepped to the map of Texas residing on the opposite wall and poked it with his finger. "We need to get a couple of Blackhawks over here from Fort Hood on the double. Searching from the air is the only way we have any chance of finding them down in that wasteland."

"Already done," Diana replied. "There will be four here just after dawn. General Owens is also sending two rifle squads as well."

He should have known Diana would take control of the situation, her professional response reminding him of her strength... one of the many reasons why he loved her. The realization snapped his mind back to the real purpose of his charging into her office.

Still facing the wall, he rested his hand the map while sorting his thoughts. In a moment he continued, determined to ask the provocative question while his resolve was high. "You know," he began, clearing his throat, "in this post-collapse world, we just never have any idea what is going to happen, Diana. I mean the world can... and does... turn on a dime."

"Oh, I know, Nick. I am worried about them, too. There is just no telling what has happened to Bishop and Terri," she rattled on for a minute, glad to have him back to share her apprehension.

The big man looked deeply into her eyes and sighed deeply. This conversation is not going the way I planned, he thought.

Diana, sensing his somewhat over the top, elevated apprehension, sought to reassure him of her plan, adding, "But we are dedicating the proper resources right away to mount a rescue, if necessary. Then again, we will probably find them out at some 4-star oasis, taking things easy, working on their tans and enjoying their second honeymoon."

Their second honeymoon? Nick thought, swallowing hard. Even that skinny-ass Bishop managed to close the deal with his lady love, and now he's on his second honeymoon. Nick slipped his top button from its hole and fanned himself with a file from the mayor's desk.

Diana noticed the glistening of Nick's skin as he broke out in a slight sweat. When he reached for the manila folder, she began replaying their disjointed conversation in her head and speculating over the cause of Nick's mildly erratic behavior. *What in the heck happened out there to turn my competent operative into a contemplative philosopher?* she wondered.

"Are you feeling okay, Nick?" the mayor asked, her level of concern rising as she began to visually assess his person for evidence of a serious injury. *Nope,* she thought. *No visible wounds.*

Someday, when the grandkids come to visit, we will remember this dialogue and laugh, he thought. *Oh, well, clearly it's now or never,* he determined. Diana appeared completely puzzled when he took a knee in front of her. "Now, back to my important discussion," he began. The true nature of the conversation finally dawned when he gently grasped her hand and looked up with the most sincere expression she'd ever seen. "Will you marry me, Miss Diana Brown?"

Tears rolled down her cheek as she stared back, almost not believing that the words she had waited so long to hear had finally been spoken.

"I will," she said, bending forward to kiss him passionately.

After they had finished, she held his face with both hands and looked lovingly into his eyes. "You just made me the happiest woman in the whole, wide world."

Terri was nodding off in the saddle when the camper finally came into view.

Seeing the familiar sight provided her with a second wind, the smile she flashed at her husband saying, "Thank you," and "I love you," in a single expression.

"I can't help you with Hunter," he explained. "I can't say why, but I think those guys behind us are close. It's just a gut feeling."

"No problem," she answered instantly. "You do what you have to do. I'm going to put Hunter down in the bat cave. If there's going to be shooting going on, he'll be the safest in there."

Bishop went to work, unloading the horses and moving the

packs into the cave with his wife and son. He made a point of making sure Terri's AR15 was ready to rumble.

He staked out the horses next to the spring, the thirsty animals wasting no time dipping into the cool pool of water.

It had been a few weeks since they had visited the ranch, the lonely stretch of property having been relegated to a second home of last resort. Terri's work kept her mostly in Alpha or traveling on the road. The same could be said of her mate's recent responsibilities.

On his last visit, Bishop had noticed several of his trip lines and early warning devices had succumbed to wind, weather, and wild animals. He'd been slacking off.

But there wasn't time to repair them now, he determined. If the men on their tail arrived while he was bumbling around in the desert, he might be caught unaware, and that wouldn't be good.

Terri appeared, carrying a wrapped sandwich. "It's not much, but the best I could do in a rush."

The Texan kissed her cheek, "It's perfect. Thank you."

"What can I do to help? Hunter's asleep. I built a wall of ammo boxes as an extra precaution to keep him safe."

"I want you to get some rest," Bishop ordered. "I don't know if we'll have to move, or when, but for right now you need to get some sleep. I'm going to stay out here and make sure nobody sneaks up on us. You stay with Hunter and keep your rifle handy. They may pass us by or might not be able to find our trail."

"Okay, if that's what you think is best," she answered. "And hey, don't forget that I love you. And more importantly, you still owe me a vacation," she winked.

"I love you too, babe. Now go catch some shut-eye. I'll yell before I come in. If they don't show up before dawn, then I'll assume they've lost us or given up. We'll ride on into Meraton tomorrow, and I'll splurge for a room at the Manor."

She hugged him tight, spinning away without another word and heading off to the bat cave. Bishop watched her go, wishing the world were a different place, or at least that they were some place safer.

Deciding to set up his vigil at the mouth of the valley, he selected a large, truck-sized boulder as cover. Arranging the extra magazines from the bat cave, he settled with his back against the cold rock and waited.

"Those are my horses," Mr. Culpepper declared, lowering the binoculars and handing the optic to Whitey. "They've got some sort of camper back in that valley. We've got them pinned."

"So what do you intend, sir," the foreman asked, studying the layout in the pre-dawn glow from the east.

"I want to take the woman and child alive. The husband, I couldn't care less about," came the steely response.

Whitey was at the end of his rope, frustrated and confused by the entire affair. With a tone bordering on insubordination, he asked, "Why, Mr. Culpepper? I need to know why. I know you better than to believe this confrontation is all over a couple of horses... or somebody sneaking out on you. So before I order our men into a very dangerous situation, I think I deserve an explanation."

A harsh rebuttal filled the old man's throat, but he checked the reaction. After a few deep breaths, he said, "Because that woman down there can win the war for us. While I was visiting the triple-8, I found out she's the head honcho of a very, very powerful group, and she controls more resources than we'd ever need to defeat the Tejanos."

"We're so desperate that we have to resort to kidnapping?"

The look on Culpepper's face made the man look old and sad. "We're losing, Whitey. We can hold out a month more, maybe two. I'm not going just to let my ranch – and everything I've dedicated my whole life to – go without a fight. Think about it. You know damn well I'm telling the truth."

Something in his boss's voice touched Whitey. He'd been in Mr. Culpepper's employ since he'd left high school, the man beside him the only person who'd ever given him a chance.

"If you think it's the right move, then I'm with you all the way, sir. I ride for the Culpepper ranch, and so do the men with us."

The statement of unwavering loyalty moved the old man, but he had never expected anything less. No matter how troubling the circumstances, it was a time-honored tradition in the West for a man to pledge his gun and his life to the outfit.

"Take them all alive if you can, but for sure, bring me that woman. It will be the end of our war, and the only chance I can see for the future."

"Yes, sir. We'll hit them at dawn," came the reply, and then Whitey was gone, moving off to rally the men and set up the assault.

The sunlight hitting Bishop's face made him sneeze, that involuntary reaction followed immediately by a yawn.

He glanced up at the cloudless sky, trying to decide if the remaining miles to Meraton would be bearable in the heat, comparing that option to traveling at night. He gave up, accepting that he really didn't have any choice in the matter. They had to get back to civilization sooner rather than later.

Standing gingerly, he stretched wide and hard, spreading his arms and flexing every muscle still under his command. He'd give it one more hour, and if the men behind them didn't show their faces, he'd saddle up the horses and head into town before it got too hot.

It was the slightest color out of place that snapped him alert, a shadow just a hair too long, a rock that hadn't been there before. Bishop bent low, carefully studying the canyon he knew so well, trying to decipher what had drawn his eye.

The first rifle shot pinged high off the boulder to his front. Before he could react, a full volley of incoming fire drove him to the ground.

They're here. There are a lot of them.

The rain of lead stopped immediately after he had disappeared from sight, giving Bishop time to replay the last few seconds. His mind worked hard, attempting to calculate angles of fire, distance, sound, and the likely position of the shooters. But it was too much, too quick; his then-groggy mind unable to reconcile all the input.

One thing was for certain; he wasn't in a good position, and when outnumbered, fighting was like real estate - location, location, location.

Bishop reached into his bag of goodies, extracting two long canisters. It took only a few moments to extract the pin and toss the smoke grenades.

Confined by the canyon walls and lack of moving air, the mouth of the valley soon filled with a thick fog. Hefting his bag and bent low, Bishop launched from behind his cover, sprinting for all he was worth in retreat.

He leaped behind a smaller rock, his new shelter one of the last boulders before the flat, open area in front of the camper. Beyond the temporary, aluminum-skinned home was the dead end of the steep canyon walls, an unscalable barrier while taking fire.

"It's now or never," he hissed, bracing his rifle over the top of the rock and waiting for the smoke to clear.

He didn't have to wait long.

Culpepper's men thought he was still behind the big rock, one of them exposing his head in an attempt to gain a better vantage. Bishop's optic centered, his first shot of the battle drawing blood.

But now they knew where he was hiding, dozens of bullets chewing into his rock cover... shards, sand, and lead filling the air.

Bishop was more alert now, ready for the return fire, his mind snapping detailed mental images of muzzle flashes and movement. He waited low, letting them blast away at his granite shield.

It was obvious he was in trouble. The enemy held a strong list asymmetrical advantages, including firepower, maneuverability, longevity, and tactical position. I'm essentially stuck with a shit sandwich, Bishop realized. It was 20 rifles to 1; he was pinned inside of a dead end kill zone. They could pick the angle of attack, take more losses, and they held the high ground.

His only hope was to inflict as many casualties as possible and pray they would rethink continuing the assault. Unlikely, but desperate men had held on with less.

When their fire subsided, the Texan popped up, spraying three quick shots where his memory indicated a target would be. There wasn't time to see if he did any damage, a hailstorm of whizzing bullets splitting the air just as he crouched low.

They were everywhere, at least 20 men. Some were up high, firing down into the valley from the canyon walls, others were spread out across the entrance and using the same field of boulders as cover.

It occurred to Bishop that the shooters on the walls weren't the primary concern. The sheer faces of rock prohibited those men from doing anything but covering for their comrades down on the floor. That's where the assault had to come from, up the mouth of the formation, and into the teeth of Bishop's defense.

He started focusing on the people at his own level, hoping the loss of a few of their own would make the survivors pause. Ignoring the men up high, Bishop's next series of rounds concentrated on the force working its way toward his position.

The M4 sang its deadly song, Bishop staying exposed longer than was prudent, but it paid off. He heard a howl of pain and then saw another man fall.

That pissed them off, the duration and amount of returning lead far more intense than previous exchanges.

Bishop knew he was fucked. He could get lucky, picking a man off here and there, but the outcome wasn't in doubt. He was simply outnumbered and would eventually fall under the weight of their attack.

A turmoil of self-doubt rampaged through his head. He cursed himself for every bad decision, starting with the horrible idea of taking a vacation, and ending with his placid attitude that very morning. It's no wonder you're going to die, he thought. You've messed up every step of the way.

The two sides exchanged salvos several more times, Bishop rising up to spray half-aimed shots, the Culpepper riders responding, pushing him back behind the rock.

But then they finally wised up. A constant stream of suppressive fire started striking his boulder, keeping Bishop pinned low while granite shrapnel stung his skin, and zips of lead passed overhead. They were taking away any chance he had to raise up and hold them back.

Bishop chanced it anyway, moving to the other end of his hide before exposing himself, but only managing two shots before they adjusted their aim. During that brief glimpse down the valley, he recognized two teams of men moving toward him on both sides. Smart, he hated to admit, finally a professional move.

With his face pressed into the dirt, praying none of the bullets found his body, Bishop wasn't surprised the cowboys had figured it out so quickly. While they may not have the benefit of first-rate military training, they had been involved in a shooting war for several months. Men learn in combat, reflexes are honed; the smart ones survive.

Anger began to well up inside the Texan's core, a fury aimed at Culpepper and his self-centered, single-purposed campaign to win his little war, no matter who he hurt or what price in human life was paid. He rose up again, almost uncaring as he stayed and sprayed.

The bullet that grazed his forearm sent a wave of pain, and reality, back into his rage-driven head. Injured and scared, Bishop dropped back down. Another session of internal criticism followed. What are you trying to do? Make it easy for them?

Movement to his right caused Bishop to look, Terri's pale face peeking out from the heavy metal door of the bat cave. She appeared there only for a second, but it was enough to re-energize Bishop and fuel his need to survive.

Reaching into his bag, he pulled out the only two hand grenades in his possession. The small, military issued explosives were leftovers from the skirmish in Brighton, stored in the bat cave out of concern for their safety.

He waited, trying to judge how bold the men moving up the valley would be. After what seemed like an eternity, Bishop pulled both pins, rising to throw one left, the other right.

He waited low, the loud crack and rumble of the detonations launching a cloud of rising debris into the air. Bishop was up and running, making for the camper's wheels and his last line of defense.

The screams of wounded men came through his heavy breathing as soon as he slid behind the metal rims, desperate cries for help drifting through the still-settling clouds of sand raised by the grenades.

Bishop actually managed a smile, pleased that at least one of his tosses had found flesh.

He raised the M4, waiting for a clear target. A form appeared, rushing forward as if to help a downed comrade. Bishop practically cut the man in half.

It was a short-lived victory. After being surprised by the grenades, the cowboys regrouped quickly, if nothing else, doubling the ferocity of their advance.

From Bishop's perspective, a solid wall of lead slammed into the camper, shredding the thin metal skin like a freight train cutting through fog. He tried to return fire, but the air was filled with fragments of the trailer, erupting fountains of dense smoke and geysers of sand and dirt. The Texan's eyes burned, and his lungs suffered for air.

Just when he thought it couldn't get any worse, he felt a heat pouring over his body. It took only a moment to realize that much of the smoke surrounding his position was because the camper was on fire. A quick glance confirmed the flames were spreading quickly, the inferno threatening to engulf his position. If he didn't move, the blaze would turn him into charcoal before Culpepper's men ever had a chance to shoot again.

But there was no place to go.

He was parallel with the bat cave, his situational awareness screaming that he'd never make it across the open ground between the camper and the rock shelter. Besides, he'd been trying to draw the assault away from Terri's hide, not lead them to it.

The flames grew more intense, his neck feeling like someone was pouring hot oil over his head. The heat was becoming unbearable.

The constant chorus of the rancher's gunfire suddenly changed, a new voice of violence sounding in his ear. Bishop chanced rolling away from the camper and its curtain of smoke, his heart stopping at what he saw.

Terri was against the bat cave's exterior wall, her AR blasting away at the attackers. He watched in horror as she would fire several shots and then duck back, just as rounds would strike and splinter the surrounding stone.

He had to get her back into the cave.

Bishop managed his feet, leaving his now empty bag behind and tucking his carbine into the nook of his arm. It was the fastest he could ever remember running, sprinting across the open spaces and waiting for the bullets to knock him down. His mind conjured up a childhood nightmare, visions of snarling, snapping wolves chasing his legs as he moved in slow motion across the unprotected ground.

He was halfway there when Terri popped out, raising her rifle to give him covering fire. She no more managed to shoulder the weapon when her body twitched, shuddered, and then she went down.

"Nooooo!!!!" Bishop screamed as he slid to a stop over his wounded wife, trying to shield her body with his own.

Relentlessly and without mercy, another broadside of fire snapped at Bishop as he grabbed Terri by the shoulders and pulled her back into the safety of the bat cave. In a whirlwind of crazed movement, he slammed and barred the heavy, steel door, and then dropped to his knees at Terri's side.

The desert surrounding the ranch suddenly became silent.

Despite having just come off an exhaustive mission, Nick couldn't keep the other members of Bishop's SAINT team off the Blackhawk. When Cory, Kevin, and Grim had heard their leader might be in trouble, all three had been waiting at the airfield before dawn.

It had taken far too long to get the pilots up to speed on the search grid he'd laid out the night before, even longer to convince the Army lieutenant commanding the two rifle squads that his SAINT team would be just fine on its own.

They'd finally taken off from Alpha fifteen minutes ago, the wasted time frustrating all concerned. Despite still being several minutes from the designated search area, all four of the Alliance men were scanning the desert passing beneath the airborne machine. Kevin was using his sniper optic, Grim and Cory intensely searching with binoculars.

It was Cory who noticed the smoke.

"Got something burning over here, Nick," he shouted over the passing wind and rotor wash. "Can't tell what it is. Sure seems awful big to be a signal fire."

After scoping out the large column of black smoke, Nick ordered the pilot to change course.

They were over a mile out when Nick realized they were approaching Bishop's ranch. He'd only visited there once before, but the layout had impressed the big man. The camper had been torched, ash and flame reaching to the sky, a good indicator they had found the missing couple.

The images of men carrying rifles didn't become distinct until they were a half-mile out, their presence confusing all aboard.

The pilot spotted a flat area that was suitable for landing, only a short distance away from the fire. As they began to descend, Nick noticed the round patterns of grenade blasts in the sand. It was too late to avert the already-committed touchdown. "This place is hot!" he screamed over the engine noise. "Shoot anybody you see moving."

Grim leaped off the platform while the helo was still five feet in the air. He was firing before his boots hit the ground. Nick was right behind the contractor, jumping out the other side and rolling away just as geysers of sand exploded next to his head.

Kevin glanced at a very frightened Cory and shrugged his shoulders, following his father into the fray. Cory, having no desire to remain alone, bailed as well.

Random shots sparked and pinged off the Blackhawk's skin as it pulled away, the copilot wasting no time in calling the other birds to the location.

Realizing they had just dropped into the middle of a hornet's nest, Grim and Nick unleashed a fury of violence against the yet unidentified foe.

The Culpepper men, already bloodied by the extended fight with Bishop, began to fall back.

Fighting against a lone defender was one thing, taking on a military aircraft full of very aggressive reinforcements another. It was all over in less than a minute, the SAINT team quickly finding themselves without any targets.

But where were Bishop, Terri, and Hunter?

Nick almost shot the Texan, the squeaking protest of the metal cave door prompting the big man's rifle to take aim.

Lured into the open by the sound of the helicopter, Bishop came into view, his shirt covered in grit and blood. "'Bout time you showed up," he sputtered weakly.

"You hit? You okay? That your blood?"

"Terri's been hit, but not bad," came the reply.

Cory was the first inside, finding Terri sitting against the wall, her arm wrapped in bandages. Her easy smile let him know she was okay. Nick didn't want to take any chances, getting on his radio and ordering their Blackhawk to return for a medical evacuation.

The big man then entered the bat cave, finding Grim and Cory fussing over Terri's wound. "Bishop and you will be able to sit around and compare your battle scars to entertain the grandkids," Grim teased.

"It doesn't look like the bullet hit anything critical, but you better go and have it checked out anyway. Infection can be a nasty thing. The chopper is on the way," Nick reassured her.

The copter hadn't gone far, the roar of the aircraft's descent soon filling the canyon walls. It seemed like everyone was trying to help Terri to the Blackhawk.

They loaded her on the helicopter's deck, Bishop climbing aboard. Nick ordered the pilot to make all haste for Fort Bliss, but Terri overrode the command. "Belay that order. I'll be fine with the doc in Alpha. Take me there; this injury is not that bad."

"But ma'am, the hospital at Fort Bliss is still the best facility in the Alliance. You should go and make sure there are no complications," Cory protested, concern written all over the young man's face.

She glanced over at her husband, memories of that horrible day when he was shot in the chest. That helicopter ride to Fort Bliss had been one of her worst nightmares. "Take me to Alpha," she told the pilot.

With a look of horror, Bishop reached out and grabbed Nick's arm. "Hunter!" he shouted. "Hunter's in the cave!"

"Don't worry about him," Nick yelled back. "Diana and I will take care of that young whippersnapper."

Nick stood next to Grim as they watched the bird lift off. "I sure wouldn't want to be those cowboys after she gets that arm looked at. Bishop's got to be pissed to the extreme."

"It's not Bishop I'd be worried about," Nick replied. "He's a fuzzy pair of bunny slippers compared to his wife. Come on, Uncle Grim, we've got a babysitting job to do."

Mr. Culpepper saw the helicopter return and lift off, but didn't react. Turning, he spurred his horse to catch up with the dejected line of men riding back to the ranch.

More than anyone, he felt the foul fog of emotion covering their withdrawal.

For the first hour of their ride, he seriously considered taking his own life. The loss of men suffered at the hands of Bishop had been bad enough, but when he saw the woman go down, the old rancher knew it was all over.

Something about the vision of a woman falling to gunfire initiated a wave of remorse that shook his soul. He knew the rest of the men felt the same way. She had been an accidental target, appearing out of nowhere, surprising his boys with an unexpected entry into the fight.

Despite his depression and sense of loss, he still had to wonder what type of woman will pick up a rifle and willingly join such an intense battle. Probably thought her husband was about to fall, he considered.

As they plodded along the open desert, Culpepper wondered if the military men would hunt them down for revenge. He didn't care, completely dejected by the loss of life and the failure to save his ranch.

"I'm sorry, Daddy," he whispered to the sky, the apology going unanswered.

Whitey, his arm wrapped in a handkerchief bandage from a shrapnel hit, came alongside. "What now, boss? We lost 8 men back there and have another 4 or 5 out of commission."

"I don't know, son," the rancher replied. "I fear I've lost everything. Give me some time, I need to think it through."

Whitey peered over his shoulder, thinking about the arrival of the helicopter and the unbelievable resistance they had just encountered. I hope you have some time, he thought. I have a feeling we just kicked a hornet's nest.

Chapter 13

The sound of nervous whinnying woke Mr. Culpepper, years of coexistence with the animals giving him an ear tuned to their language.

He remained still, barely breathing, listening to their conversation. What was making them so skittish?

He didn't need a clock to tell the time, the view of the eastern sky out his window letting him know the sun would be coming up within the hour.

There was no anger in the man as he swung his legs over the edge of the bed. Sleep hadn't been a companion since the battle at the camper. For a brief moment, he wondered how many days his ancient body could endure the insomnia before his heart gave out. I hope not many more, he thought.

The single action Colt revolver laid on the bedside table, the weapon's primary purpose having changed since they had returned from the gunfight with Bishop. Until that point, it had been a defensive piece, loaded and ready should a Tejanos assassin make it past his men. Now, he eyed it every morning and night, trying to work up the guts to use it on himself.

The only fortunate news had been a sudden lack of activity by his enemy. Bunkhouse morale had been at an all-time low since their defeat, and any large-scale engagement with the Tejanos would have surely meant the end.

Yet, for some unknown reason, his foe on the other side of the river had been unusually quiet. A blessing? The calm before the storm? Only God knew.

He pulled on his pants, then boots, moving to the window. A renewed round of chatter from the corral redirected his thoughts to the stock.

There hadn't been a mountain lion in these parts for years. Coyotes were too shy to approach the structures, too heavy with the smell of men. For a moment, he wondered if the Tejanos had finally arrived, ready to murder them all.

He walked calmly to the front door, pistol at ease against his leg. In the early morning's light, he could barely make out the profile of the barn.

He opened the door, stepping lightly onto the front porch, grip tightening on the pistol.

"Good morning, Mr. Culpepper. Please put down the gun," came a voice from the darkness.

He started to raise the weapon, expecting to see a crazed Tejano charging from the night, but the voice's owner was right next to him, pinning the old Colt against his leg. "Please, Mr.

Culpepper, don't make me take your life."

He released the sidearm, a quick hand from the stranger catching the barrel before it could fall to the wooden planks of the porch.

"Please walk to the corral, sir."

As he stepped down onto the packed hardpan bordering the house, he sensed another presence from behind. Silent. Stealthy. Ominous.

Whoever they were, he was positive it wasn't going to end well. They continued to escort him out to the corral, where he was sure a painful, excruciating death awaited. Go out with honor, he thought. Don't beg. Those animals won't show you any mercy, regardless of how much you plead. But the fear was difficult to squelch.

The pre-dawn light began to reveal strange images around the corral, odd, dense shadows that hadn't been there before. He couldn't quite make them out.

He was guided toward the gate, one of his captors gently pushing his arm in the right direction. It was difficult to put one foot in front of the other, his legs weak with terror, the sweat of fear forming on his brow.

The vague outline of men began to come clear to the rancher as the light increased, their shapes oddly distorted – almost ghoulish in nature. They didn't seem human, odd bulges, malformed heads, and thick chests.

He then could identify other figures, dozens of shorter outlines against the corral's fence. A female voice sounded from the darkness. "Good morning, Mr. Culpepper."

He knew that voice, but from where? The fear was inhibiting his thought process, making cognitive reasoning nearly impossible. Just kill me, and get it over with, he prayed.

He was steered to the corral's oak plank fence, a strong hand pressing down on his shoulders. "On your knees."

Finally, he reasoned, finally, they are going to put a bullet in my head.

He closed his eyes, whispering the Lord's Prayer, readying for a sharp pain. Would there be pain? he wondered. What was it like on the other side?

He stayed there, partially aware of movement around him, the shuffling of bodies, whispered commands, and the brush of cloth. He kept his eyes closed, praying the pain wouldn't be too intense.

After a while, the prayers changed. Culpepper pined for another chance, entreating his maker for a fresh start. He promised to do better, not to make such a mess of what he had been given.

The female voice was back, interrupting his holy wish list. "You can stand up now, Mr. Culpepper."

He did as instructed, opening his eyes that had been squinting tight from praying. The sun was almost up; he could see clearly.

Dozens of soldiers were on his ranch, men with helmets, night vision goggles, body armor, and combat vests. All of his men were there as well, on their knees, against the corral fence. It was clear to the old rancher that most of them had been taken by surprise, rounded up just like he was shortly before sunrise. Few had their hats; many were in long johns, or merely wearing skivvies.

"I wish I could say it was nice to see you again, Mr. Culpepper, but that would be dishonest of me. The last time we met, you, or one of your men shot me."

He spun around, staring blankly at Terri's smirking face. "So you didn't die in the shootout. Thank God."

She tilted her head, not quite understanding his meaning. He tried to clarify, "We never intended for you to be harmed. That would have flown in the face of my ultimate goal… of leveraging you and your people into helping us defeat the Tejanos."

"I see," she replied coldly. "And this is supposed to make me feel all warm and fuzzy?"

"Perhaps," he replied. "I just don't want anyone thinking I would ever deliberately hurt a woman."

"How honorable of you, Mr. Culpepper," Terri said, her voice thick with sarcasm. "I am sure the widows in the Tejanos village appreciate your kindness."

"War is war," he countered. "All is fair."

Terri shook her head, already tiring of the conversation. "I'm not going to run around in circles with you, sir. I'm here on official business – putting an end to your little war."

Spitting on the ground, Culpepper's voice was full of hate, "There can't be any peace with those animals. You can just come down off your high horse, Missy, and forget about it. Never going to happen."

"I don't think you grasp the situation as it currently exists. Perhaps it's too early. But I assure you, I'll make it all crystal clear in a few minutes."

A distant thumping noise sounded over the nearby hills, progressively getting louder and turning into a steady, powerful rumble. All eyes turned to the west as a line of Blackhawk helicopters appeared over the ridge.

Raising her voice over the din, Terri glanced at the rancher and announced, "Ah, our other guests are arriving. Please follow me."

197

Culpepper hesitated, having no desire to corporate.

Terri noticed his reluctance and turned to one of the huge men that were obviously her bodyguards. "Butter," she said sweetly, "I think Mr. Culpepper's legs aren't functioning properly, and he requires your assistance. Could you please throw him over your shoulder and bring him along?"

The muscular young fellow nodded, his expression making it clear the rancher was going to accompany his boss, voluntarily or not. Culpepper decided to forgo the embarrassment, stepping forward on his own two feet.

"That was wise, sir. I'm not in a trifling mood this morning, and my large friends are convinced that you tried to kill me three days ago at our ranch. They love Hunter and would hate the thought of seeing him grow up without a mother."

Without waiting for a reply, Terri turned to watch the first helicopter land, a wall of dust and sand rising into the air from the downdraft. In they came, one after the other, each depositing soldiers, and then Bishop's SAINT team appeared through the airborne debris.

After the copters had lifted off, she made for her husband, taking careful note of the tall man with a dark complexion and Latino features. The stranger was bound, Grim keeping a vigilant eye on the prisoner as he trailed behind Bishop.

"Terri, I would like to introduce you to Rocco, the undisputed leader of the Tejanos," Bishop said. "He's still a little upset that we rousted him out of bed this morning, but not nearly as mad as the señorita who woke up to find six armed operators in her bedroom."

"I've never heard a woman scream so loudly," Grim chuckled. "It was like she'd never seem a bunch of guys surrounding her bed with night vision goggles before."

Rocco didn't acknowledge Terri. Instead his eyes were busy, boring into Mr. Culpepper with hurled bolts of hatred and spite.

"I see you two already know each other," Terri commented. "Good. Now let's get down to business. Please follow me."

She led the sizable entourage toward the big stable, her large, official motorhome parked on the other side. Butter moved on ahead, opening the door for Terri and her guests.

Nick was waiting inside, a water pitcher and glasses sitting on the main salon table. Terri indicated the two hostile leaders should sit on opposite sides.

After Terri was seated, Butter took up a position behind her, ready to protect his charge if any of the visitors felt frisky. No one seemed to notice Sheriff Watts, the tall, thin lawman standing like a statue in the corner. His uniform was perfect in every detail, including white Stetson hat, polished badge, mirrored sunglasses, and spit-shined boots.

Nick and Bishop rounded out the meeting, each Alliance man taking a chair to keep the two antagonists separated.

Terri pulled two single pieces of paper from the table, sliding a copy of the document in front of each captive. "There are the terms of your surrender. Please read them carefully. Both are identical, both contain the exact same wording in English and Spanish."

"Surrender!" Culpepper exclaimed. "I haven't surrendered to anyone!"

Nick grunted, indicating the corral with his hand. "Sir, I have all of your men on their knees. I have confiscated all of their weapons, horses, and your property. I have 300 assault troops on your ranch, and can call in gunships, artillery, and front-line armor, if necessary. You, Mr. Culpepper, got your ass kicked this morning, and we didn't even have to fire a shot. You've lost; so deal with it."

It was Bishop's turn to address Rocco. "The Tejanos shared the same fate. One hour ago, we took down the villages, every one of the surrounding sentry posts, and all patrols. While there were shots fired, the enemy casualties were limited to three wounded, and one mule killed in action. At this time, the main village is occupied by 350 soldiers from the 7th Cav."

"This is outrageous!" Culpepper exploded. "I am on sovereign US soil, a freeborn citizen of the United States of America. I can't be invaded… or occupied… or whatever you want to call it."

Terri sneered, shaking her head. "The United States of America no longer controls Texas, sir. Nor has the Alliance incorporated your land. In addition, five days ago, you committed an act of war by attempting to murder an elected head of state, me, and two of our citizens, my husband and son. You invaded our territory with an armed force. We are completely justified in our actions. Consider yourself conquered."

Bishop looked at Rocco, "You're in the same boat. You've admitted to crossing the Rio Grande numerous times with an armed force. We found several of your outposts on this side of the river. In addition, you held one of our citizens, Reed, against his will. We invaded Mexico this morning and now claim all territory under our control."

Rocco didn't respond, his face remaining neutral. Mr. Culpepper, on the other hand, was indignant. "So what? Are you going to kill us all? Throw us in a prisoner of war gulag? This is ridiculous."

Terri pointed to a piece of paper no one had bothered to

read. "My terms, which are non-negotiable – I suggest you both read them. As for your question regarding your future, if you don't agree to my demands, I will have you incarcerated for the crimes I have already enumerated, and you will spend the rest of your days working on one of Sheriff Watt's chain gangs," she said, indicating the silent lawman in the corner.

Before Culpepper could spout off again, Nick added, "Of course, if you would prefer a firing squad, that can be arranged as well. We're trying to keep our prison population at a minimum."

Culpepper reached for the paper and began reading. Bishop pulled his knife, cutting Rocco free from the nylon tie that had been securing the captive's hands.

"This says that we agree to become citizens of the Alliance of West Texas, to abide by all of its laws and regulations," the old rancher stated, looking up in surprise. "That's it? That's all you want?"

Terri nodded, "Yes, that's it. If you have a dispute, claim, issue, or are the victim of a crime, then call Sheriff Watts or other law enforcement. We are going to leave both sides with sufficient radio and communications equipment to stay in constant contact with our authorities. If you have a beef with the Tejanos, then file a police report and let professionals do their jobs."

She then shifted her focus to Rocco, "If you feel like Mr. Culpepper, or anyone else, breaks the law or acts against you or your people, then by all means file a complaint. We have a system of courts and judges. If folks commit violent acts, they will face arrest and imprisonment. It's really that simple."

"None of this will keep them from treating us like animals. Their racial hatred and bigotry will still exist, and my people will suffer," Rocco protested. "Nothing will change."

"Really?" Bishop interjected. "In these times, you're really worried that some gringo is going to look down on you because of your skin color? I think you'll find what God you worship, or the pigmentation of your hide doesn't matter a hill of beans to most residents of the Alliance. We're too focused on putting enough food on the table, and making sure babies survive at birth. If Culpepper hates you because of your race, then just go around him. You don't need him. Let it be his loss."

Terri smiled at the Tejanos leader, adding, "The Alliance isn't going to get into equal rights, fair housing, or anti-discrimination governance. The concept of trying to implement any sort of affirmative action in a post-apocalyptic society is just plain silly. Yet, crime is crime, and all people will be treated equally under the law. We don't see any need to resurrect any of the pre-collapse exercises in social justice. They seemed intent on forcing people of different backgrounds and races to like each other. Quite frankly, our government could care less if you like each other. None of our business."

"Then things will be the same," spat Rocco. "We will be denied equal standing due to age old prejudices and ancient bigotries."

Terri disagreed. "The world outside your little valley has changed, Rocco. Go to Meraton or Alpha, and do business with folks there who want your goods and services. I'd be stunned if someone treated you differently because of your skin color or native language. Nobody has time for that anymore. Life is difficult enough without adding on the layer of additional hate you're referring to. People simply don't have the energy. And if someone does look down upon you, then to hell with them. Our leaders won't discriminate, our government won't allow institutional prejudice, and our police won't act with bigotry. In the end, that's all that matters. All men are created equal. All men are equal under the eyes of our law. What they do with that equality going forward is up to the individual."

Mr. Culpepper still didn't get it. "What's keeping those animals from sneaking across the border and stealing my salt or cattle or worse?"

Sheriff Watts stepped forward, "Then you call my people, and we'll handle it. You have the right to defend your property and life, just like before the collapse. But if you go taking other matters into your own hands, then you'll be considered a vigilante and a criminal, just like before. There will be a civil society in my jurisdiction, gentlemen. That's my job, and I take it seriously.

Nick added, "I'm going to maintain a significant force in this area, at least until things cool down. We won't tolerate vigilantes from either side of the Rio Grande."

"Bottom line," Terri concluded, "We are going to have rule of law. No ifs, ands, or buts about it. Either play by the rules or go to jail. Every man and woman on both sides of your dispute will be required to sign the document in front of you. This war is over gentlemen, so you're going to have to find someone else to hate."

She then produced two pens, sliding one across to each man. Both signed.

The council chambers were filled to capacity, word having spread quickly that today's meeting was extra special.

Terri entered the room last, dressed in a mid-length, blue skirt and conservative white blouse. She carried a single piece of paper, taking her usual seat at the head of the table.

Bishop was behind her, holding Hunter, who was completely occupied with a brightly colored pacifier.

Pete called the meeting to order, nodding at Terri to open.

"Thank you all for attending, I know everyone's schedule has been extremely difficult these last few months. I would not have called a mandatory meeting were it not for an urgent matter that affects all of us."

She paused, looking around the room, smiling at every face. After completing the circuit, she turned over the sheet of paper and said, "I would like to read this to all of you. Effective immediately, I hereby resign my position as President of the Alliance Council."

Sounds of shock and surprise rippled through the gathered onlookers, as well as those seated at the council table. Diana started to say something, but a glance from Terri stopped her short.

"It has been my greatest honor to serve with this esteemed body. I count all of you as friends and adored colleagues," she continued reading. "My reasons are simple and honest. I want to spend more time with my family, be a factor in my child's life, and get back to a simpler existence. God bless each and every one of you. God bless Texas."

She looked up with a smile and a single tear rolling down her cheek.

"Terri, why don't you take some time off and think this over," Diana suggested. "We need you now more than ever. I know it's been especially difficult on you the last few months, but things will get better. Take a break and recharge your batteries. Then make this decision."

Several heads around the table nodded their agreement.

"No, thank you, but no. Bishop and I have talked this over extensively, debated the pros and cons until the wee hours of the morning. I want to be with my husband and son; I want to rebuild our lives. The Alliance is strong and growing stronger. I've done my best to contribute, but the time for me to move on is now."

Protests and small conversations broke out all around the room, the din increasing until Diana called out, "Order! Order! We will have order in these chambers."

Pete waited until things quieted down, his voice solemn and clear. "I don't blame you, Terri. Not one bit. Let me be the first to express my support. I'm sure this was a difficult decision. If there's anything you and Bishop need, just let me know. I wish you both all the happiness in the world."

Using a handkerchief, Terri dabbed at her watering eyes. "Thank you, Pete, that means a lot to me," she said softly.

One by one, the council members expressed similar sentiments, their words of love and support bringing everyone's emotions to the surface. There was hardly a dry eye in the room; even Nick's throat grew tight as the acknowledgments of Terri's service and sacrifice were verbalized.

Throughout it all, Bishop stood behind his wife, holding Hunter with one hand, the other lending comfort on his wife's shoulder.

And then she rose, flashing her warmest smile around the room, and made for the door.

It was D.A. Gibson who stood first, her hands coming together in applause. Moments later, the entire gathering was on its feet, clapping loudly as Terri left the room, not daring to look back.

She rushed down the courthouse hall, a plethora of emotions welling up inside. Bishop was there, as well as Hunter, ready to comfort or support. Terri stopped midway to the exit, leaning against the wall as if she couldn't walk any further.

Bishop knew she was full of resolve to resign, the idea having been hers from the beginning. He also understood that didn't make it all any easier. She rested her head against his shoulder, intense sobs racking her frame.

Hunter reached over, his tiny hand touching her head. It was a cute, wonderful gesture of love and concern. It made both of them smile and broke the spell of Terri's remorse.

Still sniffling, she reached for her son, taking him in a tight embrace. "I have a surprise for you today, young man," she cooed. "You've never tasted ice cream, and I know where there's a hidden stash."

It was Bishop who got excited by the announcement, "You what? You know where there's ice cream?"

"Sure do. Now if you both behave like good little boys, mommy will share," she teased. "Come along now. Look both ways before crossing the street outside, blow your nose, and don't run with any sharp objects in your hand."

Chapter 14

Bishop stood looking at his garden plot, what should have been a mini-oasis in the center of the arid wasteland. For some reason, he just couldn't get anything to prosper. "I've got a black thumb," he confessed to the struggling row of beans.

Hunter's laughter echoed across the canyon, Terri pushing the boy on the new swing Bishop had secured to the overhang. He'd even installed a seat belt at his wife's request, mom worried that her son was still too young to properly hang on.

His thoughts drifted back to gardening, the frustrations over what he considered a "black art," were nearing the point of asking for help. "I'll just drive through Alpha until I spot the best looking patch, kidnap the owners, and then force them at gunpoint to divulge their green thumb secrets," he mused.

Another bout of squealing happiness erupted from the swing, Hunter's latest thrill being a ride in his mother's lap while she pumped higher and higher.

With an adoring smile, Bishop watched them together for a few minutes. Finally deciding he was thirsty, the Texan turned and headed toward the huge motorhome now parked where the old camper had once resided.

Diana and Nick had demanded Terri accept the RV as a gift, calling it an "earned severance." Terri had finally agreed, but only on a temporary basis. Bishop and she already had an appointment with an architect in Midland Station, the talented man agreeing to design the perfect home for their canyon retreat.

Bishop intended to build as much of the new house as he could, hoping to reduce expenses. They were starting over, after all.

It had taken two bulldozers an entire day to move enough boulders so the behemoth motorhome could fit. Bishop had been melancholy when one of the tracked earthmovers had connected a chain and pulled the burned-out shell of the original camper into the desert. There, the tractor had excavated a trench and buried the smelly carcass. He pondered erecting a monument over the gravesite, but decided he had better things to do.

There was also a brand new pickup sitting beside the RV. Again, Nick had been adamant that Bishop accept the vehicle, noting how many times the Texan had used his own personal wheels on official Alliance business. "After all, you're still leading one of our SAINT teams, and you never know when we'll have to call on you for a mission," the big man had reminded him.

Entering the RV, a blast of cool air washed over his face.

They had consistent electrical power now, courtesy of the underground diesel tank installed while the bulldozers were handy.

He pulled a pitcher of water out of the fridge, relishing the cold liquid while wondering how they'd ever survived without refrigeration or air conditioning. Now if he could just get pizza delivered and Monday night football on TV, life would be perfect.

Terri's voice brought him back to the here and now, something in her tone indicating she was worried. Thinking the swing had come loose and she might be hurt, he rushed for the door.

He didn't have to ask what the trouble was, the distant rumble of a helicopter the unmistakable origin of her concern. "Were you expecting Nick?" she called across the canyon.

"Nope. There's no one on the guest list today."

The sound grew intense, both of them peering around the rim of surrounding rock, trying to pinpoint the machine's direction.

Bishop ducked, and Terri yelped when the Apache gunship soared overhead, the low flying warbird not more than 50 feet off the ground. They both watched as the machine slowed over the mouth of their valley, coming to a hover, and then whirling to face the stunned couple.

"What the hell," Bishop hissed, moving for the bat cave and waving for Terri to do the same. She hadn't needed any prompting, already clutching Hunter close, and moving quickly toward the rock room's entrance.

Bishop was halfway there, already thinking about which rifle he was going to use to defend his property and furious over the need to do so. He paused when the second helicopter roared overhead, this one an unarmed Blackhawk. The Texan noted several faces staring down at him, all the visible men inside wearing helmets and combat gear.

A string of curses was just forming in his throat when a third bird appeared, another transport unit slowing to hover at the mouth of the canyon.

Bishop rushed into the bat cave, pulling his favorite M4 off the wall, grabbing and stuffing magazines into his pockets. Terri threw him a worried look while she helped him into his armor. "Who did you piss off now," she joked, trying to lighten the moment.

"I don't know, but he must be one powerful dude. Maybe it's your boyfriend, and he's sick of waiting for me to move on."

He exited the bat cave just in time to see several troops pouring out of the first Blackhawk, the rifle squad-sized unit spreading out, heading directly for Bishop's new RV. They must want the truck, he mused. It is the latest model, and that color is difficult to find these days.

Then came the second transport, men in casual dress slacks and sports coats jumping out first. There was too much dust and dirt flying through the air for Bishop to see much detail. The hovering, evil looking gunship was still perfectly visible, however, standing guard over the ground-level deployment.

Bishop didn't know what to make of the whole show. If the visitors were hostile, it was already over. Throwing Terri a questioning glance, Bishop shrugged and kept his rifle barrel pointed low.

It was a man in a sports coat that approached first, stepping through the skirmish line of what Bishop now could see were United States Marines.

A few steps closer, and the Texan recognized the familiar face of Agent Powell, United States Secret Service, and once in charge of the president's protection detail.

Bishop tensed, remembering that the agent and he hadn't exactly parted on good terms. In fact, the last contact the Texan had with the man involved a rather serious brawl. I should ask him how his nose is doing, the Texan considered, but knew Terri would scold his lack of manners.

Powell stopped short, glaring around the canyon walls with mirror-covered eyes, acting like he was still guarding the Commander in Chief. He didn't even smile at Bishop. Sourpuss.

More men came into the area, the whole gaggle looking like a presidential protection detail to Bishop. And then another figure appeared, similarly dressed, but shorter and older.

A huge grin broke out across Bishop's face as soon as he recognized the Colonel, his stocky ex-boss marching directly to the Texan and extending his hand.

"How are you, sir," were the only words Bishop could come up with in the moment.

"I'm well, Bishop. Where's Terri? And your son?"

Terri came out of the bat cave entrance, Hunter in one hand, her AR in the other. Bishop motioned for her to put the rifle down, the weapon obviously making the surrounding agents nervous.

Hugging their visitor like he was an expected uncle arriving for the holidays, Bishop watched as his wife greeted the Colonel, still having no clue why the man had dropped in without warning.

"Sorry about coming by unannounced," the Colonel began, as if reading the Texan's thoughts. "I've actually been in Alpha on official business, and when I asked about you, I was informed there was no way to contact the ranch. So I decided to stop by, just like the last time."

Chuckling, Bishop couldn't help himself, "At least your

landing was a little softer this time, sir."

The Colonel grinned, "No shit. You know, that airplane is still lying beside the highway. We flew over it on the way here."

Bishop started to say something about Mrs. Porter's grave and the council's vote to leave the plane as a memorial, but decided against it.

"So what brings you to our little corner of the world, Colonel?" Bishop asked, moving away from what was sure to be a sensitive topic.

Terri immediately swatted his shoulder, "Bishop! Where are your manners?"

She then turned to their guest and said, "Would you like to step inside out of the heat? I can offer you a cold drink."

"No, thank you for the offer, but I can't stay long. I really just wanted to stop in and say hello, make sure you were all doing well."

One of the agents approached, trying discreetly to gain the Colonel's attention. "Mr. President," he said, "I hate to rush you, sir, but the schedule...."

The Colonel acknowledged the man with a curt nod and then offered his hand to Bishop. But the Texan remained stock-still, surprise written all over his face. "Sir... Sir... did he just call you, Mr. President?"

Shyly, the Colonel answered, 'Yes, I was sworn in by what's left of the Senate and the Supreme Court just a few months ago. After the previous chief executive was assassinated, there was absolute chaos in Washington. For a while there, I thought the military was going to take over. But then someone found a signed letter in the president's desk. It stated that he had appointed me to become the Vice President. There was a lot of bickering, but finally most everyone agreed – I was next in line to occupy the Oval Office."

"Congratulations!" Terri said, again extending her arms to hug her guest.

Bishop finally regrouped enough to offer his hand, "Very pleased for you, sir. I can't think of anyone more qualified to run the country."

"I heard you just stepped down, Terri. I guess I was becoming a head of state just as you were leaving a similar post. I hope you're still pleased with your decision."

"Oh, absolutely, sir. It was time for me to move on. Bishop and I have been very busy. We've got grandiose plans, and I'm enjoying my new role as domestic goddess every single day."

Bishop remained silent and observing, not believing for one second that his old employer had "just dropped by." His feeling was compounded by the announcement of the presidency.

Sure enough, the Colonel finally got around to the real reason for his visit.

"Look you two, I confess to having an ulterior motive for stopping by. I'm facing one hell of a mess and could use both of you as advisors. I want to model our recovery after what you people have accomplished, and when I heard you were no longer actively involved with the Alliance, Diana granted me permission to stop by and offer you a job."

There it is, thought Bishop. The man's becoming a politician already.

The couple exchanged looks, a silent communication passing between them. The Colonel sensed a negative response was on the way and spoke quickly to head it off.

"Before you answer, I just want to say I only expect the occasional need for your services. I'm not asking for full-time dedicated commitment or even a formal agreement from either of you. But, if something special comes up, I'd like to know I can count on your advice and support."

Again, Bishop and Terri exchanged glances. It was Bishop who answered since the Colonel was his ex-boss. "If you really, really need us, Colonel, errr... Mr. President, Terri and I would always be willing to listen. We would have to evaluate each situation independently, sir."

"Of course, of course," smiled the Commander in Chief. "I wouldn't think of asking any more of you."

The agent approached again, his voice more urgent, "Mr. President, we have to be going, sir."

The president spread his hands wide, "You'd never know I was in charge," he teased. "Thank you both for taking the time to talk with me. I hope to be in touch soon."

After another round of hugs and handshakes, he was off, surrounded by Marines and agents.

Terri and Bishop stood and watched the procession's exit, both of them taking a moment to digest everything they'd learned from the visit.

After the noise from the last helicopter had faded, Bishop turned to his wife and commented, "I thought they'd never leave."

Terri, grinning widely, responded with, "He's your family, Bishop. I'm just the in-law. Next time, tell him he can't stay so long."

"But he always sends such nice Christmas cards," he responded with a straight face. "Besides, I hear he's rich, and we might be in the will."

They laughed hard, the outburst encouraging Hunter to offer a huge, toothless smile.

Terri then brightened, "Hey, our little monster will be going down for the night pretty soon. Want to meet later in the hot tub? I hear it's bathing suits optional tonight."

"You've got a date, pretty lady," he grinned, eyebrows bouncing up and down.

The End

CPSIA information can be obtained at www.ICGtesting.com
Printed in the USA
LVOW04s1051130115

422588LV00019B/443/P

9 781939 473271